PRAISE FOR MEAGAN CHURCH
THE MAD WIFE

"In a quietly devastating wink and nod to *The Bell Jar*, set firmly in thriller and suspense territory, Meagan Church delivers a piercing portrait of a young mother unraveling in the grip of 1960s suburbia, where Jell-O molds collapse, dishwashers invade, and card games with neighbors turn into emotional battlefields. With razor-sharp insight and aching lyricism, *The Mad Wife* traces a woman's descent through sleepless nights, domestic disillusionment, and buried guilt, capturing a haunting tension between what is said, seen, and silently endured until she no longer can."
—Lee Kravetz, author of *The Last Confessions of Sylvia P.*

"I devoured *The Mad Wife*, bite by savory bite. Church's novel expertly captures the paradox of being a 'perfect' housewife in the 1950s, all while drawing a subtle parallel to the plight of the 'ideal' woman today. The suspenseful unraveling of women's secrets—not to mention, their minds—kept me turning pages late into the night."
—Kristen Bird, *USA Today* bestselling author of *Watch It Burn*

"*The Mad Wife* is a propulsive story of motherhood, societal expectations, mental health, and resilience that is set during a time when women were often misunderstood and underserved. It's a book that does what I love best about historical fiction—illuminates a unique time and place that is new to me while exploring universal themes that hit close to home. A must-read for women of all ages."
—Adele Myers, author of *The Tobacco Wives*

"A vivid novel that deftly places you into the mind of a seemingly normal 1950s housewife, exposing the demands of motherhood and societal exceptions, while at the same time unraveling a tale of mystery and unexpected sorrow. A surprising narrative so cleverly crafted you never see the twist coming."

—Serena Burdick, author of *The Girls with No Names* and *A Promise to Arlette*

"*The Mad Wife* is a gripping and heart-wrenching portrait of a 1950s housewife at her wits end, struggling with the alienation and claustrophobia of midcentury suburban life. In this one-sitting read, Church offers unforgettable characters, a beautiful window into life in the fifties, and a stirring tribute to the strength of women. This should be at the top of every book club's list this fall."

—Ashley Winstead, *USA Today* bestselling author of *This Book Will Bury Me*

"Once again, Meagan Church deftly lights a dark corner of the past. At its heart, this story is an unflinching and evocative portrait of a woman—a wife and mother with a carefully crafted life—gradually losing herself and seeking a way back. Powerful and achingly real, *The Mad Wife* will linger with you long after the last page."

—Kelly Mustian, author of *The River Knows Your Name* and *The Girls in the Stilt House*

"Meagan Church's *The Mad Wife* is a story that is both historical and pointedly of-the-moment when the old adages assigned to hysterical women abound yet again. With an unflinching eye,

Church shines a light on the sorrows, secrets, and shames lurking behind the carefully curated lives of 1950s wives and mothers—and the quick and terrible consequences of so-called cures for what ails them. Lulu Mayfield is a courageous character whose important story will speak to mad women everywhere."

—Kimberly Brock, award-winning author of *The Fabled Earth*

"In a world where a woman can attain local fame for her Jell-O salads, what wife dares to complain that a dishwasher isn't the gift of her dreams? A rigid version of suburban propriety haunts the women of *The Mad Wife*, with their private griefs and their public smiles. But just when you think you know exactly what's going on, Meagan Church slips the area rug out from under you and tumbles you into a new understanding of the ways love can surprise you."

—Mimi Herman, author of *The Kudzu Queen*

"A gripping portrait of 1950s suburbia with a sinister undercurrent, this novel peels back the manicured lawns and perfect smiles to reveal the secrets we bury—and the strength it takes to unearth them. A haunting, hopeful tale of resilience, reckoning, and the redemptive power of truth."

—Sarah Penner, *New York Times* bestselling author of *The Amalfi Curse*

THE GIRLS WE SENT AWAY

"With beautiful prose and delicate precision, Church transports readers to the tumultuous Baby Scoop Era of the 1960s, providing a well-crafted and researched look into the struggles of women during this dark period in history, and evokes a lasting impression of empathy for young Lorraine. Heart-wrenching and thought-provoking, *The Girls We Sent Away* is a captivating novel, impossible to put down and one that will be remembered long after you turn the last page."

—Terah Shelton Harris, author of *One Summer in Savannah*

"In this stunning novel, Meagan Church weaves historical research and compelling narrative into an elegant tapestry that brings 1960s North Carolina to life. Lorraine Delford is an endearing and relatable heroine whose indefatigable spirit is sure to win readers' hearts. Even as others try to direct the course of Lorraine's future, she is determined to wrest back what control she can. A memorable portrait of a tumultuous time period, I highly recommend *The Girls We Sent Away* for fans of historical fiction."

—Heather Bell Adams, author of *Maranatha Road* and *The Good Luck Stone*

"Meagan Church's *The Girls We Sent Away* is such an important and vital story. With exquisite writing, Church exposes a murky little pocket of history and a reprehensible practice that surely had a generational impact on families. Through her captivating and thought-provoking scenes, I became wholeheartedly invested in the outcome of her remarkable heroine, Lorraine Delford, cheering for her all the way."

—Donna Everhart, *USA Today* bestselling author of *The Saints of Swallow Hill*

"Readers will be entranced as author Meagan Church steadily peels away the veneer of the era, revealing the dark underbelly of a secretive and unforgiving society."

—Tracey Enerson Wood, international bestselling author of *The Engineer's Wife* and *The War Nurse*

"Heartbreaking and heart-stopping, *The Girls We Sent Away* is a beautiful exploration of what it means to be human and how resilient the human spirit is. Meagan Church weaves the absence of choices with the desires of the heart together in another page-turner."

—Leslie Hooton, award-winning author of *The Secret of Rainy Days* and *After Everyone Else*

"Meagan Church paints a harrowing picture of one woman's experience during the Baby Scoop Era. Timely and emotional, *The Girls We Sent Away* depicts both the devastating loss of faith in those who are supposed to protect us and the ability of the human heart to trust again."

—Laura Barrow, author of *Call the Canaries Home*

THE LAST CAROLINA GIRL

"*The Last Carolina Girl* is a heart-wrenching and authentically rendered glimpse into the portal of a state's secret dark culture, family ties, and the fierce strength of a young girl's grit and resilience. Church is electric in her delivery of loss, longing, and place. Unforgettable, this a powerful debut to savor."

—Kim Michele Richardson, *New York Times* bestselling author of *The Book Woman of Troublesome Creek*

"Meagan Church has written a compelling and aching debut. *The Last Carolina Girl* is both a story of love and a tale of abuse set in the shadow of the Depression. There, a girl's blind obedience to her circumstances—a kind girl uprooted by her tender daddy's death—comes with a devastating price. Leah's life as an orphan takes her far from the comfort of sand and sea, yet she is armed with tenuous hope and a plan. Gradually, she puts together the puzzle pieces of her fractured life and uncovers truths: family can deceive and betray, but love offers salvation."

—Leah Weiss, bestselling author of *If the Creek Don't Rise* and *All the Little Hopes*

"This spirited coming-of-age debut whisked me straight to the heart of the Carolinas in the 1930s. I couldn't tear myself away from Leah's journey, from the piney, isolated woods of her childhood to an often bewildering life in the foreign world of the suburbs, where appearances are everything. Church so beautifully interweaves the connections between Leah's deeply sunk roots in the rural South with her search for belonging and her bravery in the face of unspeakable loss.

This is a story that will stay with me; I knew little about the eugenics programs that had taken hold in American culture in that time period, and Church's tale left me wanting to research and understand more of this broken, devastating piece of America's history."

—Lisa DeSelm, author of *The Puppetmaster's Apprentice*

"Fans of *Where the Crawdads Sing* and *Before We Were Yours* will find much to love in this evocative and thought-provoking debut. Church reaches into a shameful and little-known pocket of the past to give us a heroine who is plucky, tender, and determined to fight for her autonomy and dignity against insurmountable odds. This book will change the way you feel about the simple question of 'Where is home?'"

—Kim Wright, author of *Last Ride to Graceland*

"*The Last Carolina Girl* is lyrical and atmospheric, a true masterpiece of Southern fiction that will earn its long-standing place among greats on our bookshelves, both for its exploration of a horrific piece of history often overlooked and for its insistence on hope. Church's debut is a must-read."

—Joy Callaway, international bestselling author of *The Grand Design*

"While readers will surely find all of the characters in Meagan Church's debut compelling, the true beating heart of *The Last Carolina Girl* is its fourteen-year-old protagonist: a girl tied deeply to her natural landscape whose abrupt uprooting after the death of her beloved father comes with devastating consequences. Leah Payne and her indefatigable spirit will break your heart and put it back together again. I tore through this haunting and emotional story."

—Erika Montgomery, author of *A Summer to Remember*

"Leah's story is both humbling and inspiring. Church's ode to the natural world, to the often elusive feeling of home, and to the friends who become family provoke profound reflection. A dark spot in history warps Leah's path, but her resilient and unassailable character prevails. *The Last Carolina Girl* is a breathtaking read and Leah Payne an unforgettable character."

—Lo Patrick, author of *The Floating Girls*

"In this piercing novel, Meagan Church depicts one of the most disgraceful episodes in American medical history: forced sterilization. As a physician, I am deeply ashamed of the real-life actions of the medical community fictionalized so eloquently in this book, but as an author and a reader, I'm grateful for the opportunity to envision it. *The Last Carolina Girl* is a powerful and thought-provoking story."

—Kimmery Martin, author of *Doctors and Friends*

"Set in the mid-1930s in the Carolinas, the book explores lesser-known aspects of American poverty and classism and how the now-discredited ideas of eugenics caused lasting pain… Shines a light on a part of American history that deserves to be better understood."

—*Booklist*

"A dynamic and wrenching tale of family secrets and eugenics. This author is off to a strong start."
—*Publishers Weekly*

"[A] stirring debut…highlighting the true meaning of family."
—Shelf Awareness, Starred Review

ALSO BY MEAGAN CHURCH

The Last Carolina Girl
The Girls We Sent Away

The Mad Wife

The Mad Wife

A Novel

Meagan Church

sourcebooks
landmark

Copyright © 2025 by Meagan Church
Cover and internal design © 2025 by Sourcebooks
Jacket design by Kelly Winton
Jacket images © GraphicaArtis/Bridgeman Images, Robyn Mackenzie/Shutterstock, Andrey_Kuzmin/Shutterstock

Sourcebooks and the colophon are registered trademarks of Sourcebooks.

All rights reserved. No part of this book may be reproduced in any form or by any electronic or mechanical means including information storage and retrieval systems—except in the case of brief quotations embodied in critical articles or reviews—without permission in writing from its publisher, Sourcebooks.

No part of this book may be used or reproduced in any manner for the purpose of training artificial intelligence technologies or systems.

The characters and events portrayed in this book are fictitious or are used fictitiously. Apart from well-known historical figures, any similarity to real persons, living or dead, is purely coincidental and not intended by the author.

All brand names and product names used in this book are trademarks, registered trademarks, or trade names of their respective holders. Sourcebooks is not associated with any product or vendor in this book.

Published by Sourcebooks Landmark, an imprint of Sourcebooks
1935 Brookdale RD, Naperville, IL 60563-2773
(630) 961-3900
sourcebooks.com

Cataloging-in-Publication Data is on file with the Library of Congress.

Printed and bound in the United States of America.
VP 10 9 8 7 6 5 4 3 2 1

To Mom,
for your love and encouragement,
even in the shadow seasons of life

A NOTE BEFORE BEGINNING

Stories have a way of finding us at just the right—or sometimes the most fragile—moment. This one is steeped in history, woven with grief and longing, and tangled in the complexities of the human mind. It explores the weight of silence, the ache of the unseen, and the shadows that linger in the spaces between what is known and what is lost.

If you find the pages growing heavy, if the emotions press too hard against your heart, please know you have permission to set the book down. Step away, take a breath, and return only when you're ready. Stories will wait. May this one meet you in your time.

A WEEKLY CHECKLIST
to become the *perfect housewife*

THE GOAL: Try to make your home a place of peace and order where your husband can relax.

MONDAY *Kitchen*
- ○ Clean sink
- ○ Clean counters
- ○ Wipe appliances
- ○ Sweep
- ○ Scrub the linoleum until it shines like your fake smile

TUESDAY *Bedroom*
- ○ Change sheets
- ○ Wipe all surfaces
- ○ Straighten closet
- ○ Declutter
- ○ Sweep
- ○ Scream into a pillow

WEDNESDAY *Bathroom*
- ○ Clean mirror and vanity
- ○ Clean toilet
- ○ Clean shower and bath
- ○ Sweep
- ○ Mop
- ○ Avoid the shadows

THURSDAY *Living Room*
- ○ Wipe all surfaces
- ○ Declutter
- ○ Dust cobwebs
- ○ Sweep
- ○ Stare out the window and ponder how you ended up here

FRIDAY *Weekly*
- ○ Declutter entryway
- ○ Water plants
- ○ Clean out car
- ○ Clean out purse
- ○ Stop smelling colors

WEEKEND *Other*
- ○ Meal plan
- ○ Grocery shop
- ○ Clean fridge
- ○ Straighten up pantry
- ○ Spot-clean floors
- ○ Quit tasting sounds

DAILY *Tasks*

	S	M	T	W	T	F	S
Make bed	○	○	○	○	○	○	○
Load of laundry	○	○	○	○	○	○	○
Pick up clutter	○	○	○	○	○	○	○
Wash dishes	○	○	○	○	○	○	○
Wipe counters	○	○	○	○	○	○	○
Stay sane and smile	○	○	○	○	○	○	○

"Masks are the order of the day—
and the least I can do is cultivate
the illusion that I am gay, serene,
not hallow and afraid."

—Sylvia Plath,
The Journals of Sylvia Plath

PROLOGUE

Remember.

Henry said it with such earnestness. His hand cupped mine, his fingers frigid, as was everything in that facility, the winter chill snaking through the cracks, crevices, and paper-thin window panes, finding every possible way to slither inside.

He leaned close to me, his face inches from my own, his eyes fixed on mine. I used to lose myself in those eyes, the irises so deep brown they bled into his pupils. I could smell his aftershave, the undertones of sandalwood, the hint of a musk that reminded me of how Daddy smelled on Sundays.

See? I can remember.

I remember Daddy, all those years ago, and Mama and Georgie—how he used to love to run. And how he couldn't help himself from giggling as he sprinted, when he still could.

I remember when Henry and I met at the university, our first date, the restaurant with the tablecloths, my back so sore from sitting up straight, and how he made me believe in the possibility of love at first sight when all I hoped for was someone to belong to.

I remember our babies, the first cries and the ones that would ring out at all hours of the night.

I remember silence, too.

Henry stood to leave, his hat in his hand, his eyes on the asbestos-tile floor. That place, and the circumstances that had brought us there, had stripped away any warmth we had once shared. He offered no kiss, nor embrace. I used to find comfort in his arms that he would wrap around me, pull me in to him, as I rested against his chest and listened to his heart flutter a melody meant just for me: *Lu-lu, Lu-lu, Lu-lu.*

But over time that tune had changed, and his voice now drummed my name.

Lulu, remember.

I do! I wanted to shout. But I knew better. I knew to be sweet, as Mama always said. I had forgotten for a moment, but it had come back to me. For now, I needed to stay quiet. Smile the smile. And save the screams for the hours when the others slept.

Part One
THE WINDOW

"She stared at her reflection
in the glossed shop windows
as if to make sure,
moment by moment,
that she continued to exist."

~Sylvia Plath, *The Bell Jar*

CHAPTER ONE

I suppose it was in the darkness of the morning before the sun peeked over the horizon that I first came to believe that a home has a soul. That's not something I would share with others, especially not Henry. He would probably give me that look he gave Wesley the time our son tasted the neighbor's dog food. But how else do you explain the house across the street? Unlike the rest of Twyckenham Court where the original owners still held the keys, that one couldn't keep the same family for much longer than a year.

That sprawling ranch with the large picture window and shutters without a purpose was the same as all the others on the street, a flipped floor plan of our own, but otherwise a replica. If I had been the one to choose our house, I probably would've picked that one, mainly because of the sycamores out back. They weren't large, sprawling oaks like I preferred, but I would've taken any trees as opposed to the barren yard that the builders left us. Of course, Henry didn't ask me what I wanted. He never had to. He surprised me. And I smiled as a good wife should. As I always did.

The For Sale sign had gone up a week ago, just before Christmas. The Donahues had been there for more than a year. We thought they might be the ones to stay. I had hoped so. In those twelve months, Emily had become my closest friend, so close, in fact, that she had given me a key so I could let myself in to borrow sugar even if she was out on an errand. But it was only a matter of time before the house shook them loose and sent them packing, no matter how much I begged her to reconsider.

Each family offered a different reason for leaving: to be closer to relatives, a job relocation, a job loss, as was the case with the Donahues. Maybe that house was restless, anxious, like a mouse caught in a cat's shadow, and never let people feel at home. I sometimes wondered the same about our own house when I'd turn on the light over the kitchen sink and it would flicker before settling on. Even after five years of living there, I knew to expect the flutter before the light glowed steadily, but that didn't stop the shiver from tickling up my spine.

I thought about our house as I fixed Henry's eggs—over medium, with just enough yolk to dip his toast in—a task I had perfected over the last couple thousand days. But who's counting? This home had been full of firsts for us beginning the day Henry carried me across the threshold. Then there was the afternoon nearly four years ago when we brought Wesley home, followed by his first diaper blowout, the first time he slept through the night (that was a good one), when he took his first steps, said "Mama" between babbles and drool.

There were the other firsts, too, like when he had a fever and I didn't sleep for two days; when he closed his finger in the slider door; when I locked myself in our closet and cried when all he wanted was to be held, but all I needed was a moment to myself without being touched. *Babies are blessings*, they say. But what often goes unsaid is that blessings aren't always what we expect. And sometimes when we focus on the light they bring, we miss the shadows that lurk behind.

Lost in recollection, I nearly overcooked the eggs. "Are you okay?" Henry asked as he wrapped his arms around me and kissed my neck. His aftershave was so strong it caught in my throat. I typically liked the smell, but that morning my stomach soured.

I coughed and forced out, "Fine," not wanting to say more as Henry ate his breakfast, fixed his tie, and breezed out the door to the office.

Finally, I was alone. But not really.

With our annual New Year's Eve party the next evening, I had a lot to do in preparation. The list unspooled in my brain: vacuum the carpets and the drapes, mop the linoleum, a quick dusting to make sure the furniture shone. And then there was the food. But I couldn't shake the cobwebs from my mind enough to focus on any of that quite yet. So, in the hour between when Henry left for work and Wesley woke up, I counted stamps, the kind I got each time I shopped. Gas, grocery, clothing, even aspirin purchases rewarded my loyalty with those S&H Green Stamps. Tearing, licking, and sticking them into the redemption booklets had become one of my favorite pastimes, especially when I needed a moment to get lost in a rhythm.

So far, those stamps had earned us a lamp for the living room (three-and-a-quarter books), a framed painting for the front hall (two books), a tricycle for Wesley (two-and-a-half books), the Longines wristwatch Henry wore every day to work (nineteen books), and a cookbook for myself that was apparently supposed to bring me joy (two books). Rumor had it that a woman a couple of towns over had saved up enough to take her entire family to Weeki Wachee Springs to see the mermaids. Talk about patience! I considered that for a moment, but something else always caught my eye as I flipped through the merchandise catalog.

Perhaps I was trying to put some soul into our house with the items I earned. Or at least remove the spirit that had infected it before we moved in. Mrs. Mayfield—yes, my mother-in-law insisted I call her that—had taken it upon herself to furnish our home, from the living and dining rooms to the very bedroom where her son and I slept. Apparently, she felt that if she helped us with the down payment, then she also got a say in how to decorate. I had spent the last few years purging her haughty pieces in an attempt to create something of my own—one stamp, one covert shift of wall decor, throw pillows, or dishware at a time.

Sitting at my kitchen table in my winter flannel, willing myself to keep my eyes open and my coffee down, I thought again of the house across the street: all the ways I would decorate it, all the items I could get from the catalog. It would take weeks, months, years of saving and planning my shopping trips according to where I would receive the most stamps for my patronage. I could fill the necessary redemption books and then go to the store at Second and Main, redeem my treasures, and create my own home like my great-grandparents had done. Though I wouldn't build this from the ground up like them. If I was really dreaming, it would be a combination of my grandfather's handmade furniture and modern finishes: an oak dining room table atop plush carpeting, surrounded by floral wallpaper and lit by an overhead pendant lamp.

But why would I need a place of my own? This one was fine; Henry made sure of it. He had chosen this specific floor plan with four bedrooms for our growing family and upgraded the appliances, choosing the Frigidaire with the auto-defrost feature to make my life easier. He still regretted not getting a dishwasher, but I told him it was fine. We had all we needed in that home in Greenwood Estates, with its wide sidewalks and surveilling streetlamps, only minutes from the A&P. We had a son full of health and curiosity and a marriage where we sometimes still held hands, plus Henry had a good job with a steady paycheck and the promise of a promotion. My mother would say we had more than enough. So, what else could I ask for?

Well, the Kodak Duaflex camera, for one thing. I had a perfectly fine camera, I suppose, but Henry was always telling me to take up a hobby, find more ways to fill my day, and photography was the closest I had to one. For months, I had planned to redeem my stamps for that camera, but something else always came first. There was the chrome grill for the cookout Henry wanted to host (seven-and-a-half books) and the electric hair clipper set so I could trim Wesley's curls (three-and-a-quarter books). It might do me good to consider the stroller. But just the other day the percolator gave out, so I supposed that would be the practical choice.

I thought Henry might give me a camera for Christmas, but

instead he surprised me with house slippers. "Because your feet are always cold," he told me. I smiled at him and said thank you. I had never had slippers, a fact that still astonished him. I wore them for the rest of the day, the rubber soles scraping across the kitchen linoleum as I made dinner, sweat forming between my toes. Now, nearly a week from receiving that gift, I had already pushed them beneath the bed, preferring to feel the stiff carpet fibers, pretending that I had my toes curled in grass.

And what did I give Henry? I knew what he really wanted, what he had been hoping for since Wesley had turned two. I thought I wanted that, too, but I remembered things that Henry didn't. So instead, I gave him a fishing rod (two books) and tackle box (one book).

I could've used the slippers as my feet touched both cold and crumbs on the kitchen floor while I sat at the table, looking through the catalog, feeling queasy from Henry's aftershave. Or something more. I read the camera description again: Kodet lens, aluminum case, plastic trim, twin lens reflex finder, fixed focus.

Fixed focus.

I thought of those words and wondered what I might see through the lens of that camera, as the fluorescent light emitted a constant, unrelenting electric hum. I suppose I would see Wesley get taller, our family grow, new neighbors replace the Donahues, unknowingly taunting the soul that lurked within the house.

I took a drink of coffee, hoping it would wash away the sour tang of the chemical glue that clung to my taste buds. My body begged for more sleep. Instead, I sat at the table, the cold seeping through my bare feet as I flipped through the stamp catalog page after page after page. I didn't remember feeling so weak the last time. But perhaps I had forgotten. At least, that's what I told myself.

I suppose I got carried away that morning and lost all sense of time, because I was still at the kitchen table with those stamps when the doorbell rang.

"Here it is!" Nora announced as cigarette smoke curled around her strawberry hair, styled in a poodle clip like Lucille Ball. She took a drag and then continued, "Good God, Lulu. It's nearly lunchtime and you're still in your pajamas?"

She was right. I had meant to change after Henry left. Or before I got Wesley up. Or after he went out to play. I pulled the collar higher onto my neck, as if modesty would save me from her scrutiny.

"I suppose I lost track of time." Maybe I should get myself a new wristwatch (eighteen books).

Nora shrugged, dropped her Lucky Strike on the front step, the tip of it tinted with her Fire & Ice shade of Revlon. She stamped it out with her ballet flats, the ones with the pleated fans for a little extra touch. Leave it to Nora to have to be dressed to the nines just to lend a neighbor a dish.

"You're sure we can't bring anything tomorrow night?"

I waved away her offer. "You know I've got it covered."

"You always do." Nora looked at the drapes I hadn't fully opened, Wesley's Lincoln Logs spread over the davenport and onto the floor, the kitchen table full of stamp supplies. "Are you okay, Lu?"

Her look of concern, along with the question, made me regret my morning, my lazy start, my stamp booklets.

Shortly after we moved into Greenwood Estates, Nora shared with me the key to being a good housewife—or at least a decent one, she said. It was the *Good Housekeeping* cleaning schedule, and apparently everyone on Twyckenham Court followed it. Except for me. But they didn't know that.

The copy Nora gave me still hung on my fridge, as overlooked as a sunset during mealtime. Look through any living room window on any given day, and all the other Greenwood wives could be seen moving in perfect synchronicity—a shared broadcast across matching windows. Arms raising in time to dust the highest shelves, skirts twirling around hot-water buckets and mops, the choreography perfectly timed to the hum of the vacuums. It was as if the schedule was embedded in their programming, the timing absolute like the beat of a metronome (two books).

> Mondays: Grocery and kitchen
> Tuesdays: Laundry
> Wednesdays: Bedrooms and bathrooms
> Thursdays: Linens and living room
> Fridays: Defrost the fridge, groceries, dining room and halls
> Saturday: Family day
> Sunday: Rest

When we first moved, I had no idea a suburban housewife's life came with such a schedule. Of course, we always had chores to do on the farm—some daily, such as feeding the horses and mucking the stalls, while others were seasonal like harvesting and canning. But my parents never had a printed schedule that told them how to spend each day. Never had the peering eyes of neighbors to contend with.

When I first looked over the schedule, I asked Nora, "What if you don't feel like doing laundry on a Tuesday?"

"Feel like it?" She squinted as if she had never considered that possibility, before sighing at my inexperience. Ineptitude. Indolence. "The point is so you don't *have* to think about it. You just do it."

What a blessing not to think.

Sometimes, when the days elongated and the schedule lorded over me from its spot on the fridge, I had to remind myself that I hadn't picked this fate. I simply chose Henry, and this was part of the package. Years prior, when I had still allowed myself to dream, I imagined running the farm alongside Daddy and Georgie, if he wanted to. I pictured myself driving the tractor, tilling the soil, harvesting the peaches, spending my days outside, not trapped indoors like Mama. But that possibility died with a final breath in the night, and without other options, I had a lot to learn about being a good suburban wife.

I gave the schedule a try. I really did. I followed it closely for the first few months. I got out of bed, looked at that list, and vowed to complete the tasks. But some days, despite Nora's insistence, I just didn't feel like it. And as long as I kept the house in decent order, Henry didn't notice if it didn't meet *Good Housekeeping* standards. Or at least he didn't say he noticed. And based on all other outside appearances, I was like the rest of them.

But from the look on Nora's face, she saw the truth.

"You're sure you don't need more than this empty dish?" she asked.

"I'm sure."

"Have you started on the food yet?" I'd meant to, but before I could answer, she continued. "I can whip up one of those gelatin salads. I mean, I might not do it as good as you, but my last one didn't turn out too bad." I felt a prickle of annoyance.

Since moving to Greenwood, my dishes had become the talk of supper parties and carry-ins. It started with a recipe I found that set sliced bananas in cherry Jell-O. And it grew from there. Now I had an array of sweet and savory recipes, some with fruit, vegetables, meat, and even one with tuna.

It wasn't just the ingredients that surprised people. It was also the shapes themselves, how I could mold them into towers, crafting sculptures of congealed foods. *How does she get them to stand so tall?* I would hear the neighbors whisper. *And the things she fills them with! I never would've thought!*

Neither would I. In all honesty, some of the combinations repulsed me, but I swear these people would eat anything I put in front of them, especially if it was carefully shaped, painstakingly sculpted. A new invention. The less it resembled food, the more quickly they gobbled it down. But this was who I had become in Greenwood: the Queen of Molded Food. It wasn't a role I had planned for myself, but I accepted the title, even if I didn't eat half of what I made. I wasn't even sure half of it could be considered food. "Digestible" and "good" didn't always go hand in hand.

"I was just getting ready to start on it," I told Nora, which wasn't exactly a lie. And I did need to get the food going so the gelatin would have time to set. I would clean later.

Thankfully, Nora moved toward the door. She never was one to overstay her welcome, which I appreciated, especially in that moment, as a wave of nausea hit. It was probably all of the stamp adhesive on an empty stomach. Nora told me I was a fool to lick them instead of using a sponge. I didn't tell her that I liked the taste. Typically.

"I should get home," she said. "Make sure James and Marjorie haven't torn apart the house."

As she opened the front door, the daylight poured into the foyer. I squinted as my eyes adjusted, and shivered when the cool breeze blew over the sweat that had begun to accumulate on my face.

"Are you okay?" Nora asked.

I smiled and tried to brighten my eyes. I really should've gotten dressed, done my hair, put on some blush. I had phoned Nora the day before, asking to borrow the mold, but I had forgotten that she would be stopping by. I needed to get her out the door so I could get something in my stomach.

And so she didn't have time to guess my secret. Not yet.

I hadn't told Nora, nor anyone else, not even Henry. I needed some time to adjust before anyone else knew. Before others got involved.

I knew Nora would be happy for us but with a caveat. After all, she remembered. We never talked about that day. I don't know how she found me. Maybe she heard my cries from the street. God, I hope not. But somehow, she knew. She came into the house, not even knocking before entering. She ran down the hall to find Wesley on the changing table, flailing his limbs in the jerky way newborns do, as I sobbed over the spilled laundry hamper (three books), having given up hope of finding a sock that could pass for clean.

"Lulu," she'd said as she knelt beside me. "What is it? What do you need?"

Snot and tears had poured down my face, over my lips, dripping past my chin. I hiccuped a few breaths before I could respond. Only two words would come out: *a sock*.

I don't like to recall that moment, one so absurd, so weak. There I was, a grown woman, on the floor of her child's bedroom, beside herself because she couldn't find a sock. If I had only done the laundry that Tuesday, I wouldn't have been in that predicament to begin with. But I had been so tired.

Had Henry found me like that, he might've laughed. And I wouldn't have blamed Nora if she had done the same. But she didn't. She got to her feet, walked to the dresser, and said, "How about we find a sleeper with footies instead?"

Nora changed Wesley as I sat on the floor, numb. She handed him to me and said, "Babies are hard." Of course she was right. But I hadn't known until I had one. Maybe Georgie had also been that way. Perhaps I should've remembered, since I was eight when he was born. But I spent most of my days outside the house, running around the farm, chasing after kittens, sitting in my tree, leaving Mama to tend to things alone.

That morning at the end of 1954, as the breeze blew cool over my clammy skin and my stomach begged for a soda cracker to settle it, Nora stepped onto the front porch and lit a cigarette. She took a puff and exhaled a stream of smoke as she mumbled, "At least put on some lipstick, Lu. I still can't believe your mother didn't teach you that." There was a lot my mother hadn't taught me. "Call me if you need anything." She waved her hand in the air, dispersing the first haze that curled around her. "But of course, you won't."

I thanked her. Then I closed the door, stood in the dimness of the foyer, and told myself that this time would be different. I would know what to expect; it would take more than the cries of a newborn to break me.

Through the window, I looked at the uninhabited house across the street, the sign in the yard, the half-open curtains Emily hadn't tied back before they left the final time. The sense of peacefulness in its emptiness. These Greenwood Estates homes weren't as weathered and worn as my childhood one. Like the people who lived there, these houses had far less history and fewer ghosts. With time, that would change. For some of us more than others.

CHAPTER TWO

I didn't mean to keep the secret from him. I knew he would be excited, and maybe that's why I hesitated. What was the harm in waiting a few weeks to tell him? Though by then, it had been over a month. Every time I thought I would tell him, part of me still wanted to wait, still hoped I would be more excited like I was with Wesley. Sure, I had some hesitations, but this time was different. This time I knew how much work a baby took, how incompetent I could feel, how thin I could be stretched.

As I got ready for the party, my stomach pushed against the girdle, fighting the restriction. I needed to tell Henry soon, especially because of the nausea, but also because my stomach had begun to round. *After the party*, I told myself. I would start his new year with good news. For tonight, it would still be my little secret.

"You're not going to be done in time," Henry said. Though I had my eyes closed, waiting for the false lashes to set, I still knew what he was doing: adjusting the Windsor knot on his tie for the umpteenth time. I swear he could tie that in his sleep and it would look just the same, but he always fidgeted with it until the last possible minute. It was a good thing he was born a man, because if he also had to apply makeup, pin an updo, and slink into stockings without snagging a run, he would never get anywhere.

The neighbors would be there soon enough, ready to start drinking and celebrating the start of 1955. We had hosted the New Year's Eve party every year since we had moved into Greenwood—Henry's favorite tradition carried over from his youth, when he watched his parents throw grand parties while he peered through the crack in his door. Now Henry relished being in the swing of the festivities, throwing the perfect party year after year. By this point, I knew what I was doing, but Henry still worried I was running behind schedule.

"Trust me," I said as I blinked and adjusted to the weight of the lashes. I had managed to get all the food prepared, carpets vacuumed, and the bar ready to go. Did he not trust that I could also get myself ready in time?

"You put Wesley to bed?"

"Yes." Though it hadn't been easy, especially since I had to tuck him in earlier than normal. He asked multiple times if he could come to the party. I reminded him that it was only for adults. He asked that I do our nighttime routine a couple of extra times and I obliged, taking his hand—still squishy with baby fat—into mine. Brushing my index finger across his palm just lightly enough that it tickled, I recited his favorite poem that I had written for him:

With a circle and a pat
And a heart on top of that,
I give all my love to Wes
With not a single smidge less.

Typically, I only said it once before bed, but that night I spent a few more minutes lingering with him, reciting the poem on repeat until his giggles turned to cackles and his eyes teared from the tickles. I knew I had other tasks to complete before the guests arrived, but time was what he needed and I gave it to him. Especially before a sibling came along and stole the attention he had been bathed in for the last four years.

Henry continued his questioning. "You told him to stay in bed, right?" I widened my eyes at him so the lashes tickled the skin beneath my brow line. "Just checking," he mumbled.

"If you continue checking, I won't be ready in time." Henry slipped his hand into my robe as he pressed his chin onto my shoulder and stared at me through the mirror. We had been married for nearly six years, but those eyes could still soften even my sharpest edges. We met his final year and my first at the university, when I was on assignment with the school newspaper. He seemed charming enough as he flashed his smile and I snapped a picture for the front page article about the rowing team's winning season, but so did so many of those boys at that school. All with a sense of entitlement, as if the world and all it contained was theirs for the taking. I didn't want to be taken, but I let it happen anyway.

I lost myself in his embrace for only a moment before his hand slid from my side to my stomach. I could've told him then, but instead I scooted out of his grasp and said, "I won't be ready in time if you do this."

He pouted his lips and drooped those brown eyes of his—a perfect reflection of our three-year-old son. "Fine," he said, before kissing me on the cheek. "You've got five minutes." But I knew it was more like fifteen.

With minutes to spare, I slipped on the off-the-shoulder fit-and-flare I hadn't worn in more than a year, hoping that I had a bit more roundness to make it work. Until recently, my body didn't fill the hourglass style. The dress typically hung from my spindly frame instead of clinging to the contours as it should. I sometimes wondered what Henry saw in my slenderness, too tall for most men, too thin for others, too harsh and lacking the soft, nurturing curves a mother should have.

"Look at my girl," Henry said as he glanced my way moments before the first guests arrived. I wondered if he had really looked at me. If he noticed my clavicle's angles, how my breasts still fell flat beneath the bodice. The dress tried its best to give me a waist and bit of hips, but I was no Marilyn Monroe. Nor Nora Gray, who had been blessed with a buxom physique. Her ample bosom tested even modest necklines, her curves always evident. I wished our frames were similar enough that we could share clothing, borrow dresses, double our wardrobes, but I would have to find a new friend for that to happen. Maybe someone who didn't adhere to cleaning schedules. Who didn't apply a full face of makeup before leaving the bedroom each morning. Who also understood that sometimes hiding in the walk-in closet for a few minutes helped get you through the rest of the afternoon.

I took a final look around the house. All was set. All those hours spent prepping had led to this moment, and it would all be over soon enough. *Enjoy it*, I told myself. But there was still more work to do: drinks to fill, dishes to replenish, photos to take, conversations to have before the cleaning started. Then the weary could rest.

"Let me look at you," Nora said when she and Dennis arrived that night, her heels clacking across our vinyl foyer, the same flooring that she and most of the other neighbors had. Before handing me her mink stole, she made me twirl as she examined the dress for herself. "Not your typical cut." She squinted her eyes, searching every inch of my body, and I stiffened, wondering if she had detected my secret. "I like it. And if you weren't such a string bean, I'd demand to borrow it." I forced a smile and deposited the coats in our guest room, taking a moment longer than normal.

Our friend Hatti arrived a short time later carrying a cake saver (one book). Because of course she did. A good housewife always brought a dish, even when asked not to.

"Hatti Brooks!" Nora scolded. "Don't you know by now that you don't bring a dish to Lulu Mayfield's?"

"I know, I know." Hatti blushed, her round cheeks reddening to the color of her swing dress. "But my mama always told me not to go anyplace empty-handed."

I took the dish from Hatti, smiling despite my frustration. "You know I won't turn down your chocolate cake. Let's make room for it on the table."

"Oh, I have to see this spread," Nora said, grabbing Hatti's hand. The two gasped as they saw the table laid out before them.

For days, I thought about the menu, and in the rush of the last day and a half, I executed it all. There were bananas wrapped in ham and doused in hollandaise sauce, a Monterey soufflé salad with olives and tuna, a seafood mousse shaped into a smiling fish, a bologna and cream-cheese cake stacked a foot high, and a meat and vegetable loaf frosted in mayonnaise. Then, in the center of it all, standing taller than the rest, was the perfection salad: gelatin mixed with vinegar, lemon and apple juices, filled with shredded carrots, sliced celery, finely shredded cabbage, chopped green olives, and paper-thin radishes. A motley combination of ordinary ingredients molded for presentation, much like us.

"The Queen of Molded Food's reign continues," Nora declared.

"All hail, Queen Lulu!" Hatti giggled and they both curtsied. I smiled as I placed the chocolate cake in the corner of the spread.

Nora first gave me that title one afternoon as we tested vodka martinis in my living room and the kids ran around outside. A few drinks in, I admitted out loud that maybe I'd like to be known for something other than shaped salads. She had said we all had parts to play and then reminded me that it could be worse.

She was right. We did have our roles.

Henry was the all-American boy, brimming with optimism and a can-do attitude.

Hatti was the ideal mother, caring for everyone, sometimes at the expense of herself.

Nora was as funny as a sitcom and beautiful to boot. Every man's dream and we all knew it.

Her husband, Dennis, was the restless yet adoring spouse, overcompensating for his wandering eye.

And I could make impressive salads.

I begged Hatti and Nora to stop praising me. Little did I know that when I showed up to that first neighborhood carry-in with eleven layers of ribbon Jell-O, it would come to define who I was. By now, it was too late to change. It was who they expected me to be. So I played along. I bought more molds (one-and-three-quarters books), tried new recipes, and even made up a few of my own. I told myself that it was a game to see what all I could get them to eat. But in truth, I was molding myself into someone I hoped they would see as one of them.

"Please, eat," I said, handing them plates. "I don't want leftovers at the end of the night."

"Yes, Your Royal Highness." Nora curtsied again and then took a plate. We all knew she wouldn't eat much. She never did. She had her measurements to adhere to. Every morning, she measured her waist, thighs, arms, and breasts, and kept the results in a journal. If the number was higher than an acceptable maximum, she reduced her food intake and increased her cigarette habit. Nora still put a few scoops of salad onto her plate, though I knew it would be scraped into the kitchen trash when she thought no one was looking.

"Lulu, did you see what Eddie gave me for Christmas?" Hatti's face glowed, partly because she had gone heavy on the rouge once again, but her eyes danced as she pulled at the gold heart necklace. She opened the locket, revealing a tiny photo of her three children, one that Eddie had asked me to take for him as a surprise. "Now I can keep them close to my heart all the time." Her sentiment was even sweeter than the icing on her chocolate cake, sure to cause a cavity.

"It's beautiful," I told her. She was so proud, so different from me. What did she have that I didn't? What made her long to be with her kids all the time instead of desperate for a few moments away? I tried to squelch the questions, to blame them on the champagne fog that typically clouded my mind during parties like this. But I hadn't had a sip of alcohol all night.

I excused myself to grab my camera. No party happened without at least one roll of film to document it. While Bing Crosby crooned from the RCA, I captured photos of men puffing out swirling clouds of cigar smoke in the den, women sipping champagne as bubbles effervesced, and couples clinging to each other as they waltzed across our living room carpet, while the dark night loomed outside the windows, a house so full of vitality, across the street from one that still sat vacant.

I watched it all through the viewfinder as I snapped photos from a distance. All was in order. The guests seemed to be enjoying themselves and the food was a hit, but all I could see was the perfection salad in the center of the table moving, jiggling, swaying from side to side, looking as if it might fall at any minute.

I did my hostess duties, but as the clock dragged toward midnight, my insides felt like they were oscillating along with the salad, at least as much as they could, given the girdle restraints. I needed some fresh air, so I escaped to the backyard, welcoming the quiet and solitude despite the bitter cold. A sliver of a crescent moon hung overhead that night, a white curve in the sky, providing little light.

I sat in the darkness and watched the party through the sliding door. I saw the conversations, the laughter, how Mrs. Reilly piled her plate high once again despite the doctor's advice to drop a few pounds. I saw the way Dennis had his arm around Nora while he looked across the room at Maureen—the youngest wife in Greenwood, her eyes and breasts so full of perk. I could tell from his sway how many drinks he'd had and that he wouldn't remember most of the party come morning. I don't know how long I sat there, but eventually I saw Hatti leave without saying goodbye, probably desperate to get home and check on the little ones she couldn't bear to be away from for too long.

It seemed like all of Greenwood was there that night, but passing headlights reminded me that we hadn't invited everyone. We may have thought we did, but of course there were neighbors we hadn't yet met, names we didn't know, families we didn't choose to invite over to parties for a whole host of reasons, I suppose.

I had known most of these people for the last five years. On the surface, I would call them friends; they were more than acquaintances. But who within that house did I *really* know? And who really knew me?

As I sat in the darkness, the cold pricking my bare arms, Wesley found me. Of course he did.

"What're you doing up?" Henry must not have seen him, or he would have taken his son by his arm and directed him back to bed. I should've done the same, but instead I let him climb onto my lap.

"It's too loud," he said, his tongue still not cooperating, so the *l* sounded more like a *y*. It bothered Henry and his mother so much. I told them my brother, Georgie, used to talk like that and assured them that our son would outgrow it, but they didn't seem to believe me. Or at least Mrs. Mayfield didn't and Henry followed suit.

"You need to go back to bed," I said, but I let him stay. I suppose my mother-in-law would say that was another way I spoiled him. I stroked his hair, stretching his curls out straight before they bounced back as I released them. He looked so much like Georgie—those curls, the long eyelashes, the freckles across his cheeks. Did Georgie still have all those freckles? Or had they begun to fade?

Wesley pushed his body against me, taking as much of my lap as he could. He didn't know yet that soon his world would change.

Our world.

My world.

Henry would be so pleased with the idea of having a complete family. But did he remember what a baby was like? How some days I was so exhausted I would forget to eat? How Wesley cried for hours every evening? How my nipples chafed from the baby's constant need to nurse? Of course he didn't. I didn't bother him with those details when he got home from the office. After all, I was the mother; caring for the baby was my job.

And I hadn't told him that sometimes I still woke in the night, swearing I heard a cry. Only a few nights prior, I was nearly out our bedroom door on my way to quiet the sound, when I woke enough to realize there was no baby. No noise at all.

I missed the countdown to the new year as I tucked Wesley into bed for the second time that night. When I rejoined the party in the living room, Henry pulled me to him.

"Where've you been?" The syllables slurred into one long word before he pressed his lips to mine, his whiskers poking into my skin. He had shaved just before the party, but those whiskers never stayed hidden for long. "You missed the toast."

He tried to hand me his glass of champagne, but I told him no thank you. The room was already beginning to spin. The last thing I needed was a drink.

"Are you okay?" he asked.

"Just tired." I told the partial truth and hoped it was enough, but what I needed then was for everyone to leave before the room spun even more.

In that moment, I don't know why I did it. Maybe I was trying to hold on. I wished I would've had a glass or something to occupy my hands, because as the neighbors chatted and some began to say their goodbyes, Henry looked at me. Even through his champagne haze, he saw my hands reach for my stomach, my subconscious attempt to comfort what had been gripped by my girdle for far too long.

"Lulu—" he began. His eyes widened. I hoped he was too drunk to put the pieces together—the nausea I had failed to hide from him that morning, the curves that better accentuated my dress that night, my hands upon my stomach. "Are you—"

"Henry—" I tried to interrupt him. Yes, I needed to tell him, but not there, not in front of everyone. Plus, wasn't it bad luck to tell people before the end of the first trimester? I may have been close to that, but I wasn't through it yet. "Listen—"

I tried to use words to distract him, but apparently the look on my face had given everything away. He couldn't listen. Not then. The party. The friends. The champagne, all of it numbed him to my pleas. He turned from me and began to clang his wedding ring against the goblet (one book for a set of six), demanding the room's attention.

"What're you doing?" I forced the question past the lump of fear that had lodged in my throat.

"Making a toast."

"Please, not now," I begged, but I struggled to find words as my heartbeat quickened.

Henry slumped his arm across my shoulders. "A toast," he began, "to good neighbors, better friends, and—" He turned to look at me as he said the next words, his eyes sparkling. I couldn't look. I buried my face in his chest. With my ear pressed against him, I could hear our hearts beating at different rhythms, his slow and steady, mine thumping, panicked. I wanted those beats to drown out what he said next. "And the most perfect wife."

Did I hear him correctly? Had he listened to me? He tightened his arm around me and kissed my forehead as the thump of my heartbeat slowed. I thought he was done. We all did. A few glasses clinked. Some people took a sip. But then his voice rose higher, above the chatter that tried to resume. "And to the year our family is finally complete."

An invisible current pulsed through my veins like an electric charge. I prayed they were all too drunk to understand. But he wasn't done. To get his point across, he removed his arm from my shoulders, placed his hand on my stomach, and pressed against it.

Unfortunately, the neighbors understood. They gasped and cheered as I wanted nothing more than to dissolve into the carpeting, let it act like a sponge and soak up every part of me. Instead of disappearing, my body began to shake as heat rose from my toes to my cheeks, a storm of unease brewing inside me.

Henry's words slurred together as he continued, "A-dream come-true."

That's when Dennis lifted his glass and toasted, "To dreams!"

"To dreams!" our living room echoed his cheer, as men kissed their wives and neighbor toasted neighbor all over again.

But Nora didn't cheer. She watched me from across the room, her eyes locked on mine, her lips pursed shut. I nodded my head in recognition. She held a hand to her heart and raised her goblet in my direction before Dennis grabbed her and kissed her.

To dreams, the toast echoed through my mind as the final moments of the celebration continued. Those words replayed as I handed the neighbors their coats on their way out the door, as they kissed me on my cheek and congratulated us, even as Nora reminded me that the baby blues don't happen every time. It whispered to me as Henry went to bed and I gathered the dishes, tossed the empty champagne bottles, and placed the leftovers in the Frigidaire.

To dreams.

Of course, sometimes we forget that dreams and nightmares are two sides of the same coin.

CHAPTER THREE

Few things are watched as much as a house for sale in Greenwood Estates. We had all seen potential buyers come and go over the last six months. Nora hoped the older couple with the wood-paneled Ford would move in, thinking that perhaps the woman would offer to watch our kids. Hatti wanted the family with the twins, but Mrs. Reilly countered that those kids might be too loud, like too many others who were already in the neighborhood. I held out hope for a nice couple with a son Wesley's age. And a friend for me.

None of the comings and goings kept me from imagining the place as my own. During Wesley's quiet time, my mind would wander about the house, filling it with a crescent-shaped sofa with olive-green upholstery and tapered wooden legs that faced the console television, and with a walnut-veneered elliptical coffee table nestled in its center. Don't forget the bookcase room dividers and telephone bench in the hall. I would hang artwork, trying different pieces in different places, considering what my own photographs might look like, my own memories on display for all to see. I made sure to remove the bathroom carpet, add a few more cabinets in the kitchen, and plant more trees throughout the yard. I played with the dollhouse of my mind when I couldn't sleep at night, and sometimes I would visit it in my dreams.

The day of Wesley's birthday party, yet another car pulled into the driveway with yet another couple ready to take a look. And of course we all watched with interest, but perhaps I was the only one who secretly hoped it remained vacant, a place for my imagination. Even though I knew the house would never be mine, with each month it remained empty, it seemed to belong to me a little bit more.

Other than for Wesley's first birthday, we had never made it a point to invite others to celebrate, but that year I thought we should do something special before he was no longer the only child. A mother like Hatti would've planned ahead, but I called our parents on Wednesday and asked them to come for a visit Saturday afternoon, along with Nora and her son, James, who would stop over for cake.

With swollen ankles and a taut belly, I fought through the exhaustion and discomfort for Wesley. When I asked him what he'd like at his party, he requested a "tall cake." So I baked, stacked, and frosted a four-tier chocolate sponge—one layer for every year he had been with us.

"That's a lot of cake," Mama said when she saw it, shaking her head at the wastefulness in front of her. She had come in her Sunday best, the same floral dress she had worn to our wedding, the same black oxford lace-up shoes she wore every day. The same short haircut she'd had since Daddy got sick and she couldn't be bothered to fuss with her hair any longer.

"There was a special," I told her, though it wasn't the truth.

On the other hand, Marian—in my mind, I referred to my mother-in-law by her first name—had asked what bakery I had bought it from.

"Lulu baked it herself," Henry informed his mother as he put an arm around me and drew me in to him.

"How nice!" she quipped as she touched her index finger to the whipped chocolate frosting. She squinted a smile in my direction as she licked her finger clean.

"Grandma!" Wesley protested. "Mama said we have to wait!"

"I won't tell if you won't." She winked at her grandson as if sharing a secret. Though we all saw her do it—everyone except Hank, my father-in-law, who dozed on the davenport that she had picked out and he had paid for.

"You're right," I said to Wesley. I didn't crouch to his level or speak in a child's voice like she did. "How about we get this fixed, and then you don't have to wait any longer."

As I walked into the kitchen to grab a spatula to fix the slash she had cut into the icing, I wondered if she had ever asked her son to keep secrets, too. Maybe that's how she endeared him to her. I couldn't help but wonder… If they hadn't been placed together as mother and son, would they have found each other as friends, as if their connection would've brought them together in some way?

As I fixed the cake, Mama walked back into the living room and sat next to Georgie. He had changed in the months since

I had last seen him. The stubble along his chin made him look more like a man, but the faint freckles across his cheeks reminded us that he was still a boy.

It had been a struggle to get him there that day, according to her. When I had called to invite them, she warned me that it would be hard. She told Henry it had been an exhausting morning when she knocked on the door and asked him to help get Georgie into the house. "It's not easy," she said as my brother's crutches clicked across the sidewalk. Nothing for her was ever easy. And she reminded us of that often. But I still hoped that being there to celebrate her only grandchild might make it worthwhile.

I watched as Mama straightened Georgie's shirt and he reminded her that he was fine. I don't know that she would've found me had she not been my mother, but I had no doubt that she would've searched far and wide for him.

"How about we light this thing up?" Nora pulled out the lighter I had given her for Christmas (imitation ostrich with gold finish, one book). I nodded my approval, and she flicked the flame to life. Once the candles were lit, I carried the cake to the coffee table so we could all sing to Wesley.

Henry's mother held Wesley on her lap, singing directly into his ear as the rest of us acted as background chorus. She kissed him on the cheek before she told him to go on and make a wish. He didn't rush to extinguish the flames. He squeezed his eyes shut, and a closed smile grew across his face as he concentrated on his wish, taking this opportunity seriously.

As I watched him concentrate, the baby jolted inside me, as if wedging a foot under my rib cage. This one had been less active than Wesley, but it still had its moments of stretching and shifting. I hadn't anticipated how differently they would feel even before birth. All I had known were Wesley's quick flutters. How some days it felt as if he was taking after his father, an athlete in frequent motion. Yet, as active as Wesley was, he hadn't hurt me; he simply wiggled with enthusiasm.

This one didn't move often, but when it did, it felt different. Harsher. Sometimes poking outward and inward, as if trying to break free, as if needing more room, tired of feeling constrained, never fully comfortable. As Wesley made his wish, I did, too: for the baby to curl up and go to sleep.

After Nora snapped a few family pictures for us, everyone except Georgie and me went outside to watch Wesley throw his new football. The house quieted so that the only sound left was the ticking clock on the wall. Finally able to get off my feet for the first time in hours, I feared I would fall asleep if I sat for too long. The empty house across the street had never looked quieter, better, a place where I could curl up and nap as long as I wanted to.

I inhaled with a yawn and swore Georgie smelled just like Daddy used to. I wondered if he remembered that, but I doubted he did. Thanks to age and circumstances, he had spent less time with our father. While I could go to the barn to find him or sit alongside him as the tractor made pass after pass tilling the field, Georgie couldn't, not since he had needed those leg braces when he was just older than Wesley. What if Wesley had only a couple more years to walk and run without any hindrances?

I shook the thought from my mind and stretched my arm

across the back of the davenport. Reaching for Georgie's hair, I took a curl into my hand and elongated it, only to release it and watch it bounce back to its original shape.

"I was always jealous of these curls," I told him.

"You can have them."

"I'll take them," I said, but the truth was, I wanted to take more than just his curls. Not that I wanted to trade places with him, but I wished I could take it all away. Redo that day entirely.

"How's Mama doing?" I asked.

"Same as always." He shrugged. "She's got it in her mind that she's taking me to another hot spring once school ends."

I shifted, trying to get comfortable. "Those places are expensive." Of course Georgie knew that. I had no doubt that Mama would drive herself into the poorhouse in pursuit of fixing him.

I'd never thought of Mama as a hopeful one. She was practical. She knew when to plant the garden after the last frost, despite false starts to summer. She made sure the chores were done before sitting, resting, reading, or any other sort of dillydallying was permitted. She also knew Daddy needed a doctor even when he protested, even as he struggled to walk but insisted he didn't have time to take a break, especially not during harvest season. She planned his funeral and greeted the guests when I was too shattered by grief to help in any way. Hope hadn't saved her husband, nor her son, but hope was exactly what she sought in those hot springs.

"Does she have the money?"

"Enough," he said. "She's still renting out the farmland and just sold off the last of the orchard."

I didn't love the fact that the orchard no longer belonged to us, but Mama was resourceful, and that land was the only resource she had at the moment.

Georgie reached for his legs and repositioned them with his hands. He rubbed at his knee for a moment. I knew his braces weren't comfortable and that's part of why Mama didn't like going places. She knew that too much time in his braces put him at risk of sores, but I also knew that Georgie would run that risk if it meant getting out of the house and seeing people other than his mother.

Just then, a blue Chevy sedan pulled into the driveway across the street. I watched the driver's-side door open and a man emerge. I sat up a bit straighter, no longer reaching for Georgie's curls, no longer tired.

"What's going on?" Georgie asked.

"Potential buyers across the street."

Georgie reached for his legs and repositioned himself to better see out the window.

The man was already walking around the car, stretching his back and arms as the wind waved the flap of hair on top of his head. "He better hang on to that hair of his." Georgie laughed. "He doesn't have much more to lose."

"You know, that could be you someday," I teased.

"Nah, I don't plan to ever lose this." He ran his hand through his hair and flashed a smile of confidence, but we both knew fate would deliver whatever outcome it so wished.

I shushed my brother so we could watch in silence as the passenger door opened. I waited to see who would emerge. Would this person be someone who I could play cards alongside, share recipes with, borrow clothes from? Someone I could talk to. I leaned in closer, as if a few inches would give me a better view.

A gloved hand reached from the open door. I didn't know if house hunting was an occasion for glove wearing, but my mother-in-law would agree with this woman. Then a black oxford, much like my mother's, touched the concrete driveway. Again, not my particular taste, so perhaps we wouldn't be exchanging clothing. The woman emerged in true Harriet Nelson style, her blouse tucked into her high-waisted skirt, giving her an hourglass shape without revealing too much. Brown curls formed a nest for a half bonnet that, unlike her husband's hair, seemed unbothered by the breeze.

The woman turned toward our house, a smile spread across her tightly closed lips. Though her husband waved in our direction, apparently spotting Henry and the others in our front yard, the woman offered only a subtle nod, all the while holding the same unflinching grin.

"Hi ya!" the man called across the street before he reached for his belt and tugged his pants up high along his midsection, so high that his socks showed below his slacks.

From the front yard, Henry offered a hello and a wave before the man turned to the house and paused to spit into one of Emily's rosebushes. His wife remained standing in the same spot, a statue gripping her pearl-strapped handbag as her ankles wobbled in her oxfords.

"He forgot his wife," Georgie said as the man walked into the house. The husband caught the storm door before it fully latched and called to the woman, who finally broke her pose but not her smile. As I watched her stroll toward the front door, I wanted to stop them from going in, from exploring what had been Emily's house, what I imagined as my own.

"Is this what you do for fun all day?" Georgie teased. "Watch people out your window?"

"Sometimes." I shrugged, then ruffled his curls.

"Is it some sort of suburban hobby?" Like Mama, he didn't know why we would choose to live so close to other people, where we could look out our windows and see each other's business.

"How else are we supposed to entertain ourselves?"

"Well," Georgie started, "maybe it's time we finally do it. You know, sell the farm once and for all and move in across the street from you."

I saw the mischief sparkling in his eyes, and I surprised him with my reply. "I wish you were closer."

"No, you don't." He laughed. "You wish *I* was closer, but not her."

He was right. I did wish he could be nearby. But I wished a lot of things for Georgie: that he didn't need those crutches, that his legs worked like they used to, that he could be running for the football on our front lawn, that he could play sports and walk the school halls like others his age, that everyone could see him as capable regardless of what his legs looked like.

"I just wish—" I started to say, but Georgie interrupted.

"Here's what I say about wishing." He reached for both of my hands, repositioning them so my palms faced upward. He tapped on one hand and said, "Wish into this one." Then he tapped my other hand. "And shit into this one and see which one fills up first."

"George Alan Oscuro!" His full name escaped me, along with a laugh that shook every part of me. "The mouth on you!"

Georgie laughed along with me, his shoulders shaking just like Daddy's would do. "Don't tell Mama."

"Your secret's safe with me."

As our laughter quieted, we sat together, watching the others through the window. We saw Henry show his son how to throw a spiral and everyone cheer when Wesley threw a wobbly pass. We could hear him as he giggled each time he ran. As much as I wondered what Georgie thought as we took in the scene together, I didn't ask. He never wanted me to feel sorry for him, but that never stopped me from doing it anyway. So instead, I pulled my attention to the house again, to the man and woman exploring the inside. To light after light flickering on and off, testing the soul of the place.

Mama and Georgie were the first to leave, as was usual, and Henry's parents followed closely behind.

"Remember, just four weeks until we leave for the summer," Marian said as she hugged Wesley goodbye.

"What?" I asked.

"I thought I told you," Henry said as we stood together in the foyer, his arm around my ever-growing waist.

"Yes," Marian joined in as she pulled her long hair from inside the jacket and draped it over her shoulders. Her hair was still as sandy brown as her son's, not streaked urine-gray like my mother's, who happened to be a few years younger than her. "Henry and I spoke. I know it's not ideal, but if we don't go, we could lose the cottage for next year. Not to worry. We'll be back soon enough, and we'll spoil that baby rotten! Plus, this is your second. You know what to do now. You don't need me getting in the way."

For once, we agreed on something.

Mrs. Mayfield walked toward me and kissed me on both cheeks before putting a hand on my stomach. I swear I felt the baby jolt from the touch. "Do you know what it is yet?"

"We can't know those things," Henry reminded her.

Marian looked at me, her eyes the same cocoa brown as Henry's gazing into mine, searching for truth. "Oh, we can tell, can't we?" She called for Hank and then walked to the door. "I knew you were a boy from the first time I felt you kick." She pinched his cheek and kissed him on the lips. "A mother always knows her baby. It's our intuition. Right, Lulu?"

I smiled and nodded, playing along instead of admitting that I thought the day mother's intuition was being handed out, I must've been absent. I swore Wesley would be a girl, but look at him. This pregnancy did feel different, so maybe this one was a girl, but I didn't trust myself enough to make a prediction.

Hank kissed my forehead and told me to rest. Then he shook Henry's hand and said, "Good luck with the promotion. The pay increase is good. Maybe the travel will be, too."

"Travel?" I asked.

"I told you that," Henry muttered in a tone that said we could talk about it later. I remembered him telling me about the possible new job title and pay raise, but he had said nothing about travel. I would've remembered that. I would've remembered wondering how I would manage two kids without him in the house. I may have been the one to feed, clothe, bathe, and change them, but I still needed those hours when he was there, another adult presence in the house. "It won't be much, but I may need to travel some."

I wanted a better understanding of what "some" meant, but we could discuss that later, after his parents left. But how many times had we said to each other that we could talk later and then we never did? We still hadn't decided on baby names. One had come to me, and even though it wasn't a family name, something about it still felt right. Maybe this was intuition. If this baby was a girl, then her name would be Esther. Of course, Henry would have to agree, but first we would need to discuss it.

I couldn't help but think of how different we were then as opposed to when we were first together. When we first started dating, it took a while for me to get used to how Henry wanted to hear about my day, what I was working on for the school paper, how classes were going, if I had spoken to my mother. Admittedly, I was typically better at listening than talking, especially after we got married, when he had plenty of tales to tell about the office, what Mr. Ellis had said about his proposed floor plans, which secretary was leaving for matrimony or motherhood. I could tell him about the clang of the washing machine, the article I had read about Dr. Spock's child-rearing advice, or how Nora had told us that she saw Mr. Reilly sneak an empty vodka bottle into the trash bin early one morning. As the years progressed, our conversations grew fewer, our time interrupted and distracted. I suppose change likes to be subtle, sneaking in even when we think we're paying attention.

Even after everyone left, we didn't talk about anything. Henry sat down to read the newspaper as I cleaned up after the party and kept an eye on the couple across the street.

"Do you think they'll be the ones?" Henry asked from behind the paper.

"I don't know. They've been there a long time. But I hope not."

Henry lowered the paper. "Why's that?"

I don't have a good feeling, I wanted to say, for no reason other than it was true. But instead I told him, "I was hoping maybe there'd be a friend for Wesley." *Or me.*

"Who's to say they didn't leave the kids behind?"

"Maybe, but they seem older, too old for a child Wes's age."

Henry straightened the paper and turned the page. "You never know."

He was right. There was a lot we didn't know, but something about that couple—the balding man and his hiked-up pants, his wife with the stale smile... I knew enough to hope that the soul of the house showed them the door before they could move in.

CHAPTER FOUR

Labor started differently than it had with Wesley, sharper and with more intensity. Up until then, the pregnancy had gone smoothly. But Esther's wasn't an easy birth. The contractions started sooner than expected, so unrelenting as I waited for Henry to come home from work to rush me to the hospital, where I begged for twilight sleep, for that cocktail of drugs that would make the pain go away. They say women forget, but we don't. We tuck away the throes deep in our bones, forever carrying the memories in the recesses of our bodies.

We drove home from the hospital a few days later on the summer solstice, the longest day of the year. Though every day had been the longest since she was born, especially thanks to a dull but incessant headache. My body hurt in new ways, so deep that all I longed for was sleep that could whisk me away for days. Maybe even weeks. Months.

When we arrived home, a moving truck was parked across the street.

"Looks like we're finally getting new neighbors," Henry said as we turned into our driveway.

"I should make them something." I spoke without thought, as if the etiquette book's advice had become a reflex, which was probably what my mother-in-law had hoped when she gave it to me at my bridal shower. At the time, I didn't realize it was only the first set of instructions that would come with being a modern housewife. According to the book, I needed to properly welcome these new neighbors.

Henry parked the car and reached across the seat, putting his hand on my thigh as I held the pink bundle to my chest (Pepperell crib blanket available in blue, yellow, and pink; one book). "When you're ready," he said. "Don't rush it."

"I know," I told Henry as I began to gently rock so the baby wouldn't wake. I didn't tell him how I thought through each index card tucked within my recipe box, wondering what we had on hand and what I could whip up when he returned to work the next day, the first day I'd be left alone postpartum.

I spent most of the rest of the day in Esther's bedroom, cradling, soothing, sitting in the rocking chair Henry had bought for me. I had wanted the one Great-Grandpa had made. He had tried to get it for me, but apparently Mama insisted she needed it, that she couldn't bear to part with it quite yet. So he bought me a new one. It was beautiful, the wood so smooth and perfectly stained. It didn't creak like Mama's did. And maybe that's why it never felt just right.

As I sat and rocked, I watched out the window, waiting for

the new owners to arrive. Soon enough, the same blue Chevy sedan we saw during Wesley's party pulled to the curb across the street. *No, not the man with short pants and the wife he left behind.* I stood slowly, gingerly, and walked to the window. And there she was: the same lady in the same black oxfords, standing on the same wobbly legs, her hair pulled into a tight, unflinching bun.

With one hand holding the bundle to my breast, I reached for my hair. It lay limp and flat, having not been brushed that day, nor previous ones. I wondered what I looked like, embarrassed by what the nurses must've thought, but I had been too tired to care. But now, with this woman in front of me, I cared.

I watched as the back door of the car swung open and a little girl emerged. Not a boy, as I had hoped, but she looked to be close to Wesley's age. She pointed at the rosebushes and began to run for them, but the woman grabbed hold of her arm and held on to her wrist. Then she stood still, unnaturally so, holding on to her pocketbook. A yard ornament in a full-skirted swing dress. She looked across the street at our house. And she kept looking. Directly at me.

Or so it felt. I stood and stared back, entranced, hoping the window acted as a one-way mirror.

By then, Esther had settled, so I put her in the crib, careful to tuck the blanket beneath her, before I returned to the window and continued watching. The woman remained paused, still holding on to the girl's wrist. Finally, the man with the flap of hair across his bald head called them into the house—my house. Or what I had imagined to be my own. But now boxes and lamps and a davenport in the most awful pattern I'd ever seen in my life were being moved into the space I had been creating as my own over the last several months. If it were mine, one thing was for sure:

I would not have chosen that davenport.

I was so tired the next day. Esther's cries had kept me in her room most of the night. When they quieted, I tried to tuck her into the crib and doze in the rocking chair, but it hadn't ended with much sleep, only a crick in my neck. Home again and getting back into the swing of the day-to-day life, I forced myself to start the pot of coffee (four books) and fry Henry a few eggs for breakfast, regardless of the fact that our baby's needs consumed my every thought.

Wesley, now somehow taller than when I had left for the hospital, headed out to play in the yard as soon as he finished breakfast. He was a boy who didn't like being bound by walls and a roof. I can't say I blamed him. I used to be the same way, when I could be. On the farm, I rushed through my chores so I could run through the woods to where the creek divided our land from the neighbor's. Those were my happiest times, listening to the water wash over the moss-covered rocks as the breeze swayed the tallest branches of the trees, and the squirrels and birds acted as my only companions before Georgie got older.

Now I remained inside, looking out. My duties kept me within the four walls of our home in Greenwood Estates. Four walls that seemed to crawl closer by the minute.

I still remember the first time Henry drove me to the neighborhood. He'd been so excited to show me where we'd be living, where we'd raise our family, where we'd grow old together, him with a briefcase in his hand and me standing firmly beside him on the front porch steps. It hadn't been the home I had imagined when I was a child. Maybe it wasn't even the one I would choose if I could. But it was where our life was.

As Esther slept, I wanted to rest my eyes for a bit, but that damn book kept nagging at me, reminding me that the new neighbors' presence meant there was no time for such frivolity. Now was the time for good first impressions and obligations of neighborliness, not naps.

That book had a way of haunting me. I knew making a dish was a nice thing to do. I didn't need a book to tell me that, but somehow I felt its judgment, as if it were watching me, waiting for me to be the good neighbor. Mrs. Mayfield thought it could turn me into the wife I hadn't been taught to be. Maybe the book had taught me how to be a good housewife. Or maybe it had shown me how to wear a mask.

Truth be told, despite the sense of obligation and the full-body exhaustion, I wanted to take a dish across the street because then maybe I could see inside.

When the phone rang, I ran for it, grabbing the receiver off the hook as quickly as possible before the ringing roused Esther's cries and I'd spend the next few hours attempting to quiet them.

"Lulu, honey." Nora hesitated, as if she had forgotten why she had called. "God, I've missed you. How are you?"

"Fine," I said. "Tired."

"I imagine." She paused again before continuing. "You're sure you're—"

"I'm good, Nora." The socks were all clean, and I hadn't cried into a laundry hamper yet.

"I hope the hospital treated you well. I mean"—Nora paused

for a moment before her voice rose—"with royalty in their midst."

"I'm not sure they realized that." I smiled, always thankful for her humor and the fact that she had called to check on me.

Then her voice dropped. "Did you see the new neighbors?"

"I did. Three of them."

"No. Five of them." I assumed she hadn't been watching out the window as closely as I had been, but before I could correct her, she continued. "I already stopped by. They have two boys, a bit older than the girl, but they're away at school." Leave it to Nora to already have the gossip on the new family, but I couldn't help but wonder what she had told them in return. "No one should have more than two kids. That's simply obnoxious. And Hatti's on her fourth. Bless her heart."

I laughed, finally feeling awake, my head throbbing a bit less for the first time in days. Leave it to Nora to pull me out of my fog. She had been my first friend in Greenwood, ever since the day Old Man Reilly got locked out of his house when he was getting the paper and Nora called to make sure I wasn't missing the scene unfolding across the street. Of course, Nora was friends with everyone, or at least friendly. She believed in keeping her friends close and her enemies closer, swearing she got more dirt that way.

"And did you see that davenport?" I asked as I moved around the kitchen, testing the length of the phone cord so I could gather the ingredients for the welcome dish.

"Awful. Can't imagine the drapes that go with it." Nora laughed, that deep bellow of hers ringing out so that I had to pull the receiver away from my ear. "Are you taking them one of your famous salads?"

"Of course." She knew me well, but since I hadn't made it to the grocery store, my options were limited. I had settled on a creamy lime Jell-O with fruit cocktail, but then I wondered if I should double the recipe in case the boys came home. With the phone firmly lodged between my ear and shoulder, I got on the floor and dug the mold out of the back of the cabinet, trying not to make too much noise.

"So glad the queen has returned," she said. We both laughed.

The crick in my neck tightened as I tried to hold on to the receiver. Needing to stretch and focus on the recipe, I attempted to say a quick goodbye.

"Lu?" She was the only friend who called me that. "Get some rest, and I'm here—"

"I know."

And I did know. I knew she was nearby if I needed anything. I also knew that she had her own two kids, plus dinner to make and a house to keep. We were all nearby one another, close enough to lend a hand, yet far enough apart to blanket ourselves in the illusion of isolation.

CHAPTER FIVE

I saw Mrs. Reilly waddle her way across the front yard, her hair still in rollers as she beat me to delivering her welcome gift. But of course she did. She seemed to believe that neighborliness was built on competition. To her, the shortest clipped lawn, the most squared hedge-bush, the handiest husband were all indications of the best Greenwood residents. And all just so happened to belong to her.

Shortly after breakfast, I watched her carry a casserole across the street, knowing she must've pulled it out of the freezer and thawed it in the oven to make it seem fresh. My offering took more time. But I didn't want to wait too long. So, that afternoon, I took the salad out of the fridge and placed a platter on top like a lid before flipping it upside down.

Normally, the salad would slide right out. Sometimes I might need to give it a little jiggle or a few pats to encourage it. This time none of that was necessary. I had tested the top with my finger. It had the right resistance. It shook and shimmied as gelatin should. But as I pulled up on the mold, a waterfall of green liquid and chunks of canned fruit cascaded from the plate onto the counter, soaking my apron, the dress beneath, and my shoes. I stood frozen in the kitchen with half-congealed goo dripping down the front of my body.

I couldn't believe it. That had never happened before. I tried to figure out what I had done wrong, how I had failed. I suppose I had rushed it. Maybe I had miscalculated when doubling the recipe. Or perhaps I had been too tired and distracted, always anticipating Esther's cries.

I thought about cursing, screaming, maybe throwing the mold against the wall. Perhaps I could shatter that kitchen clock that ticks too loud at night or tear apart the stamps that sat waiting—mocking my inaction—on the sideboard, rip them to shreds and watch the confetti rain down. But instead I wiped at the couple tears that slipped out and stored the rest deep within the ever-growing reservoir.

I looked at the clock and forced myself to come up with another plan. Reaching into the freezer, I took out a peach pie I had baked in the weeks before Esther was born.

As it thawed in the oven, I changed myself for the second time that day. The first time was when my breasts, so full of milk, leaked through my bra and soaked my top. Feeling the fullness starting to build again, I shoved a few tissues into my bra, hoping they would absorb a potential leak. I looked in the mirror and barely recognized the woman looking back at me. My skin was pale and my lips were still chapped from the stale hospital air.

I tried to fix the things I could, but no amount of makeup

could hide the dark circles beneath my eyes. I ran a brush through my hair and attempted a simple French twist, but the bobby pins pressed into my scalp, exacerbating the dull headache that had been lurking beneath the surface. In a final effort to look presentable, I dabbed on a bit of mascara and looked away before I became too self-conscious to even leave the house.

I didn't put much thought into the shirt dress I grabbed from the closet before I hurried across the street. I felt like a stranger standing in front of the house I knew well. Before ringing the doorbell, I took a deep breath, trying to settle butterflies I hadn't expected. I had only seen this woman and her frozen smile from across the street. Perhaps she wasn't as old as her shoes and furniture choices let on. Maybe the way she clutched her purse and daughter's arm showed earnestness. Maybe I shouldn't judge too quickly and from across the street.

Standing on the doorstep, I began to regret my outfit, its buttons pulling across my chest and stomach. I certainly had more curves now but not in all the places I wanted. The dress stretched across my midsection, showing off the softness in my stomach. After having Wesley, I was surprised by how long it took for my stomach to return to its previous shape, how I still looked pregnant for months afterward. Of course this time would be no different.

As the door creaked open, I smiled and did my best to brighten my eyes. "Welcome to Greenwood," I said with forced cheer.

The woman stood in the open door. She was even shorter than I had thought.

"Thank you," she replied with dimples firmly divoted into her cheeks, a smile plastered across her porcelain face. I waited for her eyes to meet mine, but they focused on my nude, scaly lips instead. I had forgotten to put on lipstick—an unforgivable sin, according to Nora.

I waited a moment for her to say more, but she held a distant stare, watching my lips, so I filled the dead air before the silence became too awkward.

"I'm Lulu Mayfield." She continued staring at my mouth, saying nothing. I wondered if she noticed the cracked, peeling skin. Or maybe she was reading my lips. Maybe she was hard of hearing, so I began to slow my speech, raise my voice, elongating each syllable. "From across the street." I pointed in the direction of our house.

She reached her hand toward mine. "I'm Bitsy Betser."

Her voice was quiet, understated. I leaned in and asked, "Betsy?"

She cleared her throat and said with more volume, "Bitsy." She emphasized the vowel as we shook hands. Bitsy's palm felt small and cold, perhaps partly because mine was so warm from holding the steaming pie. I waited for her to invite me in, in part to set down the pie, but more importantly, so I could take a look. I wanted to see what she had done with the place. I felt it urging me inside, pulling me to step across the threshold, but I resisted for the moment.

"Welcome to the neighborhood. I brought you a little something." I spoke loudly enough that the entire street could probably hear me.

"That's kind of you. You didn't have to."

Of course I did. We both knew that. It was part of what we did, of what was expected of us. And her response was part of the game: feign modesty. "I was happy to," I told her. Nothing like starting a relationship with a lie.

"Well, thank you," she said as the smile lessened. But the closer I looked, the more I realized it wasn't really a smile. Sure, her cheeks were dimpled, but they grooved even when she wasn't smiling. It was a static, forced upturn of the lips. But they remained closed, as if guarding something—perhaps conversation, because the woman didn't seem like she wanted to talk much. I wondered if Nora had gotten Bitsy to talk, but she rarely needed two people to have a conversation.

Feeling the heat of the pie and a fullness beginning again in my breasts, I decided to take matters into my own hands. "I hope you don't mind if I set this down." Bitsy didn't budge at first, but as I moved toward her, she began to step back.

"Oh, yes, sure."

She moved out of the doorway and motioned for me to come inside.

In the day I had spent creating a liquid pool of lime gelatin and fruit carnage, this woman had been making herself at home, so much so that she even had a portrait already hanging in the front hall. It's not what I would've hung there. The Betsers looked back from the picture, Bitsy in the middle, surrounded by her smiling husband and their sons. The Betser boys all looked at the camera, their eyes bright and open. Not a single hair looked out of place. Except for Bitsy. She looked different—taut skin and no gray hair. While she was surrounded by three happy family members who all looked in the same direction, Bitsy looked off to the left, her eyes dark, her lips flat, a lock of hair flipping outward, as if a flag that no one noticed.

The living room was arranged with armchairs flanking the davenport, which looked even worse up close—a putrid pattern of green, brown, blue, yellow, orange, and red floral, as if a subdued rainbow had exploded into a forestscape onto the couch. She had lamps and knickknacks arranged on side tables, and china already filling the cabinet in the dining room.

But she had done more than simply place her belongings in the house I had imagined as my own. In the short time she had been there, she had already covered the far wall in the eat-in kitchen with new wallpaper. I paused in the doorway for a moment, taking in the faint blue background, the color of the sky on a calm day as it broke beneath the cloud line. Thin, gold lines curved and intersected, creating a series of butterflies that swarmed the walls.

"Well, looks like you've been busy," I said as I gathered myself and walked into the kitchen. I placed the pie on the counter next to the Hamilton Beach food mixer (eleven books). Organdy ruffled curtains (one-and-a-half books) framed the kitchen window, while the five-piece coppertone aluminum mold set (one-and-three-fourths books) hung on a pegboard. I wondered if she used them for cooking or decoration.

"You collect stamps, too?" I asked before turning toward Bitsy, who watched me with surprise. She walked toward me and took the pie from where I'd placed it on the counter and moved it to the stovetop, as if correcting my mistake. "I'm sorry—" I began. Apparently, I had made myself too much at home. I brushed my bangs from my eyes, seeing more clearly that, though I may have known this house better than she did, it was not mine. But before I could complete my apology, a small voice interrupted.

"Who is it?" a little girl called from behind Bitsy. She spoke normally to her mother, answering my question of whether Bitsy was hard of hearing. The girl looked different from her mother, an elongated face and no dimples, though her hair was a similar shade of brown.

Bitsy reached for the girl's hand. "This is Katherine. And this is Mrs. Mayfield," she introduced us to each other. "She brought a pie."

"Peach," I told them. "Like what we grew on my family's farm."

"Oh, how nice," Bitsy said. "Did you pick them?"

Yes, from the bin at the A&P. "No, I'm afraid the orchard's out of the family now."

"Can we have some?" Katherine interjected. She was so beautiful. A satin ribbon—the same color as the gold flecks in her wise, hazel eyes—held her hair away from her face, but the ends of her long locks were tangled. I wondered if Bitsy had to sit her down at the end of the day and brush out the knots, just as Mama used to do for me, one hand on top of my head as the other pulled the brush through my hair. She didn't like it when I told her it hurt. If I ever tried to stop her by reaching back, she would smack my hand with the flat side of the brush. Standing in Bitsy's kitchen that day, I swore I could feel the pain in my knuckles as if Mama had just paddled my hands.

"Not until after dinner. After vegetables. What do we say about sugar?"

Katherine's smile faded as she recited, "A sweet tooth makes for a round belly."

I watched Bitsy's gaze go from my mouth to the pie and

then to my stomach. My hands reflexively attempted to cover the paunch that pulled at my dress. I knew I should've chosen something different to wear. The look on Bitsy's face proved it, the smile having faded as her eyes grew wide.

"I'm sure it's delicious, Mrs. Mayfield," Bitsy said.

"Please, call me Lulu. Is Katherine your only child?" I asked in an attempt to make small talk. The portrait—and Nora—had told me otherwise, but in the moment, I grasped for a way to change the subject.

"We—Gary and I—have two boys. Jake's sixteen and Larry's…" She paused for a moment, looking to the floor as her lips moved, but no sound came out. Then she continued, "Fourteen."

I waited for her to say more, to say where they were, why they weren't coming to say hello, but we simply stood in silence, me watching her as she looked at the linoleum.

"Are they here?" I pressed, glancing down the hall.

Bitsy put her hands in her apron pockets as she said, "They're away. At school."

"The academy," Katherine offered. "Getting discipline and edgy…edgu…edga—"

"Education." The word came out faint, as if catching in Bitsy's throat on the way out.

I wanted to know more—where they were, how long they had been there, if she wanted them there—but I recognized her downward gaze, the furrow of her brow, the way she stuffed her hands into her pockets. While some might dig for more information, I understood how it felt to want to remain quiet.

So I turned to Katherine and asked, "And how old are you?" The girl held up her hand with all four fingers and her thumb displaying her age. "Five. Wow! My son is almost five. He just turned four. Maybe you could play some time." I looked at Bitsy for approval. She continued watching my lips, but as the wall clock ticked in the silence, she made no attempt to add to the conversation. I took it upon myself to fill the awkward pause and spoke to the girl again. "Would you like to meet him sometime?" Katherine nodded.

As the girl began to tell me all the games she liked to play, the wallpaper caught my eye. I watched as beams of sunlight lit some of the butterflies so that they shimmered, sparkled, and even… fluttered.

I blinked and reached for the counter to steady myself. Then I dared to look back. A single butterfly caught in the sun's rays. And I saw it again, the flap of the stenciled wing.

I closed my eyes as the room began to spin. "I'm sorry," I interrupted Katherine from whatever she was telling me. "I'm afraid I need to get going."

"Oh," Bitsy said. Or maybe she asked it. I didn't hear the tone and I didn't look at her. I peeked at that butterfly, waiting for it to move again.

"I'm afraid I need to get home."

We said our goodbyes as I walked to the front door. Then I ran across the street, the world spinning around me, my full breasts aching with each step. Esther's cries called to me as I walked inside, but the butterfly haunted me as I held her.

As my milk let down and Esther nursed to contentment, I thought of the flutter that I knew couldn't have been real, a trick of the sunlight that danced across the gold lines that ignited my imagination. That was the only explanation.

And I thought of Bitsy. She looked different up close—smaller, older, even more uncertain than when I saw her stand on wobbly legs from across the street. The woman barely spoke, didn't make eye contact, shared little else other than that forced smile that seemed designed to act as a fortress. The question was: What was it guarding? What did that woman—with the butterflies trapped in the walls—have to hide?

CHAPTER SIX

I hated the quiet, the type that crept in during the dark hours of the night—the *dormiveglia*, as Daddy used to call it. It was one of the few Italian words he remembered his grandmother speaking, but he said it with a tongue born and bred in America, a fact his *nonna* both celebrated and mourned.

Dormiveglia are the veiled moments between sleeping and waking, the space in time that floats instead of hurries—a reprieve for some and an unrest for others. Daddy and I shared a lot of those moments over the years, neither of us sound sleepers. I wondered if Nonna was the same way, if that's why she used the word and taught it to him, who passed it to me.

When Daddy was still alive, I didn't mind those silken hours, having a companion to sit with me and sip milk the cows had given earlier that day—or better yet, steal a piece of pie if we had any. We didn't need to speak. We listened to the cicadas and tree frogs, the crickets and other night critters who sang their songs as others slept. We simply sat and sipped or nibbled, before slipping back upstairs to hopefully coax a few more hours of sleep to visit us.

And now, since Esther, the silence roused me each night, stirring me in anticipation of a cry to come, a need to attend to. Ensconced in *dormiveglia*, I pleaded with myself to fall back to sleep before I woke too much. I scooted toward Henry, feeling the warmth radiate off his body, willing it to act as a blanket that could soothe me back to slumber, but I quickly began to sweat and my mouth watered, thirsting for a sip of late-night milk and a dash of cinnamon. Too restless for sleep, I surrendered to the night and got up.

Our home had few sounds, at least compared to the home of my childhood, the one my great-grandfather had built—frame, floors, furniture, and all. Georgie and I couldn't even roll over in bed without our parents hearing the wood-plank floors creak beneath our bed frames, as if history cried out with each movement, especially the ones in the still of the dark night.

In our Greenwood home, the windows dampened the chirps of the frogs and crickets, the trees standing too far from our home for the hum of the cicadas to seep through the window panes. On the inside, the insulation and carpet quieted sounds. Even still, there was a creak in the floor right outside Wesley's door. I had learned quickly in his newborn days to walk nearer the opposite side of the hall and take a giant step past the door, so as not to wake him. He slept more soundly now, not having received the family curse—I wondered if Esther had—but I still took that step with caution.

Henry had forgotten to pull the curtains closed before coming to bed, so the streetlights poured orange light into the living room, bathing the davenport, darkening the corners, reflecting off the mirrors Mrs. Mayfield had chosen, transforming the room into a combination of warm light and dark mystery. The lights reflected in the gaudy mirrors, but I refused to look at them, not simply because I hated them, but because I was afraid of what I might see. Though my rational mind knew ghosts didn't exist, my imagination could be convinced otherwise.

Mirrors might hold haunted things, but windows showed reality. I moved closer to peer outside, to see Greenwood as the others slept. All the lights were off at the house across the street. With the car parked in the garage, it still appeared as if no one had moved in, as if it still sat waiting for me. If only. As if on cue, a light clicked on in the front bedroom, reminding me that the Betsers had arrived. I wondered if Katherine was a restless sleeper like me. But didn't she know to keep the lights off so she could creep through the dark hours unnoticed?

I went into the kitchen and opened the fridge, the light creating a wedge of brightness, illuminating my nightgown. I hadn't bothered to grab my robe, too hot for another layer of clothing. I welcomed the cool of the linoleum on my bare feet.

The milk was nearly gone, so I filled a tumbler (two books for a set of six, plus the pitcher) only half-full, saving enough for Wesley. I hoped he'd drink it in the morning with his breakfast. He had taken only a sip at dinner before asking to dump the rest down the drain. He typically drank two full glasses, knowing that it was good for his growing bones. But that night he had refused more than the sip. I hoped it wasn't a sign that he was coming down with something. What would happen if he got Esther sick?

I touched the glass to my cheek, absorbing as much of its coolness as I could, when I realized I wasn't the only soul awake in all of Greenwood. The cry was low, muffled. I stopped breathing and listened, waiting for Esther's wails to get louder, for her to demand my presence. But this cry sounded different.

Maybe it was Wesley. Maybe he was sick after all.

My heart started to pound with the possibility as sweat began to form and prickle along my lips, neck, and hairline. I wondered how I would take care of a newborn and a sick child. What if they both needed me at the same time?

Don't get ahead of yourself. I heard Henry's voice in my head. He always told me that when he thought I was worrying too much, as if those words would stop the racing thoughts.

And then I heard a squeak, coming from the patio door.

A cat too fat to be a stray stood on the outside looking in. She reached upward, balancing on her hind legs as her front feet pawed and screeched against the glass door. As her mouth opened and a cry escaped, I laughed, relieved that the sound came from a cat and not one of the kids.

As I opened the door and stepped onto the patio, she tried to make her way into the house, but I moved her aside with my foot, her soft fur brushing across my toes.

"Now, now, kitty," I told her, and she responded with a quiet meow.

The cat circled through my legs, making figure eights, her gray body strutting with each step, her tail high as I walked to the lounge chair. I had barely sat down when she jumped into my lap. She kept her eyes trained on me, her white mustache shining even in the darkness. I tried to take a sip of my milk, but she bumped against my hand, attempting to get her nose in the glass, wanting a drink for herself.

"This is mine," I said, reminding myself of something I would correct Wesley for saying.

I stretched to the side, moving out of her reach so I could take a sip. As the first drop hit my tongue, instead of the refreshment I had hoped for, a sour taste filled my mouth. Grocery-store milk never tasted as good as fresh from the cow, but this taste went beyond the store-bought difference. No wonder Wesley had refused to drink it for dinner.

I held the glass to my nose, trying to sniff it as the cat did the same. I hadn't been to the grocery store since Esther. I thought I could stretch a few more days, but apparently I would need to get there sooner than I had realized.

The cat didn't seem to mind the sour smell. She tried to fit her head inside the glass but could barely get past her whiskers. Her tongue lapped up what it could. No use in it going to waste, so I reached for the Flying Saucer that Wesley had left outside, turned it upside down to use as a bowl, and poured the rest of the milk into it. The cat immediately jumped down and began lapping up the milk, her purr growing even louder.

When she was done, she jumped back onto my lap, tucked herself into a crescent, and closed her eyes. I welcomed the touch of her softness, her purr vibrating my lap as she settled. But I quickly began to sweat under the warmth of her body.

Even still, I didn't want her to leave. I stroked her fur as she drifted to sleep. I had missed the feel of an animal. I had taken for granted all the animals who filled our farm: cows, goats, chickens, a few pigs, ducks, wild rabbits, a stray cat or two each season, a dog to herd the livestock. Daddy preferred the animals who served a purpose or held a job. I liked the ones that I could pet, cuddle with, take on walks along the creek, curl up alongside for an afternoon nap under my oak tree.

Remnants of milk glistened in the moonlight, covering the cat's natural mustache. I ran my fingers through her smoky-gray fur. She blended in with the night, nearly invisible as clouds passed over the moon.

"Luna," I said. "That's what I'll call you."

Luna seemed to approve of her name. She twisted her head so the underneath of her chin pointed to the night sky. Her purr deepened before fading. She slept so easily, peacefully, effortlessly.

I tried to do the same, but my mind wasn't ready to settle. I thought about the grocery store and the list I needed to make, wondered how many stamps that trip might give me, and how much closer I'd be to getting that treasure, especially since I had to start over when I got the percolator. I thought about Wesley and how much he had grown in the time I had been at the hospital. It hadn't even been that long, but the moment I walked into the house, I saw the difference. I thought that perhaps I should introduce him to Katherine across the street. Why couldn't she have been a boy so they could better play together?

Then I thought of the pie, hoped it tasted fresh, and wondered if the Betsers had liked it, if they had enjoyed the fruit swimming in thick syrup with cinnamon and nutmeg, the crust flaky. They wouldn't know this, but it tasted just like Mama used to make. And I wondered if she would be proud of me. If she could taste what I had made, would she be happy that I had figured it out, that I had worked to replicate her prize-winning dessert? It had taken trial and error and so many peach pies that Henry asked if I couldn't use another fruit, just once. But then I got it. The spices balanced. The crust golden. The peaches sliced to the perfect thickness.

Would she be happy? Or would she say, "Don't expect awards. Life rarely gives them," as she'd said countless other times? I didn't need a blue ribbon from the county fair like she'd gotten. I only wanted her to be proud of me.

It's surprising how much you can miss someone you're not sure ever really loved you. Maybe I should write her a letter. It had been a while since I had called and even longer since I had visited. A letter would be easier to manage. I could update her on Esther, how Wesley could ride a tricycle. But maybe she wouldn't want to hear that, especially since her own son couldn't do something of that sort.

Maybe I should tell her I now understood how exhausting it was to care for someone else, to be the one who must meet their constant needs. But those in my charge would grow and become capable and move on to take care of themselves. Unless they were dealt the same fate.

But I couldn't think of that then. I couldn't let those thoughts wriggle in. Henry always told me that I couldn't blame her. But she blamed me, so why not?

I tried to do like Luna. I closed my eyes, breathed deeply, and begged sleep to come. I listened to the frogs, crickets, and cicadas calling in the darkness. I felt the night breeze across my bare legs, toes, hands, cheeks, and still-throbbing head. For a moment, I thought I could will myself to join Luna in her slumber.

But then the voice whispered through the night and blew cool across my skin, *It was your fault.*

I turned to look, to make sure Henry or Wesley hadn't woken. But I was alone on the patio with the cat on my lap. I knew the voice hadn't come from them.

Your fault, it said again, filling every inch of my body, forcing goose pimples to pop along my arms and legs. I shifted in the lounger, attempting to draw my legs into my body. Luna chirped awake, her sleep disrupted by my movements.

"I'm sorry," I said, running my hand across her head, rubbing the wells beside her ears, willing her *dormiveglia* to turn back to rest, praying she wouldn't leave me, becoming jealous of how easily she fell back asleep as I sat in the silence of the night and reminded myself, *I didn't know. I didn't know. I didn't know.*

CHAPTER SEVEN

I don't know how I ended up in the camera store. The only place I needed to be was the A&P next door, but somehow I found myself being greeted by the salesperson as the bell on the closing door jingled behind me. Despite my sore muscles and desire to stay in bed that morning, I knew I needed to get to the store. So I had gotten dressed, pulled up my hair, and dabbed on a bit of makeup. Then I had stood frozen in my living room, holding my pocketbook, trying to figure out how to manage a trip to the store. I had never thought through a grocery store trip so much before that moment: how I would load the car, drive the few blocks, walk the aisles, manage it all alone.

The early days were always hardest, making adjustments, finding new rhythms, trying to make it through the day when all you wanted to do was curl up and sleep for weeks. Nora stopped by as I was gathering the courage to leave. Thankfully, this time she didn't find me in a fit on the nursery floor, though

I nearly cried when she offered to stay at the house so I could run my errand alone.

"Hello again, Mrs. Mayfield."

I snapped awake as the man behind the camera counter greeted me. Last I remembered, I had been sitting in the car as it idled in the garage. This was the first time I had been out of the house since coming home from the hospital. Feeling a tether tugging on me, pulling at a tension to bring me back inside the house, I had needed a moment before I could put the car in reverse, back out, and drive down the street. But I didn't remember doing any of that.

I clutched my handbag as sweat began to form on my upper lip, my wobbly legs aching despite the warm shower I had taken to try to loosen them. Then there was the still-throbbing in my head that pounded at the same rhythm as my accelerating heart.

"Are you okay, Mrs. Mayfield?"

That was a good question. I hesitated for a moment before responding, but quickly decided that I didn't need to let this nice man know that I didn't remember having arrived there.

After a quick breath, I smiled and said, "Yes, Mr. Perry. I was out running errands and thought I'd stop in to take another look."

"Ah, yes. It's a nice one," he said as he reached into the glass case and pulled out the Kodak Pony 135 without having to ask. "But you know that already."

I certainly did. I had looked at it the last few times I'd had film developed. I didn't need a new camera, I told myself. Plus, if I really wanted one, I could use my stamps, but the one in the catalog was not as nice as this one.

I reached for the camera, hoping Mr. Perry wouldn't see the

sweat on my hands. The plastic casing made it lighter than I always anticipated.

"We've missed you around here," he said. It had been a while since I had stopped by. I still hadn't developed the film from Wesley's party, nor any baby pictures. "Do you have a roll for me today?"

"I knew I was forgetting something," I lied. "I suppose I'll have to bring that by another time." After I'd completed the roll with newborn photos, tiny toes, and gas-induced grins. Another thing I should add to my to-do list.

For that moment, I ignored the tug of the tether that tried to pull me home. I pushed aside the nagging call of the grocery store and peered through the viewfinder. Every other camera I had ever used had a waist-level finder with a mirrored perspective. But with this one, I could hold it to my eye and see the direct view, the actual perspective of the image I wanted to take.

I looked around the store, framing various shots, focusing on other cameras, customers, and even the view out the storefront window. I watched people walking by, the clouds shifting overhead, birds flitting from one bush to another. Then I watched as a blue Chevy pulled into a parking spot and my new neighbor and her daughter exited. My heartbeat quickened. It was a Tuesday. Shouldn't she have shopped the day before? Then I watched as she held on to Katherine with one hand and pulled a pile of laundry from the back seat of her car, her bun tight and her bangs in a stiff curl across her forehead.

As they walked into the dry cleaner a few doors down, Mr. Perry pulled me back into the store. "Is today the day?" he asked, calling my attention away from the woman outside the window.

"I'm afraid not," I said as I handed him the camera. I glanced at my watch. I had already been gone too long, and I hadn't been to the grocery store yet. As the tether home pulled on me, my body tightened from my calves to my stomach and up to my mind.

"Are you sure you're okay, Mrs. Mayfield?"

"Yes, thank you for asking." And for being nosy. "I just lost track of time and should be going."

As I hurried out of the store and into the next one, I felt the pressure in my breasts begin to build. I tried to shop quickly, but I hadn't put together much of a list other than milk, bread, and something for dinner. I thought about getting some pork chops, especially since Nora said there was a sale. Or, I considered Wesley's favorite: meat loaf. I tried to make a decision, but my mind felt heavy. Hazy. I needed something simple. I suppose that's why the TV dinners caught my eye. Plus, we had never had them before. I doubted that Nora and Hatti had served them either. After all, wasn't it our job to make good, nutritious food for our families? But in that moment, something quick and easy was exactly what I needed.

I glanced around the store before I walked to the freezer section. No one I knew shopped on Tuesdays, so when the coast seemed clear, I grabbed three of each variety: beef, turkey, and chicken.

As I dropped the dinners into the cart, I swore I heard the hum of a song, not the grocery-store radio playing from the speakers above, but the same few bars of a song, whispered slightly off-key. The tune began to grow in volume, as if it were lurking behind me. I glanced over my shoulder and discovered the source.

"Oh! Bitsy." I needed to get home, and I hoped she was not in the mood for small talk. "It's nice to see you," I lied again, as I tried to figure out a way to make a quick exit. I looked at my watch. I had been gone an entire hour, nearly twice what I had hoped for, and I still hadn't checked out.

"Hello, Mrs. Mayfield," she greeted me, with the warmth of sliced bread straight out of the bag. Katherine stood beside her mother and kept one hand on the cart, her eyes barely peering over the handle.

"Please, call me Lulu," I reminded her.

For a moment I stopped and looked at her: the always-present dimples on her cheeks, the curl that hung to her eyebrows, the grip she had on the handle of her shopping cart so that the skin stretched tight across her knuckles. I imagined looking at her through that camera's direct-view finder, centering her in the frame, composing the picture, not as a portrait, but as a full-length image capturing an everyday moment of an everywoman housewife with a dutiful daughter by her side. Would the image show the deepening creases beside her eyes, the strand of hair the bobby pin had missed, the lipstick painted outside the lines, the downturned lips of her daughter's mouth?

"Are you getting snacks, too?" Bitsy asked. I didn't know why she assumed I would be getting snacks. Apparently, she hadn't looked in my shopping cart—thankfully.

"I needed to get a few things, for dinner and such." I moved in front of the cart, trying to hide the boxed meals from her. She didn't need to know what I planned to feed my family. "We were running low."

"Ah, yes." I willed myself to not look at my watch. Why was

she there on a Tuesday? Didn't she follow the schedule like all the others? Then she continued, "I was grabbing a few things. For our game tomorrow."

"Game?"

"Yes. Spades."

Spades? What was this woman talking about? Nora, Hatti, and I had been playing spades for the last couple of years, since Hatti had moved into the neighborhood. It had always been the three of us, and Emily when she was there. We took turns gathering in one of our homes as the kids napped. It was the time when we could chat about the kids, husbands, and neighbors.

But how had she found out? I certainly hadn't said anything, not to mention I didn't realize we had a game coming up.

As I was too confused to respond, Bitsy spoke again, "I'll see you tomorrow."

"Tomorrow?"

"For spades." Surely this woman was confused. "Nora invited me. I assumed—"

I assumed if a card game was happening, my good friend would have told me, but Nora had said nothing that morning when she stopped by unannounced. Now that I thought of it, why *had* she stopped by? It seemed that she had arrived to judge the state of my house, the clutter and dust that had filled the place since I had been too tired to keep up with the schedule. I saw the look on her face as she glanced around the room, trying to not be obvious, but I knew her well enough to know what she was thinking.

"Yes, of course." Trying to hide my confusion, I sealed my lips together and blinked to keep the tears in my eyes. This woman did not need to see my hurt, but apparently I wasn't hiding my feelings too well.

"Are you okay?" she asked.

Not exactly. I had just learned that my friends were planning to get together without me. How was I supposed to feel? Not to mention that I needed to get home. I had been gone too long. Esther would be hungry. Plus, I could stand another aspirin. But this woman didn't need to know any of that.

"Why, yes," I told her. Perhaps the etiquette book would suggest I go a step further and thank her for asking, but instead, I held that smile, mirroring hers, and glared at her. Then I said, "But I'm afraid I do need to be going."

Before I could walk away, Bitsy pointed at the frozen meals in my cart and said, "I looked at those. But Gary likes things home-cooked." Her voice may have been warm. Someone passing by might have thought she sounded kind. But I saw the insult drip from her tongue.

Then she started humming again as she and Katherine pushed the cart down the aisle. I stood in the frozen foods, willing my breasts to not leak, the tears to stay hidden, and the redness in my cheeks to fade before I had to check out.

The sound of the vacuum cleaner greeted me as I walked into the house. I dropped the bag onto the kitchen counter. The entire drive home, I had played conversations in my mind, trying to find the right words to say to Nora, to make it seem casual, as if I wasn't hurt about the card game, to let her feel the guilt and shame of having left out her supposed friend.

As ready as I was to expose her treason, Wesley stopped me in my tracks. As I rounded the corner into the living room, I spotted him with a dust rag, wiping off the end table.

"Look what we did!" Wesley waved the cloth in the air. "We cleaned!"

I paused the running dialogue in my mind and looked around. The toys were put away, clothes folded, and curtains open so the sunlight poured into the house. The half-empty glass of water I had put on the end table as I managed early labor was gone. The place looked so much better than when I had left.

As the vacuum turned off, Nora called from down the hall, "We didn't expect you back so soon. Let me finish up the hallway."

"You didn't have to do this," I said as I walked to the piles of clothes on the couch and realized they were sorted and organized by who they belonged to.

"I know. But I don't mind. It gave us something to do. I just need a minute—"

"Really, Nora. You've done enough." I meant for it to sound grateful, but apparently the tone didn't come out right, maybe because the exhaustion was beginning to set in, as was the realization that I needed to feed Esther. I was surprised she wasn't crying from all the noise.

Nora began, "Oh, I'm sorry—" As she should be. That was the moment I should've let her know how I felt, to tell her that Bitsy had let the cat out of the bag. But I couldn't do it.

"No, I'm sorry." I disappointed myself. How many times had I stopped myself from speaking up? But silence had been the better companion for far too long. "It's just…I didn't sleep well."

"I understand. Let me put this away and we'll get out of here, let you get some rest."

As she wound the vacuum cord, the words forced their way out. "I saw Bitsy at the store. She told me about tomorrow."

Nora paused as she put the vacuum in the hall closet, the same location she kept hers in her own home. "About that—" she said with her back turned to me, her voice dampened by the closet. As I waited for her to continue, I wondered if Bitsy had misunderstood. "I thought it would be good to get together."

Now that she had been caught, I told myself, she was going to invite me.

"Nora, you don't have to—"

"Have to what? It's time for a game. I know it's hard to get out of the house, so I thought we'd come to you."

"Here?" It wasn't my turn to host.

"That's why we cleaned, so you didn't have to do it."

I looked around the house. It looked better than it had in months. And she had done this all in the time it took me to buy a single bag of groceries.

"But you didn't even ask me."

Nora walked toward me, put a hand on my arm, and lowered her voice. "I know. But I know you, and I didn't want to give you a reason to make an excuse." She called for James and then continued before I could say anything. "We'll be here during naptime. Don't worry about snacks or drinks. Don't clean anymore. I'll set up the card table when I get here." She walked to the front door as she continued, "I already told Hatti that we'll play here. And Bitsy, too."

"Did you have to invite her?"

"Now, Lulu, I'm supposed to be the mean one." Nora winked before she turned to watch James and Marjorie run toward the road. "Look both ways!" she yelled as they paused and then sprinted across the street. "I gotta go. But please, Lulu, get some rest. No offense, but you still look like hell."

Apparently, I looked the way I felt.

CHAPTER EIGHT

I thought I would be happy when Henry got home that night. Maybe *relieved* was a better word. But the man who walked in the door wasn't the one I needed. He took off his tie and jacket before he mixed himself a drink, a habit he had gotten into when I was in the hospital and we both seemed fine with the new arrangement. He emptied that glass before he said a word. By the time we sat at the table, he had downed at least two drinks.

"Do I have to eat this?" Wesley asked as I placed the compartmentalized dinner tray in front of him. He leaned in closely, took a sniff, and wrinkled his nose.

Henry rubbed at his temples and said, "Your mother made it." Then he took a sip of his third vodka martini.

"But—"

"No buts. This is what she made, so this is what we have to eat." Henry looked at me and nodded, like I should thank him for taking control of the situation, for reminding them both that they must eat whatever I put in front of them, and be thankful for it.

"Remember?" I said to Wesley. "I showed you this when I got home. You were so excited."

Wesley slouched in his seat, his arms hanging at his sides, his shoulders slumped.

"It looked better in the picture," he mumbled before Henry reminded him to sit up straight and act right, but the kid did have a point.

What didn't look better in the picture? Go pick up any magazine off the end table and you'll find all sorts of pictures—the perfume and makeup ads, the tips for being a better housewife, the foolproof recipes, the articles on how to better love your man. All the pictures showed a perfection more elusive than we wanted to believe.

But this reaction of Henry's wasn't typical. While he believed in being firm, he was usually patient.

"We haven't tasted it yet," I reminded Wesley.

"Do I have to?"

Henry looked in our son's direction, and Wesley fell quiet. He sat up in his chair and took in a deep breath. Henry assumed he did it as a way to get his act together, but I knew that look; he was trying not to cry. After all, big boys didn't do things like that.

Mothers shouldn't either.

After grace was said, I let Henry take the first bite. He closed his lips, smiled, and gave an attempt at approval, enough to fool Wesley, who took a tentative bite. He then proceeded to nibble his way through dinner, eventually swallowing down most of the tray.

Each food tasted the same as the other, with underlying notes of aluminum. I pushed the cubed carrots around with my fork, not having the appetite to stomach the meal even though I knew my body needed it.

After Wesley had been excused, Henry and I sat alone at the table. Surprisingly, he hadn't rushed to his office to get more work done.

"Is everything okay?" I asked.

Henry chased a remaining pea around the square compartment as I waited for him to respond.

"Yeah, I mean"—he dropped the fork and pushed the tray toward the center of the table—"Jack said he wanted to talk today." I knew by the name he used that it wasn't good news. When he spoke with respect, his boss was Mr. Ellis. When he was frustrated, he called him by his first name. "He's been dangling this promotion in front of me for months now. He called me into the office, and I thought this was finally going to be it. But instead, he was pressing me on the blueprints."

"Is something wrong?"

"No, I mean, other than the clients can't make up their minds. 'We want two bathrooms, no three. Well, how about a half bath instead? And what would it look like for the garage to be on the other side? Or, how about we take some space from the second bedroom and enlarge that walk-in closet?' Nothing I do makes them happy, and Jack is apparently waiting to see how this plays out before he makes his decision." He put his elbows on the table and rested his head in his hands.

"I'm sorry."

"Alice says I'm still a shoo-in, but I don't know."

"Alice?" I asked as a jolt ran up my spine and shook me awake.

"Yeah." Henry yawned before continuing. "The new girl. I told you about her." He hadn't. "She came on when you were pregnant. She says I don't have anything to worry about, but I don't know. I just can't figure out Jack." He reached for his glass and took the final sip of the martini.

I wanted to know more about this Alice, but then again, maybe I didn't. I knew the other secretaries and saw the way they looked at him, no different from so many of the girls at college. I had never had to worry in the past, I reminded myself. But why hadn't he told me about this one?

Henry rubbed his temples again and ran his hands through his hair. "I thought maybe I could take the night off, but I guess not." Soon enough he would go into his home office, close the door, and work on floor plans while I went through the bedtime routine. Ever since the possibility of becoming a senior architect at Simon and Glasser, the evening office hours had grown longer. Longer than I had anticipated. And he had also grown quieter.

But he didn't get up from the table quite yet.

"I'm sorry," he said. "How was your day?"

"Fine," I told him, because that seemed like the easiest response, easier than asking questions about this Alice girl. But why bother him with details of how I could barely grocery shop? "Wesley got to spend some time with James, so that made him happy."

It had been a while since we had lingered together. Though neither of us were in the mood to talk, we also didn't hurry away from each other. As heavy as my eyes were, as much as my body cried out for rest, I delayed clearing and starting the dishes.

After a few minutes, Henry scooted to the edge of his chair and leaned toward me. The few moments of silence—or maybe the third drink—seemed to have calmed him at least somewhat, because he noticed me for the first time that evening. He placed his hand on my thigh as he looked at me with those brown eyes. And I thought back to before we were married, when we first met at school.

Being one of the few girls on campus, I was used to catching the boys' eyes. But few caught mine in return. I had a scholarship and, according to my mother, four years to either find a husband or learn an employable skill. I didn't blame girls for being there if their only intention was to find a guy. I just wanted an outcome other than my mother's, which was to always be stuck inside, taking care of others. As a girl, I had imagined I would run the farm alongside Daddy, but when that possibility died with my father, I needed to find something else. A degree and the promise of a job was what I had expected, but Henry found me before the skill did.

He bought me more than just a soda on that first date, more than the other boys typically did. He drove me off campus to a restaurant with candles, tablecloths, and multiple courses. My back hurt at the end of the night from sitting so still and straight, trying to be prim and proper in ways I'd heard about but never learned on the farm. All through dinner, I wondered what he would see in a girl like me. Some days I still did.

Henry kept his hand on my leg, the most intimacy we'd had in weeks. His touch felt warm as the remaining scent of his aftershave activated memories and moments I hadn't entertained in months. I began to feel my muscles relax, my body exhale for the first time in what felt like ages. He leaned in and I felt a rush, an energy, excitement as my heart began to beat with anticipation instead of anxiety. After all this time, I didn't know I could still feel this way, especially when all we were doing was sitting at the dining room table in silence, staring at each other.

And then his lips parted. I saw his Adam's apple slide in his throat as he formed words. I waited to hear his voice, hungry for what he was about to say.

"You got dressed today."

My heart thumped in my chest, but no longer from anticipation. The heat rose in my cheeks as I sat in the disappointment and the lack of the sustenance those words offered. I wanted to cry. Yes, I had gotten dressed and it had taken effort. He didn't know how long I stood with my pocketbook in hand, trying to figure out how to manage a newborn and a child as I shopped so I could put a meal on the table that night. A barely edible meal, at that. He didn't know how badly I'd wanted to stay in bed. How I hadn't wanted to answer the door when Nora came. How I'd nearly cried when she offered to stay with the children. How abandoned I'd felt when Bitsy told me about the card game.

The fact that he noticed I had gotten dressed meant he also noticed the days when I didn't.

But I didn't want to talk about any of that. So, with his hand still on my leg, I smiled and said with a wink, "Well, Mr. Mayfield, I am a big girl."

Henry tilted his head to the side. He squinted his eyes and stared straight at me. There was that look, the one he would give Wesley when he tried to make sense of childishness—when he colored on the bathroom wallpaper or kicked a ball into the

Reillys' window. The look came before he would say something like, "What were you thinking?" He never said that to me, not with his words, but he did with his eyes.

But this time, the look passed quickly. He replaced it with the flash of a smile and squeezed my leg. "There's my Lulu." Then he took his hand away and stood up. "And you cleaned the house. I'm glad you're feeling better." He leaned toward me and pecked me on the forehead before going to his office and closing the door behind him.

I sat alone at the table, still feeling a warm spot on my leg where his hand had been, wishing he was still there, touching me, looking at me, smiling with me. Not thinking of that Alice girl, but thinking of me. Not the Lulu who could barely manage a trip to the store, but the girl he fell in love with. The one we both wished I still was.

I heard Henry come to bed that night, but I pretended I was asleep. Even as the mattress shook with his movement, I lay still, waiting to hear his breathing slow to a sleep rhythm. Then I got up.

I knew Esther would be waking soon for her first middle-of-the-night feeding. How old had Wesley been when he finally slept through the night? Nora told me to let them cry, that babies needed to learn to sleep, but what was I to do when I hadn't even learned that lesson for myself?

Nora, Wesley, and James had done some cleaning while I had been away, but there was more to do to make the house presentable, especially if Bitsy was coming. It needed to shine. So I got to work.

I dusted what Wesley had done earlier in the day, polishing and buffing the furniture to a shine. I couldn't vacuum and risk waking the others, but I mopped the kitchen floor, Windexed the picture window and sliding door, and knocked down the cobwebs that had gathered in the corners. I had just begun to wipe down the refrigerator shelves when I heard the squeak of Luna's paws on the glass door.

I let her in without thinking, relishing the quiet company. The soft body that didn't demand anything from me.

After a milk snack, she curled up on the couch, her purr fading to silence as she napped. I watched her in the darkness, so content, finding a home wherever she could, calm enough to sleep despite being in a place that wasn't her own. But where was her place? Did she even have a home? Where did she spend the hours other than twilight?

I let her rest until Esther began to fuss. I put her outside, promising I'd see her the next night, having realized our companionship only existed when the others slept. Then I hurried to Esther's room, avoiding the squeak in the hallway floor.

"*Shhhhhh—*" I called as I opened the door and rushed to the crib. "Don't wake your brother."

I reached for her, pulling her toward me, nestling her tiny body in to my own. My mind still went through the motions every time I picked her up. *Support the head*, I told myself. *Get your hand beneath her neck. Pull her toward your body. Rest her against your own.*

It had only been four years since Wesley was this age, this small, this delicate, but it felt as if I was learning all over again. Hatti was such a natural, so nurturing, so loving. When she saw a baby, her eyes lit up, her arms reached out, her hands cradling just so. I envied the comfort and ease she had with them.

Esther still fussed, still squirmed in my arms, and I couldn't ignore the cries.

I sat in the rocking chair and unbuttoned my nightgown before holding the bundle to my breast. She had taken to nursing more easily than Wesley, who fought to latch and gasped every time my milk let down, as if he were drowning. After each feeding, I had to burp him until his body released every bit of gas, or he would spend hours fussing. Esther didn't need any of that; she just needed me.

It didn't take long for her to quiet, but I held her for a while, rocking back and forth. As many hours as I had spent sitting in that chair, I still missed the feel of Mama's old rocker. I closed my eyes and imagined her sitting in it in the living room of our farmhouse. In my mind, I walked through the house, reminding myself of every knotted floorboard, every chip of plaster, every crooked step that lead to the root cellar. I escaped into the halls of the home that was no longer mine.

Soon dawn would come, the light sweeping over the horizon, sprinkling onto our rooftops, waking the morning dew. But at that moment, the world remained dark, quiet, caught in its own moment of *dormiveglia*.

I looked across the street to Bitsy's house. What kind of a name was that? Bitsy? Though I suppose some could say the same for my own name. I had been Lulu for seven years now, since our first date when, at the end of the night, Henry walked me to my dorm and said with a stammer, "I really l-l-l-like you, Lu-lu."

He was a senior at the university. Under any other circumstances we wouldn't have met, but there we were, our worlds given the chance to overlap. Six months later, Henry Mayfield proposed to me underneath the maple tree in the center of campus, just after the leaves had opened in all their spring fullness.

He had a picnic blanket laid out. I had a book in my hand, but I looked above me at the green leaves. We had never discussed marriage. I wouldn't let Henry. I didn't know how the two of us would work. He was too optimistic for his own good and for our reality. His world was not mine. The fields of my childhood, the woods so deep and full, the pond with its dark water, all were as foreign to him as the need for multiple forks beside a dinner plate was to me.

He'd reached for my hand, taking it in his, requesting my attention. I looked away from the leaves to see those eyes of his. I knew what he was doing. I knew what he thought we needed to do. I knew what Mama wanted me to do. After all, that's why she let me go away. Without the scholarship, I wouldn't be there, but more than learning, she wanted me to find someone who could give me a good life because she didn't believe I could provide that for myself.

And I had found someone. She should be happy about that, especially with someone from a family like the Mayfields, not one she could relate to, but one she could approve of. I wasn't sure they would say the same of a farm widow like her.

As for Mrs. Mayfield, she had plans for Henry. We both knew it. And neither included me, regardless of what we thought had happened. So when Henry reached into his pocket and pulled out a little box, I didn't know what to think. Surely he hadn't thought at all through. This couldn't work. It wouldn't work. But then he'd proposed anyway.

I wonder sometimes, in the middle of the night, if he would

ask me the same today. Especially in those moments when he gives me that look, when he compliments me on a major accomplishment like getting dressed for the day, I wonder if he would've been so quick to propose if he had waited just another week for my monthly to start up as if nothing had happened. And sometimes in the darkness of the hour, as the Frigidaire hums from the kitchen and the streetlights cast shadows, I wonder: Did I calculate right? Did I fool him into something? Or did we really love each other?

But I stopped thinking about all that when a light switched on in the Betser house. It was the same light as before. I assumed it was Katherine's bedroom. This time, with the curtains open, I could see inside, noticing piles of boxes. Had they not unpacked her room yet? I wondered how the girl could sleep in there with all that clutter, but then I saw someone move toward the window. It wasn't the girl. It was Bitsy.

What was Bitsy doing up at that hour before the sun had even risen? She walked to the window and stood, perfectly centered in the frame. I couldn't help but notice her body silhouetted in the window, her nightgown hanging loose, not giving her outline any shape. The light burned in contrast to the darkness outside, and I wished I had my camera to capture the picture.

I don't know why she stood there or what she looked at, but she lasted only a few minutes before Gary walked up behind her. I saw her body jerk as his hand touched her shoulder. I saw her gather her arms and hug herself as he reached around her waist and pulled her away from the window. I could see her try to pull free of him before they walked out of view. The light switched off, and I was left to wonder alone in the dark who this new family really was.

CHAPTER NINE

The truth of the matter was, I wasn't like the others. I knew this from an early age. I could spend days on the farm by myself, wandering from house to barn to tree, lingering in the meadow, sitting in only the company of whatever cat followed along with me. I looked forward to the summer days, when school was out and I didn't have to be in a room with rules and kids my age. I didn't need to be needed like others did. Because sometimes being needed got us into trouble, like whatever was going on across the street.

I couldn't shake that image from my mind. Every time I closed my eyes to try to sleep, I saw Gary pulling Bitsy away from the window. What had she been doing in that room? And why hadn't he wanted her there?

With no sleep, I nearly called Nora and told her to cancel the card game. Too gripped by the vise squeezing my temples, I wanted to spend the day in bed. Of course, the kids wouldn't let me do that, and neither would Nora. I knew if I called her, she would make a big deal out of it, saying the visit would be good for me, that I needed to make more friends. But I didn't know if I wanted to be friends with Bitsy.

Regardless of how I felt, I swallowed a few aspirin and told myself I could make it through an hour. If I did, my reward would be rest, if the kids allowed it.

As I set up the card table, I heard Daddy's voice, the words he'd said one day when they thought I was outside: *She needs friends.*

Mama hadn't even stopped working the dough as she told him that I was fine. Daddy didn't seem to agree. He went on to ask about Sue Ann down the road. "They're different types," Mama told him. She was right. Sue Ann didn't come to the creek often, but one time when she did, I attempted to show her the frog I had found. She refused to touch it because she said it would give her warts. I knew that day to not believe her. If frogs caused warts, by then my hands would've been coated with them.

"There must be someone," Daddy had said.

But what was he talking about? He spent his days with the livestock, farm equipment, and crops while Mama worked away inside the house or hanging laundry on the line. We all had our roles and we kept to ourselves, exchanging few words unless absolutely necessary.

Maybe that wasn't the life he'd wanted. Maybe Daddy wanted more friends. Maybe Daddy wanted to be needed by more people. Maybe that's why he was the one who would hug me, pull me in close, peck me on the cheek before bed each night. He was the one who laughed with me, hung the tire swing and pushed me higher when I asked him to.

I hadn't thought of Daddy like that before, of maybe wanting different things. He had always been my father, the heir to the Oscuro farm, the only son who would continue working the land his ancestors had settled. I never thought to ask him if he had wanted something different.

Mama didn't need us, or anyone, in the same way. She needed to get the bread made, the floors swept, the laundry on the line. She needed to ration the food, pull together the meals, dig for every last root vegetable. And she needed to care for the kids. Of course, I needed to do that too, but what did I owe to anyone else? Friendship was nice, but it wasn't a gift to be given to just everyone. Especially not a woman who wouldn't make eye contact with me but had no problem insulting my dinner choices.

Right on schedule, my doorbell rang. Nora and Hatti arrived together, with kitchen timers in hand, ticking away the countdown to when our time would end. One of the best decisions we ever made was getting our kids on the same nap schedule so that we could get in a couple hands of spades during rest time.

As Hatti walked into my living room, I saw how much she had changed since I had last seen her. It was no secret that the Brooks had not planned this fourth child of theirs. Their three-bedroom was already bursting at the seams. Her husband told Henry they were about to have too many children for the square footage. It made me wonder if they had considered moving.

Hatti's shoulders leaned back to counterbalance her developing stomach. As much as I hated the softness, the empty pooch of a stomach, I didn't miss pregnancy. It takes a lot of a woman.

If I was being honest, I hoped to never experience that again, but of course I would never say that out loud.

For all I knew, I was alone in those thoughts. As much as Nora complained about her kids, she loved them and would probably welcome more if she could. We all knew that Hatti saw all parts of motherhood as nothing but a blessing. Though I wondered if she ever hid in her closet or the backyard or with a drink in hand.

I thought about this a lot in the dark, quiet hours, or submerged in the bathtub, or as Luna rested on my lap and the wind whispered to me. Maybe they felt those same things. Maybe I wasn't alone in all this. Maybe I needed to be the one to speak up, the first to say something, to refuse to remain silent. But what if I was the only one?

"How are you feeling?" Nora asked Hatti as they took their seats around the card table.

Hatti took a breath and looked at me before answering. "I can't complain."

But she could. We all could. The things that children do to our insides. The pressures we feel. The pain of being torn in two. Then there are the chapped nipples. The sleepless nights. The constant need to be present for this helpless child while our bodies are still healing and trying to figure out how to become their own again.

"Well," I began, "you're glowing." It was summer. Everyone who spent even a few minutes in the heat and humidity was glowing.

Hatti placed a hand on her stomach, already comforting her baby before it had even arrived. "Thank you, Lulu." We smiled our polite smiles at one another. This wouldn't be the time or place for confession, especially not with a new person joining us.

Especially with that new person being Bitsy.

As if summoned by my thoughts, Bitsy rang the doorbell a few moments later. She stood on my front step, her hair pulled back in a tight bun, her blouse tucked firmly into her A-line skirt, a belt fastened at her waist. She had overly rouged her cheeks and a smudge of pink lipstick clung to her front tooth as she smiled. She had tried so hard, a realization that both saddened and annoyed me.

But she didn't have any dark circles beneath her eyes. She didn't look like she had been up all night. Like me. Like I knew she had been. She looked fine, other than the misplaced lipstick.

"Welcome," I said. The word came out flat, nearly more as a question.

"Thank you for inviting me." *I hadn't.* I looked at the dish in her hand. "A strawberry-pretzel salad," she said. She held out the pan for me to take. I hesitated as I looked at what she had brought. Beneath the plastic wrap were sliced strawberries set in red gelatin on top of a layer of cream cheese and a crushed-pretzel crust. Of all the snacks this woman could've made, she chose a Jell-O salad. Distracted by her audacity, I at first missed the other thing she had brought.

"Oh, Katherine—" I stammered as the girl peeked from behind her mother's back. I looked at Nora, wondering why she hadn't told Bitsy to leave her at home.

"Hello, Mrs. Mayfield." Katherine's voice was quiet. While Bitsy had clearly put as much thought into the girl's attire as she had her own—a Sunday dress and ribbon to match the lavender flowers along the collar—no outfit could hide the girl's peaked complexion, glassy eyes, and flushed cheeks. "I was hoping to play with Wesley." The young girl punctuated her sentence with a sneeze.

"I'm afraid Wesley is resting. All the kids are." As the girl coughed, I looked at her mother and explained, "We put the kids down for naps so we can play uninterrupted." Bitsy looked confused, so I continued, "With peace and quiet."

"I'm so sorry I didn't tell you." Nora moved me out of the doorway and guided Bitsy and Katherine into the house.

"Oh," Bitsy began, "I couldn't leave her alone."

"We're just across the street," I pointed out. What did she think would happen?

"While the kids lay, we play!" Nora said as she took the salad from me and placed it in the kitchen.

"She won't be a bother," Bitsy explained as the girl sneezed again. And then coughed. And sniffled. Without skipping a beat, Bitsy reached up her sleeve, pulled out a handkerchief, and handed it to Katherine.

Nora told Bitsy to have a seat and then whispered to me, "Go get Wesley."

"No," I told her. "He's napping."

"He doesn't sleep anymore." She was right, but I still didn't want to disrupt the routine and I certainly didn't want him to catch whatever it was this girl had. The last thing we needed in the house was a lingering cold. "It's just this once. She didn't know."

Nora and I looked at each other. I didn't want to back down, but what was I to do? I wasn't going to argue. So I gave in, got

Wesley, and said they could play out back. Bitsy told them to stay on the patio where we could see them. As we started our first hand of cards, I longed for the timers to ding or, better yet, for these guests to leave so I could slip into a hot bath and dissolve the day away.

I told myself that I would be nice. I could make small talk for the remaining forty-five minutes, especially if it could drown out Bitsy's incessant humming. Every time the room went quiet, she would begin with a few notes, always the same, not any sort of recognizable song. Instead, it was a series of long and short spurts, as if melodically humming Morse code.

"You're getting settled in?" Hatti asked.

"Oh, yes." Bitsy looked at the fanned cards in her hand as she answered. She tilted her head to the side and smiled so that dimples recessed into her cheeks. "Didn't take much time."

"I should say." My voice came out louder than I had anticipated. I wondered if anyone else noticed. "They had everything unpacked by the next day." Had I just revealed I had been watching them? "I mean," I stammered, "when I dropped off the pie, it was clear you were already making yourself at home." All except for that front bedroom that appeared to still have boxes piled high, but I wasn't supposed to know that.

"Where did you say you moved from?" Hatti asked.

"Across town. Knollwood."

Nora shifted in her seat and spoke for Bitsy. "You moved to be closer to your husband's work?" She had apparently already learned a few things about the Betsers, which made my stomach twist. How much time had they spent talking, getting to know each other?

"What's he do?" I asked as I tossed a card into the center of the table.

"He's at Fink and Fischer."

"An architect! So is Lulu's husband!" Hatti exclaimed. She always loved making a connection.

"A project manager," Bitsy corrected.

"Ah, so they aren't the same," I said as I tossed out another card. Beneath the table, Nora pressed her foot into mine, issuing a warning for me to be nice, but I ignored her. If she wanted to invite someone new to our game, then I figured we should get to know her. "And in commercial, from the way it sounds. Henry's in residential." I kept my eyes on my cards, as though I was planning out my next move, but really I was trying to ignore Nora's glare.

"Gary would like that," Bitsy's small voice chirped. I wondered about their relationship. She seemed eager to please him, but from what I had seen in the middle of the night, he didn't have the same care for her.

"He's looking for a new job?" Hatti asked when Bitsy didn't offer more. Even then she only responded with a slight nod. From our few encounters, I already knew not to expect her to say more than a few words at a time.

"Well, I'm sure Henry would be happy to get him in at Simon and Glasser, isn't that right, Lulu?"

I refused to look at Hatti. It was one thing to let a neighbor borrow a cup of sugar, but giving them a new job was a bit much, especially when Henry was still trying to lock down his own promotion. I kept my eyes on my cards as I responded, "I'm not sure there's an opening."

"He could put in a good word." Hatti used the same singsong voice as she did with her kids, but I wasn't one of her children. The sunlight poured through the picture window, causing my head to throb as I looked at her. Sensitive to the light, I squinted in her direction as I tried to think of what to say next. I didn't want to promise anything, nor did I want to continue discussing my husband's job, but the building pressure in my forehead was all I could think about.

Before I could respond, Nora called out, "We set you!" Our win had been to Nora's credit. She always had a way of winning, almost a confidence about it, as if for her it was inevitable. Meanwhile, I could barely concentrate enough to know if I was following suit.

"My deal," I said as I gathered the cards. As I looked at the clock to see if it was time for another aspirin, Bitsy excused herself to use the restroom.

Once we heard the bathroom door click shut, Nora leaned in and offered a warning, "Be nice, Lulu."

"I am!" I said, louder than I had intended, and Nora tapped my foot beneath the table again. "I'm just trying to get to know her."

"Are you?" I thought I was. Instead of offering a defense, I shuffled the cards. Thankfully, Nora didn't press any further. Instead, she began to whisper, "You heard she's from Knollwood? Did you hear what happened? About the despondent wife?"

"Despondent?" Hatti asked.

"That's what the paper called her." With eyes wide, Hatti

and I leaned in, our silence begging Nora to keep going. "Word from the bird, this woman put her child down for a nap, shut the bedroom door, and then went into the kitchen. It was an old place—small rooms, apparently, each one with a door of its own. Well, she closed the kitchen door and then took plastic wrap and taped over it. She sealed off the kitchen, turned on the gas, opened the oven door, and stuck her head inside. Her husband got home that night, kid was crying, still in their room. Couldn't figure out what was going on until he broke through to the kitchen. She sealed it off so well, he couldn't even smell the gas when he walked in."

"She"—I could barely force the words out—"killed herself?"

Nora nodded.

"Lord have mercy," Hatti gasped. "Do you think she went…" It took a moment for Hatti to say the final word: "Mad?"

The pause grew thick over the tick of the timers.

"Don't we all?" The words slipped out before I could even register them as my own. Hatti's eyes immediately dropped, as if nervous to be associated with my confession. But Nora looked at me, taking in my reddening face. She nodded slightly, and I chose in that moment to believe she understood.

Lost in the tragedy of this stranger's story, we didn't hear Bitsy, not until her voice called from the kitchen and startled us all: "Where are they?"

"Probably out back or around the side of the house." Nora waved off Bitsy's concern.

"Or out front," I said.

Bitsy pulled open the door and stepped out back. She began to yell for Katherine, her voice growing in volume and panic each time she bellowed the girl's name. The three of us looked at each other, confused by Bitsy's urgency. When she disappeared out of view and hollered louder, we got up and followed.

By the time we had reached the backyard, Bitsy had Katherine by the wrist. She bent down to eye level and said, "You were to stay here," as she pointed at the poured concrete slab in the backyard.

The girl's already glassy eyes began to pool with tears as her bottom lip quivered and she choked out an apology.

"It's okay," I said. Wesley looked unfazed, other than being disappointed that his playtime had come to an end. "They were just playing."

Bitsy dragged Katherine into the house. As she walked by me, she muttered, "I gave them instructions."

"They're just kids," I reminded her. As long as they stayed in the yard, they were perfectly safe, so I didn't care if they stayed on the patio. Why did Bitsy? "They probably got carried away and—"

"*Katherine* knows better." She emphasized the first word, and I knew what she meant—her daughter knew better, but my son did not.

Bitsy didn't say goodbye, nor did she take her pretzel salad with her when she left.

I drew Wesley to me. I wanted to tell him to ignore that crazy woman, but Hatti and Nora were listening. Instead, I asked him what had happened.

"We were just playing." He shrugged. "She said that her mom was gone and her aunt was sick, so we had to drive around the yard to look for them. I was the taxi driver and she was the detective, and we were looking all over."

As Wesley continued droning on about their make-believe

game, I watched Bitsy pull Katherine by the arm. The girl's hair ribbon bounced as her feet struggled to keep up. I felt bad for that girl, being pulled away by a force stronger than herself, like her mother had been in the middle of the night.

Hatti and Nora decided to head home early, and I was thankful when the ticking timers walked out the door and the house grew silent again. The quiet lasted only a few minutes, not long enough for me to rest, but as I nursed Esther, I thought about Bitsy. I couldn't believe she'd brought her sick child with her, but why had she gotten so upset when they were safely in our yard? The more I thought about her, the faster I rocked. I worried that Esther sensed my irritation.

To calm myself, I tried to think of something else, but the only other thing that came to mind was the despondent woman. I wondered about her and what had led her to make that decision. She had lived in Bitsy's neighborhood. Had Bitsy known her?

Rocking the pink bundle alone in the nursery, I began to wonder if we all knew her. Maybe she had a cleaning schedule taped to her fridge. Maybe she also got tired of ironing underwear. Maybe she woke in the night and sat in the shadows, wondering if dawn would break like it did each morning. Or if, just one time, the moon would blanket the sun and the night creatures would bask in the continuing darkness. Or maybe that was just me.

CHAPTER TEN

I felt the storm brewing even as the sun shone that morning. The day hadn't been easy ever since Wesley woke up telling me he couldn't "bweathe." Of course, I knew it would happen. I feared it would. I got ahead of myself in worry, but I had been right. Three days after our card game, Wesley woke with a cough. Bitsy couldn't do like the rest of us and leave her child at home, and now we had a sickness in our house because of her.

It started with a sneeze at dinner the night before, and by morning his nose was too stuffy to breathe out of. I sent Wesley back to bed and told him to stay in his room. The last thing we needed was for him to contaminate the rest of the house and infect his sister. I thought back to the story of the woman in Knollwood and the plastic wrap she had used. I wondered if I could seal him in his room—of course not to harm him, but to keep the sickness locked away.

I phoned the doctor immediately and requested a house

call. Thankfully, Dr. Collins practiced that way, especially for his oldest clients. The Mayfields had been with him since Henry was small, so he never hesitated to come by when we asked. I had been uncertain about such an old doctor, but Henry called him seasoned, knowledgeable, more competent than a new graduate who only knew textbooks but not people.

By the time Dr. Collins arrived that afternoon, the humidity was wrapped thick around everything like a suffocating blanket while clouds shrouded the sky. "Thank you for coming." I invited him in but had to kick a few toys out of the entryway so he wouldn't trip. "Pardon the mess. It's been a little…busy around here this morning."

Dr. Collins held his bag in one hand and his hat in the other as he looked around the house. That's when I did as well. I had spent the morning catching up on my stamps—filling booklets, counting, and considering what I might get. I had nearly ten booklets completed, but I still couldn't decide how to spend them.

Instead of losing myself in the stamps, I should've been cleaning the house, but I realized this only as the doctor looked around. Toys littered the living room. I hadn't yet opened the curtains. I had barely gotten myself dressed, but I hadn't sufficiently done my hair. I was certain my cowlick was divided in the back, showing my scalp. I saw him notice it all. I saw him take it all in, his lips drawing together, his white woolly-worm eyebrows crawling toward one another.

"Please, right this way," I said and directed him to Wesley's room.

The doctor did just as was expected. He examined Wesley and declared it was only a cold.

"I can't bweathe!" Wesley told him, his tongue and nose both complicating the words.

"I know, son," the doctor said as he tucked his stethoscope back into his bag. "Get lots of rest and drink lots of water, and you'll be breathing again soon."

I waited until we were alone in the living room to ask, "You're sure he doesn't have a fever?" I hadn't wanted to question him in front of Wesley. I didn't want to frighten the boy.

"No fever. Just the sniffles. Try this recipe to help with any cough."

The doctor jotted down a quick note and handed it to me.

One teaspoon lemon juice, one tablespoon honey, and one teaspoon whiskey.

Give one teaspoon every hour as needed.

I folded the note and put it in my pocket.

"But—" I didn't mean to question his knowledge, but I knew that early detection and proper diagnosis could make a huge difference. Plus, I needed peace of mind to replace the knot in my stomach. "He felt warm to the touch this morning."

"If he did, it passed. Maybe he was still warm from sleep, from being under the blankets. According to the thermometer, there's no sign of fever, and I trust it more than a mother's hand." He blinked a few times as his lips pressed together in a closed smile. Then he asked, "And what about you, Mrs. Mayfield? Are you okay?"

I was getting tired of people asking me that. "I'm fine," I said. And I was. I had been assessing myself all morning. Of course I still had the lingering headache, and my hands had been sore since I had pulled a couple of weeds a few days ago. Plus, there was the constant exhaustion, but that was part of the newborn days. I knew that much. But I felt no signs of the cold. Not yet. What would I do if I got sick? How would I take care of everything? Nurse Esther, make the meals, clean the house?

"Well, that's good," he said, but those woolly worms scrunched together, as did his lips. "It's only been a few weeks. It can take time—"

"I know, Doctor." I'd been through it before, and I hadn't forgotten. But who are the ones who say that? The men, even the doctors. They may see certain sides of pregnancy and birth, but they don't experience it in a way that they know what it's really like. "I'm fine. It's Wesley who has me concerned."

"It's good you called. If anything changes, if he seems to get worse, give us a ring, but I anticipate he'll be running through the backyard again in a few days." I hoped he was right, but the knot in my stomach hadn't loosened.

The storm finally arrived that evening. I stood at the kitchen sink and watched the gray clouds tumble over themselves as they converged until they dominated what had been a blue sky. Henry called me out of the kitchen and into the driveway when I had been in the middle of finishing up dinner. I tried to tell him that I didn't have the time, but he insisted I come outside.

"We should get inside," I told him as the wind shook my dress and flapped my apron. "I think I feel raindrops."

"But first, I want you to meet—" he said, pointing to the man who stood in our driveway in shorts and crew socks pulled up to knees.

"Gary Betser," our new neighbor said as we approached. Henry always said you could tell a lot about a man by the way he shook hands. When Gary forced his fleshy palm into mine, I knew his type right away. It was more than his strong grip that bound my hand. It was also the way he cupped his other hand over the top of mine, suffocating mine into submission.

"It's nice to meet you," I said. He looked familiar, but I couldn't quite put my finger on the reason why. He had a long, drawn face and sloping nose. Thankfully, Katherine did not get her looks from him. I wondered if the boys did, trying to recall from my brief glance at their family portrait.

"I was just telling your husband I admire his lawn." He still held tight as his auburn hair flapped in the wind. "Best on the street, in my opinion. At least for now." He winked at me and released my hand.

As Gary blathered on about lawn height, crabgrass, and how he was considering trying a new crisscross mowing pattern, the temperature dropped. A fat raindrop fell onto my cheek and trickled down my face. It was only a matter of time before the clouds would open up. Yet we still stood in the driveway, listening to this man in his house shoes tell Henry the benefits of fescue versus bluegrass.

I rubbed my arms, attempting to warm myself as the breeze tickled my arms. I expected Henry to see the gesture and put his arm around me, draw me in close, transfer his warmth onto me. But instead he remained focused on Gary.

I tried to act as though I was listening, but a sound caught my attention. A voice carried over the wind. I looked at Henry and Gary, who didn't seem to notice. I heard the singsong sound a few more times.

"What is that?" I asked, and Henry turned his head to the side, trying to listen.

"Oh, that's nothing." Gary waved off the sound as sprinkles began to fall. "Just Bitsy."

"What's she doing?" Henry asked as her voice rang out again, repeating something I couldn't quite make out.

Gary paused for a moment and said, "Sounds like she's calling for that damn cat. Probably thinks it can't survive in a storm. Have you heard such a thing?" He looked at Henry and laughed. "It's an animal. If it's meant to survive, it'll figure it out. And if it doesn't, well, that's one less mouth to feed, right?" He elbowed Henry as Bitsy finally came into sight in their yard, crouching to look under a bush in front of their house.

I thought of Luna. Every night, that cat met me on the patio, no longer crying for my attention because she always knew I was coming. Instead of pawing at the glass, she simply sat and waited until I opened the door and joined her outside or let her in the house. For the next few hours, she would rest on my lap, and I would ignore how hot she made me as I ran my hand over her fur and let the hours of the night slip away.

I hesitated to ask, but I had to know. "What's she look like?"

"I don't know," Gary said. "A cat. One of those tiger types, I suppose." Luna wasn't a "tiger type," so whoever Bitsy was crawling underneath bushes looking for wasn't the same cat whose fur gathered on my nightgown each night, leaving traces of her presence.

Gary turned toward his house, cupped his hands around his mouth, and bellowed for his wife. It took a few calls before Bitsy heard her husband. She hesitated at first, but when he waved for her to come, she obeyed.

As Gary introduced Henry to his wife, Bitsy wiped her hands across her apron, rubbing until she thought she had wiped away all traces of dirt. Once they shook hands, Bitsy withdrew behind Gary and looked back at the house, eyes still searching for any sign of movement.

"I wanted to get back to what we were talking about earlier," Gary continued. "About your company."

"Yes." Henry turned to me. "Did you know Gary's an architect, too?"

Oh, had I forgotten to tell him that?

"You mean a project manager?" I asked. I watched for Bitsy to react to see if she remembered our conversation over spades. Nora had thought I had been too hard on her that day. But Bitsy didn't react, perhaps ignoring us, ignoring me.

Henry looked at Gary, who clarified, "Well, I suppose, yes, for the moment. I want to get back to the drafting side of things."

"And..." Apparently, this guy wasn't telling Henry all that Bitsy had said over cards, so *I* clarified. "You're in commercial."

"At the moment, but like I said, I'm open to change."

"Yes, sure, sure," Henry said. I knew that phrase, the politeness covering for the truth that he didn't really want to do what he was being asked. "I can pass your name along to Alice."

There was that name again. Heat prickled up my arms despite the breeze that blew cool across them.

"If you wouldn't mind putting in a good word."

"Yes. I'll see—"

"Well, I'd be ever so grateful."

Hoping to rescue Henry from this favor, I turned toward Bitsy. "Is Katherine feeling better?"

She didn't hear me at first, not until Gary tapped her on the shoulder, and she looked from their house to me. "What? Oh, yes. Better."

I waited for her to ask about us, waited to be able to say that Wesley was now ill thanks to her, but instead she looked across the street, her curled bangs fluttering in the breeze. She didn't acknowledge the fact that she had brought a sick child into our house. Or that she had grossly overreacted to their play in the yard—like my home was unsafe for her daughter.

"That's good. Maybe once Wesley is *better*, they can play again." I emphasized the word for her, trying to convey my annoyance, but she didn't respond. Before I could stop myself, my words turned sour. "Although, I know you weren't much of a fan of their games, so maybe it's better if they didn't." I crossed my arms, and Henry's eyebrows rose in shock.

"If the kids want to play, I'm sure it's fine." Henry chuckled nervously, shooting a look at Gary.

Bitsy's gaze finally found mine, vacant, staring, as if she didn't know what I meant. All of them waited for me to explain myself.

"They were just playing some game the other day," I began, "but Bitsy seemed bothered by it." I suddenly felt like I was tattling.

Henry leaned in to me and whispered, "Does this matter right now?"

He was probably right. I probably shouldn't have brought it up, especially not when we were in the middle of meeting our new neighbor. But that woman had a way of getting under my skin, and as she stood silent in our driveway, I was the one who looked like a fool.

"It probably doesn't," I relented. I hadn't bothered to tell him about any of this that afternoon. But when would I have told him? The only time I saw him anymore was at the dinner table, and I wasn't going to bring it up in front of Wesley. Any other time, Henry was at work or in his home office.

Then Bitsy finally spoke, her voice barely squeaking out above the breeze. "They weren't where I told them to be."

"They were around the side of the house," I explained.

"Not on the patio."

Gary cleared his throat and stepped in front of his wife as he extended his hand to Henry. "You know kids." Gary rolled his eyes, his gaze pinned to Henry as if replacing the word *kids* with *women*.

"You're right. They were playing a game and got carried away," I said. "It was something Katherine suggested, something about Wes needing to be her taxi driver because her aunt was sick and her mom was gone, and she wanted to find them."

The Betsers looked at each other. Bitsy's eyes darted away first, but I saw her hand go to her mouth as she turned away from us and tried to hide in Gary's shadow.

"Where do kids come up with this stuff?" Gary chuckled. Then he shook Henry's hand and said, "Well, anyways, sure was nice to meet you. We should be going now."

The man in the crew socks and shorts that hiked up above his belly button didn't say anything to me. Instead, he turned to his wife, grabbed her by the elbow, and led her across the street as the sprinkles turned to fat drops that gave way to a steady, soaking rain that washed over all of Greenwood.

CHAPTER ELEVEN

Sometimes I wondered what Daddy would've thought of Henry. More than anything, Mama cared most about the security Henry could provide. But I think Daddy would've cared more about how he loved me.

I thought I'd found both security and love in Henry. I suppose I had, I kept telling myself. But with each year that went by, love seemed to change. I remember those early days, that first date, the moments in the back of his car, the scare that came before the engagement. Now we rarely talked, we hardly even looked at each other, and he barely touched me.

Is he touching someone else?

I told myself not to think this, but the question lingered after Alice phoned on behalf of Henry to say he'd be home late again. Her voice was younger than I had expected, and I assumed her skirt was shorter than I would have liked.

I typically bathed later in the night, but I couldn't wait. Too many thoughts raced through my mind, coursed through my body, sprinted from my head to my fingertips and toes, sending jolts of electricity through me, my mind and body buzzing.

Baths were where I went to not think. I liked to keep the water running, flowing from the faucet and into the tub, drowning out the sounds from all around, the ones that liked to carry through the walls. But they can't when the water is flowing.

That evening, I needed a bath. I wanted one desperately. I told this to Henry as he finished his dinner, which I had left warming in the oven all evening. Well, in so many words, I said I was going to take a bath. I didn't say "need." He didn't like that sort of insistence. It wouldn't make sense to him. I simply told him that I was taking a bath and that I would clean the kitchen when I was done.

Esther and Wesley seemed settled for the night, or so I thought, and I knew that soon enough Henry would be locked in his office, putting in a few more hours before bedtime despite having stayed late at the office. *Had Alice also been there?* The question plagued me, adding to the list of things that soured my stomach. Alice and Bitsy; this mysterious sick aunt they didn't want to discuss; my husband's closed office door; Gary's hands on his wife, pulling, yanking, dismissing her back home.

I walked into our bathroom, the one that just belonged to the two of us. Mama couldn't get over a house that had a bathroom for one bedroom, not shared with others. Such an extravagance, she said. The woman who lived on a hundred-acre farm thought it was too much for us to have our own bathroom.

That farmhouse had one tub. And we couldn't linger. The water took so much effort to heat, and it cooled so quickly. One time Mama came in to find my fingers pruned, my toes shriveled, and my lips blue.

"Are you trying to kill yourself?" she'd asked.

But the cold didn't bother me. In some ways, it's where I felt most at home, most comfortable, most at peace. I suppose that's why the hot summers, the humidity so thick it felt like walking through a Jell-O salad, never felt like home to me. It's never when I felt the most comfortable. That's why I went to the watering hole every afternoon as a child, counting down until I could run along and dive into the pond, which never fully warmed despite the summer temperatures. I didn't care if others were there. I often preferred they not be. And when Georgie got to be old enough to join me, I felt I'd lost some of my own time. He was a fine brother. We got along as far as siblings were concerned, but I still wanted that time, that place, that cold to myself.

I spent whole hours floating on my back, my face to the sun, my eyes watching the squirrels that ran at the tops of the trees that branched out all around us. I wondered what it would be like to run along those branches, so high, so far out of reach. I'd watch them jump from one limb to another with a fearlessness I envied.

One day, I watched one fall. He and another had run a spiral up the tree, the other chasing him so closely it looked as though the other would nip his tail. Before he could, the first one jumped from one tree and attempted to land in the neighboring one. But he missed.

He began to fall, to plummet. It happened so quickly, so silently. No one else saw it happen. I was the only one witnessing what could be the final moments of that squirrel's life. I watched him turn his body in the air. I waited for him to grab on to a passing branch. Instead, he landed on the ground, last fall's leaves crunching beneath him. He stood stone still for a minute.

I wasn't sure if he had survived. I'm not sure he knew either, at least not for a minute. Then he shook his head and ran off. How he had survived a fall that high, taller than our house, I didn't know. I wondered what went through his mind in those seconds when he went from the top to the bottom. Had he feared what was happening?

I turned off the faucet and stretched my body as much as I could in the tub, though it didn't give me the full space I wished it would. I couldn't lie out flat and float like I wanted to. I pushed my toes against one end, bent my knees, and slid my head down into the water.

All sounds dampened other than the crackle of the bubbles that floated beside my ears. The water swayed, swishing from my movements, submersing my cheeks, splashing up to my lips, even settling between them and into my mouth. I swallowed it, drinking in the soapy taste, longing for the purity it could bring me, partaking of it as if a Communion. *These are the bubbles popped for you. Do this in remembrance of cleanliness.*

"What're you doing?" Henry's voice broke through the bubbles and bathwater.

I startled, sloshing the water so that it spilled over the edge and onto the carpet below. Why did we ever think carpet belonged in the bathroom, the wettest room of the house? It merely acted as a sponge, trapping the dampness to grow mold as if a giant petri dish.

Water splashed into my eyes. I reached for my towel to dry them, but it slipped from the side of the tub. My hand fumbled along the floor, attempting to find it, causing more water to cascade over the sides.

"Lulu! Watch what you're doing."

"Well, if you can't tell, I can't watch anything right now."

He held the towel to me, placing it in my hands so I could dry my face and finally look at him. He stood across the bathroom, leaning against the vanity. He had removed his work shirt, but remained in his tweed pants and undershirt. I looked at his arms, his stomach. Both used to be more defined, more rippled than they were now. He used to play basketball with the guys at school, help out on our farm on weekends sometimes, even row some Saturday mornings as the fog swirled along the river. He hadn't done any of that since we had gotten married and moved to Greenwood.

I sat in the tub, uncertain of what to do. I wanted to remain there, but I didn't know how long he would take, what he wanted to say, how much of an imposition he would be. I crossed my arms on the rim and rested my chin upon them, allowing the tub to shield my exposed breasts, as if I needed to be modest in front of the only man who had ever seen me naked.

"We need to talk," he said.

One night. One night I dared to take a bath before cleaning up the kitchen, and here he was talking to me as if I were a child who didn't complete her chores.

"I'll get to the dishes as soon as I'm done here." I reached for the drain plug, realizing that my bath time had come to an end for that evening. Maybe I would take one in the night, when I couldn't sleep. I had never done that before, always too afraid the running water would wake Henry. Maybe I should take one in the hall bathroom. Surely he wouldn't hear the faucet filling and draining, gurgling on its way down when I was done.

"Wait," he said as my fingers came in contact with the chain. I stopped before I could open the drain. "I think I know what's going on." He looked away from me, dropping his gaze to the pink carpet. Why was it pink? I hadn't chosen it. He pulled his fingers through his hair. He was looking more tired these days. I didn't know why. He seemed to sleep soundly at night, through everything else that went on in the house. "Lately you've seemed... I don't know how to say it. Moody. Distant. More than usual."

He continued to lean on the vanity. I hadn't realized until then what a mess it was. So cluttered with all those perfume bottles, the decorative one Wesley had gotten me last Christmas, the one shaped like a cat. He had been so excited to give it to me Christmas morning. I dabbed some on my wrists and neck, and spent the rest of the day with itchy eyes and a tickle in the back of my throat.

"I know—" I began, ready to be chastised for being rude to the Betsers, but Henry held up his hand and I stopped.

"I think I know what's going on. I should've realized it sooner, but there's been a lot." He kept looking at the floor, and I wondered if he also thought that carpet was ugly. I assumed he did, but we never talked about it. But that's not what he meant. Standing with a river of pink carpeting between us, a bath mat that looked like an empty raft floating down the center with no passengers. How I wished I could be on that raft and float away from this conversation, this room, this house, and all of Greenwood.

"But, Lulu..." I stopped looking at the carpet and met his eyes—those brown eyes. I could get lost in them. Even after years of being together, they still pulled me in. "I made a call, and we're going to have a dishwasher delivered in a few days."

"A what?"

"A dishwasher. I should've seen it sooner. I mean, we debated installing one when we moved in. We should have. It'll make things easier for you."

Henry crossed the carpeted river and knelt in front of me, placing his hand beneath the edge of my chin, encouraging it upward so our eyes met. As much as they pulled me in, I still couldn't make sense of what he had just said.

"A dishwasher?"

"Yes. I mean, at first I thought you just needed some time and then you'd come around, but it has been a few weeks now, and we've had those dinners each night, and the more I started thinking about, the more I realized. You don't want to have to clean all those dishes, so if we get a dishwasher, it'll make your job easier. Right?"

A dishwasher would solve it all; that's what he thought. He looked at me. He looked through me. He wanted the solution to be so simple, a modern convenience that could snap me back to normal. I put my hand atop his and smiled, but what I wanted most was to fall down into that water, let it engulf me, let my skin and bones, hair and nails, soul and spirit swirl down that drain, let it gurgle me up and flush me out to sea, to be absorbed into a mass of water so much bigger than myself.

"That's so thoughtful of you," I said with a smile like Bitsy's plastered across my face. Henry kissed me on the forehead and stood up.

"Really?"

"Absolutely."

It was our word. The one I'd said to him when he asked me out on our first date. The one he'd repeated when he first said he loved me and I asked him if he meant it. The way I'd told him that I would marry him. I must have believed in absolutes then.

That evening in the tub, as my husband looked at me and his eyes pleaded for me to let a dishwasher make everything okay, I thought about grace. Mama talked a lot about it. God's grace was why we were there. Why the crops survived each year and harvest happened at all. Why the war ended. Why Georgie survived. Why I got the scholarship and a husband.

But for me, I think the greatest gift of grace was that we couldn't read each other's minds.

"Listen." He looked at that ugly pink carpet instead of at his own wife. "Thursday night, we have a dinner, for work. I know it's a lot for you right now, but I've already spoken to Hatti. She'll come over that evening. And I know it's been a while, but it would be a good reason for you to pamper yourself. Get your hair done."

While grace saved me from him knowing my thoughts, I wasn't sure I could hide the look on my face, the astonishment that he expected me to get dressed up, to mingle, when I needed to be home instead.

"I can't. I don't have anything to wear."

"Go shopping."

"It has been ages since I've been to the salon."

"I'm sure they'd love to see you again."

And then, with the most honesty I could muster, I said, "It's too soon."

He looked me square in the eyes. I didn't want to look at him then. I didn't want to see the pity. What must he have thought of me? I sat in that cold water, the bubbles having long since popped so that an iridescent sheen swirled on the water's surface.

"It's time—and, Lulu, I need this." He looked away from me, and for the first time in months, I saw him. The promotion wasn't coming as easily as he had expected, assumed, hoped. He had put in so many hours. Worked so hard. He wanted this, and he needed his adoring wife by his side. She had been absent, but he was calling her back.

"Okay," I said, trying to get myself to believe what I had just told him.

"You're sure?"

I held his gaze, unblinking. He couldn't read my mind—thank God—so I looked at him with as much earnestness and compliance as I could, and I uttered one word. Our word. "Absolutely."

CHAPTER TWELVE

The day the dishwasher was delivered, I began to smell colors. Henry was at work when two guys in uniforms that smelled like black licorice knocked on the front door. They wore white gloves as evidence that they wouldn't leave a mess behind. And they didn't. Leave it to me to make my own mess. But they did exactly as they claimed they would. They delivered the appliance and installed it to its specifications. Of course, its specifications were not what I thought they would be.

Harvey and Sal, as their name tags labeled them, unboxed the large rectangle and positioned it in the center of my efficiency kitchen. Then Harvey brushed his white gloves together and said, "All done!"

"I'm sorry?" I looked at the metal rectangle in the middle of the kitchen and thought he meant they had just completed step one of a multistep process.

"She's all ready for you."

There must be some mistake. "I thought you were going to install it."

Sal, the silent one, nodded as Harvey proclaimed, "We did!"

According to their uniforms, these guys were the professionals, and yet they seemed to be missing an important step: the actual installation.

"So you're going to put it right there." I pointed. "Next to the sink?"

"Oh, you can push her closer if you want. That's the beauty of the Mobile Maid; you move her to wherever you want to. When you're ready to use her, just attach this hose to the faucet."

"And the other one, Harv," the quiet one said beneath his breath. I wondered if he had been instructed to not speak.

"Yes, unless you want a flood, make sure this end of the hose is also in the sink. Oh, and plug her in, but I'm sure a smart lady such as yourself would've figured that out." The guys both chuckled.

"But doesn't it go there?" I pointed next to the sink again. "You know, into the cabinets?"

"Ah, no, ma'am. Not this here model. Like her name says, she's mobile. You can store her wherever you like—in the pantry there if you want. And when you're ready, just wheel her out."

The Mobile Maid took up a third of the floor space in my U-shaped kitchen, blocking the flow from the oven to the fridge, the sink to the pantry, creating an island of obstruction.

"Fully automatic, with king-sized capacity," Sal muttered as if he was reading off an advertisement, but king-size intrusion seemed more like it.

"If you don't have any more questions, ma'am—"

The first time I was called that, I took a sense of pride in it. I was newly wed and had just arrived in Greenwood when the butcher at the A&P handed me the shaved ham and said, "Have a nice day, ma'am." At that time, I smiled. I still felt so much like a miss playing the part of a married woman, still wondering what I was even doing with a ring on my finger and a car of my own. Six years later, I couldn't remember the last time someone had called me *miss*, and I realized they never would again.

"No, that's all, thank you," I told the men as I escorted them to the front door.

I knew Henry would want to give it a good test that night, so I decided to make a real meal, one Wesley would appreciate. I stubbed my toe three times on that monstrosity as I chopped the potatoes and molded the meat loaf. By the time Henry got home, I was limping.

"Oh, look at that!" He ran his hands over the top of the dishwasher before lifting the lid and looking inside. "King-size capacity, they say."

I didn't think he had ever been so interested in the use of dishes before. Henry couldn't wait to start the machine after dinner, having read every page of the manual while I set the table. After dinner, the machine chugged to life, causing Wesley to put his hands over his ears and declare, "Too loud!"

"I was telling Gary about this," Henry shouted.

"Gary?"

"Yeah, ran into him at the mailbox when I got home. Was asking if I'd said anything to Jack yet." The machine paused before water began to spit out the hose and into the sink. "Think of the time you'll save!"

The Maid roared again, moving on to the next cycle, so that I had to raise my voice to be heard over it. "I thought it was supposed to be installed."

"It is."

"No, into the cabinets. Not the middle of the floor."

"I got you the mobile one. It was too much to cut into the counter, reconfigure everything. But this one, you can put it away when you're not using it."

"Where?"

He shrugged. "The pantry."

Apparently, he had not set foot in the pantry in quite some time. If he had, he would have realized there was no space for the Maid to fit in there.

"There's no room."

He shrugged again. "Just leave it where it is. It's like extra counter space."

"More like a tripping hazard."

There was a time when Henry had found me funny, when he got me in ways few others did, like Mama, who told me not to sass. He used to laugh with me more. Some of our first nights together in that house, we stayed up late talking, dreaming, laughing together. Each night we were eager to be together, happy he was home, satisfied to be in each other's company and arms, as if nothing else in the world mattered.

Henry took a drink before setting his tumbler down so hard the ice shook against the glass. "I was just trying to help."

"I didn't mean it like that."

"I remember when you used to be grateful." He was right. Once upon a time, I had been. "Send it back if you don't want it."

I had been grateful when he asked me out, when we went steady, when he proposed, and when we walked down the aisle. I was always thankful. What he didn't realize was that I wanted more than a dishwasher. I wanted him to understand that without me having to tell him. At one point, he would've recognized that truth for himself. But time has a way of changing, a subtle, secret metamorphosis that surprises us later.

That night, the smell of our pink bubblegum sheets woke me after I had only been asleep for an hour. I got up to warm myself some milk and hoped it would calm my senses. As I sprinkled cinnamon on top, I couldn't help but miss Daddy. I never thought of him in the day. Only in the darkness. After he passed, I missed those stolen moments of just the two of us. It was during one of those moments when Daddy took his last breath. Mama had gone to bed, knowing the end was near but thinking she still had time. I snuck downstairs just in time to hold Daddy's hand as he exhaled the last rattle. I waited for another intake, a gasp, a huff, something. But only silence came.

I joined Luna out back and watched the wind wave the trees in the breeze. The first tree I'd fallen in love with was at the back of our property where the creek ran. Its branches reached far, from one bank across to the other. I would spend afternoons sitting in her branches, listening to the water bubble across the slate rocks on its way to the watering hole. But I don't like to talk about that pond.

It was your fault.

Sometimes the memories we keep are the ones we'd rather

forget. But they have a way of finding us in the night, whispering along the wind so we remember.

Mama had told me not to go. But Georgie begged. Daddy was still with us then, off in the field, and Mama was putting together a pie for after dinner. We had all heard the news, but I was fifteen at the time, too full of self to listen. They had tried to tell me. I should've listened. I had seen what it did to Mary. She had been so healthy one day. And gone the next.

They told us not to be near water, that it seemed to like the water. But this was our swimming hole, the one we played in every summer on days when the heat got so high only cicadas kept on with their usual business. We had tried resting in the shade. We sat in the low branches of the tree, too hot to climb any higher. We listened to the water flow beneath us.

And then Georgie began to ask.

"Can't we please go?"

"You know what Mama said."

"I know."

"Then you know the answer."

But he kept on asking.

The more I thought of it, the more I listened to that water flowing toward a reprieve, the more I felt a drop of sweat trickle down my neck, meandering along my back and dripping into my underpants, and the more I realized he had a point. There were a lot of things Mama didn't know. This could be one of them.

We raced to the pond, Georgie giggling with every step. He was only eight years old, but he could nearly beat me already. I thought that soon enough he would be faster than me.

We heard the others before we could see them. Neighbors had

gotten to the pond first. Clothes lay on the banks, shoes kicked off in a hurry to get into the water. Georgie stripped down to his underpants, too young to be self-conscious.

The water felt cool against our skin. We splashed and dove. We laughed and held our breath. We played until our fingers pruned. Then we walked home slowly, letting ourselves dry to hide our disobedience.

But a few days later, Georgie didn't want to play. He didn't want to leave the house when Mama said he needed to get some fresh air. Mama soon realized the sweat that trickled down his temple didn't come from the heat and humidity. It came from a fever.

Mama told me to go outside. And I did. I ran to our tree and I climbed up in her branches, not knowing that Georgie wouldn't be able to climb again. Soon, polio would ravage his body, twist his legs, take away his ability to ever run again.

As the doctor asked questions, trying to track his exposure, Georgie revealed our secret from that day.

It was my fault.

I had been the one to take Georgie to the tree, the creek, the watering hole, the place we knew not to go. The place with other kids. Including Jamison down the road, who had taken to bed with polio as well.

That was the last time I remember Mama slapping me. Because then she seemed to care about me. After that day, she gave me silence, not attention.

That was when I began waking in the night, hearing Georgie cry out for Mama, thinking I could hear him even when they sent him away to the paralysis hospital. And that was when I learned to cry silently in the night, only in the dark hours, only in the quiet, so the stillness didn't betray my continual attempt at penance, my effort to be the good, obedient girl who was seen, but not heard.

CHAPTER THIRTEEN

Sometimes, I needed to get out of the house and away from its stale stenches: the lingering aroma of last night's dinner attempt or the artificial scents of the laundry. Of course, the outside didn't smell much better. Suburbia had a scent so different from the farm. It was one of asphalt, exhaust, and lawn fertilizer. You couldn't smell the corn growing, the rain coming, the deer looking for a snack.

On the days when I found myself aching for fresh air, Wesley and I would go to the tree. Mama always said the fresh air would do us good. She said that about Georgie, too. Once his fever set in, she opened our bedroom window. The sheer curtains danced in the breeze, but no matter how much cool wind filled our room, no amount of fresh air could cure him. That's when I stopped believing in the breeze, the breath of God that Mama claimed healed. But when healing never came, what else was I to think?

Even still, sometimes my body craved the outdoors. And Wesley seemed to understand. Most times he would bring paper and crayons so he could sit beneath the tree and draw. He wasn't allowed to use my camera to take pictures, so instead he would sit and draw, making his own portraits of what he saw.

"Ready, Mama?" Wesley ran to the door, ready to pull it open, when I noticed his shoes. Despite having worked with him for weeks—months, even—the kid always put his shoes on the wrong feet. I didn't know how it felt right to him. It seemed like he would feel the difference. I hesitated in correcting him. It wasn't like it really mattered what feet his shoes were on, but of course it mattered to Henry. He thought the boy should be taught right from wrong.

"Not yet, buddy. Wrong feet." His shoulders slumped in protest. I saw the pout coming, and I certainly didn't have the energy for a full-blown tantrum, so I reminded myself to soften the correction even though what I felt most like doing was snapping back at him, telling him to listen.

"Let's fix this so you can run even faster."

That seemed to do the trick. I bent down and fixed his shoes, but before I could stand, he looked at me, held his hands palms up, and said, "Do it, Mama."

"It's not bedtime," I told him.

"Please?"

How could I resist?

"With a circle and a pat," I began, using my index finger to trace a circle on his palm, "and a heart on top of that. I give all my love to Wes with not a single smidge less."

"Again," he said.

"Don't you want to go make pictures?"

"Again." I knew he wanted to get outside as much as I did, but I also knew he had a way of living in the moment, of not worrying about the past nor the future, but instead finding delight in the present. I decided to try the same.

"With a—"

He interrupted, "Faster."

I obliged. And when he said faster and faster and faster, I sped up the rhyme until the words ran together and his shoulders shook with laughter.

When I stood up, Wesley finally satisfied, the room began to spin. I steadied myself on the wall, waiting for the dizzy spell to pass, hoping it wouldn't linger.

"Are you okay?" Wesley asked.

I saw the look in his eyes, the fear that something was wrong.

"Yeah, I just need a minute."

"But what's that?" Wesley pointed at the underside of my arm. I had to twist it to see what he saw. There was a lacy, red rash spread down my upper arm. I ran my hand across it, feeling the texture. It reminded me of the time that Henry and I went to the shore, a peaceful getaway in the sun, but by the second day, a rash had broken out across my arms. Henry told me it was sun poisoning—the light so bright it had sickened my skin.

"It's nothing," I assured Wesley. Perhaps the sun had caused it again, though I hadn't spent much time outdoors since I'd gotten home from the hospital. Thankfully, the room had stopped spinning, so I swaddled Esther in her blanket and the three of us headed out the door.

Wesley tried to hurry me down the street, but my stride hadn't returned to normal yet. I still took steps carefully, delicately, clinging to Esther, recovering from the husband stitch, still healing in so many ways.

I saw Bitsy's house across the street and wondered what she was doing at that time. She probably had Katherine meticulously dressed and a matching ribbon tied in her hair. She had probably twisted her own hair into her typical updo hours ago. I don't know how she tolerated that bun every day, so tight that it pulled at her temples. Maybe that's why she smiled so much; her hair was pulled so severely it caused her lips to turn up.

My hair lay limp on my shoulders. I hadn't put on my face yet that morning and doubted that I would at all that day. Henry had started getting the mail in the evening because I didn't want to show myself in such a condition. Of course, his mother, and the etiquette book, would say that I needed to look my best for him. After all, he had been away all day, working to properly care for his family. The least I could do was meet him at the door with a drink on ice, pearls around my neck, and a smile plastered across my painted lips. Then maybe he wouldn't think anything of Alice.

Wesley knew the way to the weeping willow and ran on ahead, always going fastest past the Reilly house. He waited for me before taking my hand to cross the street. I remember when I had to reach for his, explain that he must hold mine, but now he did it out of habit and obedience, his warmth radiating into the palm of my hand. I squeezed his, not wanting to let go.

"Look both ways," he said before announcing that it was all clear. He let go as soon as we arrived safely on the other side. Someday he'd cross the street without holding my hand, without me watching nor standing nearby. Someday he'd hold my hand for the last time. Would I know the day when it came? Would I be able to recall that moment later even if I tried? Or would it blur together with so many other memories that would get pruned along the way, a heap of what my mind would deem unnecessary even if my heart would beg to differ.

He ran to our tree; that's what he liked to call her, *our* tree, as if she belonged to us.

I settled beneath the drooping branches, rocking and swaying so Esther would rest, my body in a constant state of motion as long as it was standing. I considered sitting and leaning against the tree. I wondered if I closed my eyes, could I drift off to sleep? Of course I couldn't. My mind couldn't quiet enough for that to happen.

"Mama! Look!" *Yook*, that's how it sounded. It seemed to be his favorite word. He was always saying it, always pointing to something that had caught his attention.

"LLLLLook." I exaggerated the *L* as a reminder. Truth be told, I wanted him to go on saying *yook* for as long as his little tongue wanted to.

"It's ants!" I nodded, delighting in his pure joy. "Look at all of them! Climbing in a row!" He watched the black things march up the tree, zigzagging their way through the rough edges of the bark.

I wondered what their journey must have looked like from their perspective. To us, the depth of the bark was shallow, but to them it was a valley, a deep crevice, perhaps like the Grand Canyon to humans.

"I'm gonna find the anthill!" Wesley announced before running off in search of the insects' home. I wondered how far they traveled and how they always found their way back home. Without addresses and roads, they still seemed to know where they were going.

Then a girl's voice called out, "I'll help you look!"

I turned to see Katherine running toward Wesley, the ribbon in her hair flapping in the breeze as if it were a tail wagging behind her. I looked down the street, anticipating that Bitsy would be close behind, but I saw no signs of her.

"Katherine, where's your mother?"

Children played unsupervised along our street all the time, but I had yet to see Katherine without Bitsy. And typically, Bitsy had her by the wrist, holding on as if she were a balloon that would float away if she let go.

With her attention on the anthill that she and Wesley had located, she offered only a shrug.

"Does your mother know where you are?"

Another shrug.

"Can she stay?" Wesley asked. I looked down the street, unsure of what to do. Had James followed after us, I wouldn't have given it a second thought. Nora wouldn't mind, if she even noticed he was missing. But I didn't know what Bitsy would think.

"Please?" Katherine asked. She really was a cute girl, with freckles across her nose and eyelashes I couldn't help but envy. Our time there was limited, and I figured Bitsy probably knew where her daughter was. After all, a good mother would.

"Yes, but we won't be here long. We can walk home together in a bit."

That seemed to satisfy the two of them, and soon Wesley invited Katherine to make a picture. They sat together and began drawing. Wesley sketched a mountainous anthill with a zigzagging line of spots marching to the top, while Katherine decided to draw her favorite insect: a butterfly.

The girl took her time with her drawing, carefully rounding the wings, trying to make them even before filling them in with a pink, blue, and yellow pattern. As they worked, I stood and watched, swayed and shushed. The breeze rattled the leaves overhead and the birds were extra chatty, calling to one another as they landed and lighted upon the branches. A chipmunk darted across the grass, sprinting into a neighbor's yard.

As they drew, I thought of Bitsy's overreaction the last time they had played together. And I also thought of that game Katherine had suggested with a taxi driver and a detective. Her aunt must've been quite sick if she was so worried about her that she'd created a game about her.

"How's your aunt?" I asked, but Katherine didn't respond. She looked at me, uncertain. "Wesley said she wasn't feeling well."

Katherine only shrugged. Perhaps she had made up the entire game, but I thought of how her parents had responded, how they looked at each other, so I pressed further. "I hope she's okay. I've been worried."

"She will be," Katherine finally said, revealing that it hadn't simply been a game. "That's what Father says. And do you see this flutterby? We saw one just like it in our backyard the other day. Mother told me not to chase it, but I wanted to get closer. She doesn't like it when I run. I used to run all the time." She shrugged so matter-of-factly, saying it not as if it bothered her, but as if it was simply a statement of how things once were. "But things are different."

"Do you want to run now?" Wesley asked.

"Wes, maybe she shouldn't—" Before I could finish my sentence, they dropped their crayons and began running around the tree. I thought about stopping them, but then I saw how happy Katherine was. Perhaps Bitsy was one of those mothers who thought girls should look pretty and not be adventurous. How different my childhood would've been had my mother held that belief. I saw her smiling, heard her giggling along with Wesley, and I decided to let them be, to let the girl enjoy herself.

She laughed and ran for only a few minutes. Until Bitsy found us.

"Katherine!" Bitsy ran in those oxfords of hers, her feet hitting the pavement hard as her skirt swayed with every step, and Nora hurried behind her.

Bitsy darted past me to get to Katherine. "What have we said about leaving the backyard?" she asked as she looked the child up and down, making sure she was okay. "And about running?"

No longer giggling, Katherine's eyes focused on the ground, her hands gripped in front of her. Instead of words, she responded with her typical gesture and shrugged her shoulders.

"She's fine," I tried to reassure Bitsy. "We came to get outside, and Katherine found us here. They were just watching some ants and drawing pictures."

Bitsy didn't say a word. She didn't even look at me. She put her arm around her daughter and marched her down the street.

"What was that about?" I asked Nora as we watched them leave.

She pulled a cigarette from her pocket and lit it. Between puffs, she said, "She's upset."

"The girl's fine."

"She didn't know that." Nora exhaled a line of smoke that curled toward me.

"How many times have our boys taken off to play? What does she think will happen?"

"Lulu." Nora turned toward me. "She's not us." Wasn't that the truth? "You can't take her kid without asking."

My indignation rose, along with my pulse. "I didn't take her kid." I wanted to say more, but before I could, Wesley had walked up behind us, and besides, I was too tired to argue with Nora.

Instead, I took Wesley's hand and went home. Wesley hung the drawings on the refrigerator, deciding he could take Katherine's picture to her later. As I got sandwiches around for lunch, I looked at that butterfly, the pink mixing with blue and blended with yellow to make streaks of green in some places. Her picture was so much more complete than Wesley's. It had so much more detail to it.

She seemed like a good kid, though quiet. I knew the type. I wondered about her as I stared at her drawing. Her mother seemed to keep her so close, while her older brothers were off at school, even for the summer. Could I do that to Wes? Could I send him away like that? If I did, maybe I would cling to Esther, too.

A tickle ran along the underside of my arm. I scratched at the rash, thinking it had caused the tingle, but my finger felt a lump of something that moved on its own. I smacked at myself and an ant fell to the floor. I stomped on it for good measure, not wanting the intruder in my house.

As a shiver carried through my body, Katherine's picture

caught my eye. Sometimes the late-afternoon sun trickled through that window, highlighting dust particles and causing reflections to dance. It was noontime. The sun was still high, and while daylight bathed the kitchen, the beams were not angled to play their tricks. Even still, I swear to you, as the ant flinched on the floor, the butterfly on my fridge wiggled its antenna. I know it didn't happen—it couldn't have—but as I finished getting lunch together, I felt it watch me as heat prickled along my arms and a voice whispered through the noonday light, *What did you really see?*

CHAPTER FOURTEEN

The morning of the company dinner, I woke to find the rash had grown. I ran my fingers over the bumps that dotted the undersides of my upper arms and wondered if it would be a good enough reason to not have to go to the dinner. I played every excuse in my mind and realized that Henry would not accept any of them. But I wasn't sure I could even get myself ready, not when I felt the way I did.

I hadn't listened to Henry. He'd told me to go buy a dress and get to the salon, but I hadn't done either. The salon used to be such a regular occurrence, but it had been months since I had been. It's surprising how quickly we can slip out of routines.

I'd never been to a salon until Marian sent me to one before my bridal shower. Mama had always been the one to cut my hair, and until college, the only style required was one that kept my hair from my face as I fed the animals, ran through the fields, or swung in the tire swing. A braid worked just fine.

Once I got to college, I noticed that other girls seemed to put more time and effort into their hair. The first night of freshman year, as I watched my roommate, Doreen, take her one hundred brushstrokes before putting in rollers for the night, I wondered how she knew to do that. Had she taken a class I had somehow missed? And how did she sleep with those things on her head, pushing into her, pointing her neck at an angle? She always slept on her back, a snore escaping every few minutes. I wrapped the pillow around my head, trying to dampen the sound. So far removed from the sounds of crickets and tree frogs, the silence was too loud, the snores disruptive.

I got used to it over time, as I suppose Doreen got used to the curlers as well.

"You've never used rollers?" she'd asked. She ran her fingers through my hair and decided to help me. "Do you have an old shirt? A rag of some sort?"

I gave her the closest I had to a rag, and she proceeded to rip it into strips. She showed me how to comb, section, and wrap my hair around the strips of cloth. The next morning, I removed the rags and my hair hung in ringlets the likes of which I had never seen before. While the braid would add wave, it never achieved the curl the old cloth had.

That became my style for the rest of college, until Marian sent me to the hairdresser and I was educated on how to properly care for and style my hair. Magazine subscriptions helped as well. Soon the practice became a routine.

Sometimes routine offers certainty, action without having

to give thought, a practice that doesn't require questioning. Sometimes it offers comfort. Sometimes when we lose those routines, we lose ourselves.

The previous night I had gotten out the curlers and tried to remind myself of how to use them. Wesley joined me in the bathroom, watching as I stood in my slip in front of the bathroom mirror and rolled up one section of hair after another. He seemed delighted by the transformation, as intrigued as he was when he watched his favorite program, *Howdy Doody*. Henry walked in to find him puckering his lips and testing out my lipstick.

"You shouldn't let him do that," Henry said after he sent Wesley off to play. After he had wiped every bit of the Cherries in the Snow shade from his son's lips.

"It's fine. He's not wasteful."

"This isn't about frugality," Henry said. "It's inappropriate."

"He's only four."

"Yes. By this age, he can remember things. And he doesn't need to see his mother half-naked."

If only Henry knew of the days I spent sitting on the couch, nursing Wesley's sister with my breast in full view as he played with the Lone Ranger and Roy Rogers figurines on the floor.

I told Henry that Wesley was only having a little fun. Then I reminded him that I was doing it because of him and the company dinner the next night. After that, he locked himself in his office, and I handled the rest of the nighttime routine alone.

That night, I sat awake, eyes trained on the house opposite mine. Waiting for a light to trip on, for the woman across the way to appear in the window. I waited to witness her secrets, see her flinch again, knowing she was hiding something beneath that perfect veneer, but unsure exactly what. And as the hours ticked by, my brain slipped somewhere new, somewhere distant and dark. Until the conscious world disappeared.

When I woke under the weight of Luna in the morning, I smelled colors as soon as my eyes opened. I tried to go through the motions of the day. I even tried to distract myself by counting my stamps, but I couldn't concentrate. In the afternoon, I removed the curlers, but I stood frozen in front of the mirror, my hands aching, my mind vibrating, my eyes throbbing. I made myself a drink and when that didn't seem to help, I poured a second one. But as the clock ticked ever closer to when Henry would be there to pick me up, I did the only thing I knew to do: I forced myself to be the good wife he wanted.

Despite the heat wave that hung heavy that week, I chose a long-sleeved dress to hide the rash. Henry seemed to like my choice, because when he first caught sight of me, he smiled like he did when he used to notice me. As we pulled away from the house and out of the neighborhood, my heart began to pound, thumping in my chest, beating in my ears, throbbing against my forehead. Heat rose in my cheeks, and I regretted not putting on more deodorant.

"You'll be great tonight," Henry told me. "And I can't wait for you to meet Alice."

Of all the duties I had that night, the one he focused on most was meeting the firm's new assistant, the woman he had helped hire when I was too pregnant to waddle into the office and make her acquaintance. I had spoken to her a few times by phone, when she called to tell me Henry would be home late. She sounded young, probably one of those girls who went straight to secretarial school and into an office job, another way of finding a husband. A path I might've taken had it not been for Henry.

"I can't wait," I told him as I took a deep breath and tried to calm my pounding heart.

Before we got out of the car, Henry reminded me of why I was there. "Put in a good word for me with Jack, but don't bring up his wife. She's been off with relatives for a while. And save him a dance. You know he always likes that."

As Henry walked around the car to open my door, I checked myself in my compact mirror. A different version of Lulu stared back. Someone who used to exist but had faded away over the last months, morphed into someone else. Someone not used to updos and fancy dresses, mingling and dancing, making good impressions. Maybe I hadn't morphed; maybe I had lost the mask and the middle-of-the-night Lulu was more real than the one who looked at me through the mirror.

The woman in the mirror was who Henry needed me to be that night, so I took his hand and let him guide me into the party. I smiled and waved at those I needed to. I shook hands when one was extended to me. I sipped champagne and welcomed refills. I didn't even let the smile fade from my face when Alice, with the baby fat still rounding her cheeks, told me, "It's so nice to meet you, ma'am."

I continued to smile as I told her it was nice to meet the new office girl, and I watched as she looked at Henry and blushed.

Thankfully, Mr. Ellis wanted to dance. I finished the rest of my champagne and let him lead me onto the dance floor. I placed one hand in his as his other wrapped around my waist.

"It's so good to see you out and about," he said.

"I wouldn't have missed this," I lied, but that was part of being a wife.

"Your boy's been working hard." So he had noticed. "I knew I made the right decision bringing him on board. He was young, but he showed promise."

"And the promise is paying off?"

Jack slid his hand farther down my back so the tips of his fingers rested just below the waist of my panties. "I think so."

He pulled me closer to him so his stomach pushed into me, and his plaid jacket smelled like mincemeat pie. He put his cheek against mine and hummed into my ear. His voice rattled deep, a low vibration thrumming like a hive active with anxious bees. He spun me around the dance floor, never loosening his grip. I looked for Henry, hoping he would cut in. It took a few more turns until I found him, in the corner by the bar, laughing with Alice. The static of bees grew frantic, electric in my ears, as the room tilted on its axis.

I began to sweat, certain Jack would feel it against his cheek, or on his hand pressed into my lower back. But he gave no indication. He held tight, humming with the music as he moved us around the dance floor. I couldn't look at Henry and Alice anymore. I shifted my gaze overhead to the chandeliers. But they swirled and so did I.

I tried to loosen his grip on me, create some space between us. Even with a lump in my throat, I forced out words, hoping if I got him talking, he'd slow down the dancing. "He's enjoying what he's doing." I swallowed before continuing, willing the bile and champagne to stay in my stomach. "But looking forward to what's next."

Jack had taken to me the first time we met, telling me that I reminded him of the one who got away. At the time, I had taken it as a compliment, but looking back, I thought of how his wife had looked away when he said that and then excused herself.

"Well, he's got a future ahead of him."

I breathed again, thankful to have something to concentrate on other than the spinning room. I pushed further, but knew I couldn't speak too directly, even if Jack did like me. "I know he's hoping that future comes soon."

"Mmm," his voice rumbled, as if he was thinking about what I meant. "Well, he is still young."

"Has he shown you the new plans?" He hadn't shown me what he had been working on most every evening and weekend. I hadn't asked either, but I needed to say something. "Works on them every night."

"Does he, now?"

"Comes home for dinner and then straight into his office."

"Mmm." I gave him a minute to think, to consider what those plans might look like, how they might help the company, how Henry was putting in the hours that showed his commitment, the justification for the promotion that had been slow coming. But I should've continued, because in the pause, he began to consider someone else. "Did he tell you about Gary? Gary Betser?" The bile climbed higher, burning my throat, threatening to escape. "He's got a lot of experience. Nice guy, too."

"Yes, lots of commercial experience, from what I hear. Seems like a different thing, designing for a business versus a cozy place to raise a family."

"I've seen his renderings. He's a good architect."

"But he's a project manager."

"Maybe not anymore."

I pressed my lips together and smiled as those words replayed in my mind. Was he implying that Gary was going for the promotion Henry had thought was his?

Jack tightened his arm around my waist. I looked over his shoulder, trying to find Henry. I didn't know if I could last much longer. After that song, I needed to get home. Jack continued the box step to his own rhythm, turning me despite my desire to stay still.

"You know what I always look for in an employee? Loyalty. Do you think Henry's got that?"

I took a deep breath, willing myself to hold it together. The song ended and Jack let go of me. Over his shoulder, I caught sight of Henry and Alice, standing together in a corner as he leaned close to her and she said something into his ear. The bile rose again, but I pushed it down. I tried to keep my eyes on Jack's, wanting more than anything to not smell the color of his jacket anymore. Through a painted smile, I said, "Absolutely."

Walking off that dance floor and over to my husband took my last bits of strength. I remember in the days after Daddy died, watching Mama go through the motions—dress us kids, stand beside the casket, silent and still. I did as she did until the middle of the night, and then I wondered if she heard me crying through the floorboards. If she did, she never told me, but she didn't talk a lot those days.

As I stood before Henry, I thought of her, and for the first time that I could remember, I told myself to be like her, to stand still. But instead of being silent, I spoke. "We need to go."

Henry looked from Alice to me, his expression shifting to confusion as he asked, "What?"

"Alice, it was lovely to meet you," I said as I extended my hand to her and hoped she wouldn't see mine shaking from the effort it took to keep myself together. "I'm afraid we need to call it an early night."

I whispered to Henry that I wasn't feeling well. Then I headed to the car and waited for him to say his proper goodbyes. I didn't give him time to protest, to try to talk me out of it. I knew he was too well mannered to cause a scene in front of everyone, but his first question when he got into the car and slammed the door closed was, "What the hell, Lulu?"

"I'm sorry," I said. And I was. I didn't want to feel like that. I didn't want to have to leave, to go home, to pull Henry away from what he needed to do to land the promotion, but my body had not given me a choice.

He pounded his fist on the steering wheel and said nothing to me, not even when he turned off the car and placed the keys in the visor. I didn't wait for him to walk around and open my door, as he typically would, especially on a night out like that. We both got out at the same time, and he looked at me over the car.

"What is going on?" he asked me. "Ever since—"

"I don't know." I had a decision to make: I could keep my answer at that, or I could tell him how I'd been feeling. But I looked at him as the streetlight illuminated one side of his face, and I said the only thing I thought he wanted to hear: "I'm sorry."

"God, Lulu. You don't know what it's been like." That made two of us. "I needed to be there tonight to show Jack I'm ready for more than being a junior architect. I just needed a couple of hours from you. I didn't realize that was too much to ask."

I closed my eyes and shook my head. He didn't know that what he had asked was more than a couple of hours of me smiling beside him.

"I danced with him. Isn't that what you needed?"

"You know it's more than that."

"And do you know he's looking at Gary?"

"Yeah, to be a project manager. I introduced them."

"No. Not a project manager." I put my hands on the hood of the car, trying to steady myself as the night began to swirl around me. "It's you or him; do you know that?"

Henry pounded his fist on the car. "Shit." As he leaned over the hood, I saw Luna sitting at the corner of the house, ready to head to the backyard, to sit on the patio and wait for me to let her into the house. She didn't come closer, as if knowing to stay only in my line of sight.

I lost her in the darkness as my vision began to fade. I should've had more than Wesley's sandwich crust that day. The pounding in my head grew louder as the black of night swirled around me and my body fell to the driveway.

I think I was only unconscious for a moment. All I know is that as I came to, Henry told me not to stand. He picked me up in his arms and carried me into the house, like when he carried me over the threshold the day we moved in. This time, we didn't laugh. He didn't spin me around the living room. Instead, he carried me down the hallway and placed me on the bed before he went out to the living room and whispered to a concerned Hatti.

I did the only thing I was capable of at that moment. With my hair still pinned in a chignon and while still wearing my sheath dress, I rolled onto my side. I didn't bother to remove the red lipstick that, by the time I'd wake a few hours later, would be smeared across my pillow. Streaks of Revlon blood from the battle I'd lost.

CHAPTER FIFTEEN

Henry called Dr. Collins the next morning. Who am I kidding? He probably had Alice do it once he got to the office. All I knew was that after I cooked and served him his eggs that morning, he said, "You're not well, Lulu."

I couldn't argue with him. Somehow I had avoided the cold Katherine had given Wesley, but something had turned my stomach the night before and caused me to faint in the driveway. Plus, there were all the strange ways I had been feeling since Esther was born. Maybe I was imagining some of it. I knew it had taken time to feel like myself after Wesley, but this felt different. It was best if we got to the bottom of it.

Dr. Collins arrived during naptime, having had to run through an afternoon downpour to get to the front door. The day had started full of sunlight, but by afternoon, the gray settled overhead until the clouds became too thick and heavy to hold back the precipitation any longer. I wondered where Luna was, if she had a shelter to keep her out of the rain.

"I spoke with Henry," the doctor said after he folded his umbrella and placed it in the stand in the foyer. I spent two books worth of stamps on the stand shortly after we had been married. It seemed like an item a good hostess would have, but it rarely got used.

Dr. Collins motioned for me to sit down on my own davenport. "How's about telling me what's going on?"

What was going on? Didn't Henry tell him? Or at least tell him his version of it? I suppose I should've been happy that the doctor wanted me to tell him. I was tired, sometimes nauseous. I wasn't sleeping well. I got hot when I left the house. Some days I had headaches. Sometimes I smelled colors. But I knew how all that sounded, so what did he want me to say?

"I suppose Henry told you about last night?" That seemed like a good place to start, but before offering him more details, I waited for him to respond, wondering if that was as much as I needed to say.

"Mmm-hmmm. Henry mentioned that." The doctor seemed distracted. He looked around the living room instead of at me, his caterpillar eyebrows twitching downward as he squinted. "Do you mind if we turn on some lights?"

Perhaps I should've thought of that. The house was dark that day, especially since the rain had started, but I hadn't bothered to turn on any lights. As I said, the day had started bright, sunny, with birds chirping outside until the storm rolled in. It reminded me of that Sunday afternoon back in 1940 when the moon eclipsed the sun. The day had started so bright, but everyone knew what was coming.

After church, we'd all headed home and didn't visit with neighbors or family like we usually did on the Lord's day. Instead, we sat in the house and waited. They told me not to look at the sun when the eclipse started, and I listened, too afraid of losing my sight to not obey. Mama and Daddy stayed inside, and Georgie wasn't born yet. I went out back and sat beneath my tree, watching the shapes of the leaves change to crescent moons as the sky darkened, the birds quieted, and the crickets sang their nighttime song in the middle of the afternoon.

I wondered if Henry saw that eclipse. We never talked about it, but I imagined he did. Everyone seemed to take notice, at least in our town, but maybe he'd had better things to do that day.

I clicked on the lamps and sat back down on the davenport as I started to tell Dr. Collins how I'd been feeling. "I've been pretty tired lately." He nodded like he understood, so I kept going. "I suppose I haven't been getting the best sleep. It's hard, you know." He assured me that he did understand. "Not much of an appetite for a while. Oh, and sometimes I've been getting headaches." His woolly-worm brows scrunched together, so I stopped.

"And passing out? Was last night the first time?"

"Yes." As much as I wanted to feel better, I didn't like the look on his face, the downward turn of his lips, how his eyes squinted. I know doctors are meant to help, but they don't always bring the news we wanted to hear. "I'm guessing it's a touch of something. Thankfully, I feel better this morning." Hopefully that meant I wouldn't be getting anyone else sick.

"Henry said you had some champagne." He opened his bag and pulled out a stethoscope.

"Yes." Who hadn't had a few drinks at the party? But I was the only one who seemed to feel sick.

"Perhaps it was a bit too much?"

"I don't know that I'd say that."

"You are still postpartum." He held the stethoscope to my chest and told me to take a deep breath. "Have you been drinking much in that time?"

Did he expect me to breathe or answer? "No."

"Maybe your body's adjusted and last night was too much, too soon." Perhaps he was right. "Tell me more about how you've been sleeping since—"

"Not well. But after Wesley"—and my entire life—"I expected as much."

"Mmm-hmm." Dr. Collins asked me to lie down. "Of course, this isn't like Wesley."

I suppose every baby is different. Look at me and Georgie. Mama said he had such an easy disposition, so different from my own.

He pressed on my abdomen and asked, "Is it possible that you're—"

"No." I was certain that pregnancy was not a possibility, and he seemed to agree, because he changed the subject.

"How many hours of sleep are you getting at night?"

I wanted to be honest. But I knew I couldn't tell him the truth. Even Henry didn't know how little sleep I got. Even I didn't, because I didn't want to know for myself. I would start off with a couple of hours, but then my body would rouse, my mind would wake, and there was no returning to sleep after that. Sure, I would stare out the window and maybe drift off for a few minutes. But sometimes it felt more like passing time than drifting off.

I crossed my ankles and folded my hands across my stomach, my fingers gripped tightly. "I'd say six hours." I couldn't look him in the eye. But, really, what could this little white lie hurt?

"Six?" he asked.

I nodded.

"How do you feel throughout the day?"

"Tired."

"And would you say you feel happy?"

I didn't mean to laugh. Only a short one escaped before I caught myself. What kind of a question was that? Was I happy? Were Nora and Hatti? Was Bitsy, with her wobbly ankles and flinching shoulders? Was the woman with her head stuck in the oven? Was anyone well and truly happy?

Yes, they were. They had to be. It was me; I was the problem.

At one point, happiness was all I thought I needed. I'd felt so smart saying that to Mama one day, as if I had found some true search in life that no one else had thought of. But really all it did was reveal something about my family: The idea of happiness was so foreign that I assumed no one else had thought to strive for it.

All Mama wanted was security. A good husband. A good farm. A good harvest. A good son to take over when the time came. A good daughter who would settle for the boy down the road. "There's no chasin' happiness," she said to me when I begged her to let me go away to college.

But I knew people believed in it. Look at Hatti with her kids and Bitsy with that smile always on her face. Then there was Henry, thinking that happiness was something he could conquer and achieve. Perhaps for him, it was. A house with all the modern conveniences—the Mobile Maid, the car in the driveway. A beautiful wife with an easy smile and desirable body. A job that came with promotions, promise, and a steady paycheck. He did have something to work for, a way to find happiness. He somehow thought that was possible for us as well. When it didn't come easily, he made sure to find ways to make it happen.

I remember rolling my eyes at Mama that day in the kitchen when she dismissed my hope for the future. That woman never seemed to understand me. Now I see that she was only trying to teach me. I thought I was so much smarter than her, heading to college, an opportunity she never had. But she didn't need to go away, read a bunch of books, and listen to professors speak to packed lecture halls. She already knew the truth of the matter: Happiness was a fool's errand.

I paused long enough that I didn't need to answer Dr. Collins's question. He proceeded to give me the standard once-over, checking my pulse, looking into my eyes and ears, rubbing his cold hands along my neck.

"What you're dealing with here is nothing new," the doctor began. "Physically, you're fine. Right as rain, from best I can tell, but sometimes we see this."

I swallowed hard, waiting and yet also not wanting to hear what he had to say. Daddy's diagnosis had not been unusual. Though they never told me what it was, they always acted like it wasn't too much to worry about, but look what happened to him. Did I want to know what was wrong with me? Though the bigger question was: Could Dr. Collins fix me?

"We call this hysteria." He said it so matter-of-factly. I didn't feel hysterical, and I wanted to tell him that, but I feared that anything I said would only prove his point. Instead, I smiled and nodded. He packed up his bag and continued, saying, "I see this in women such as yourself all the time, this housewife syndrome. You're a bit tired, doing a lot around the house. Not really feeling like yourself. Finding yourself a bit moody like your kids. The good news is that we can treat this. I'm going to write you a prescription for Miltown. Take it twice a day, morning and evening. It will take a few days to get into your system, but then I think you'll be happy with the results."

He tore off a prescription and handed it to me. I looked down at the scribbles.

"A pill?"

"Yes. I like to call it 'emotional aspirin.'"

"That's all I need?"

"This is pretty common. And Miltown is better than the stronger tranquilizers we used to use. I write a prescription for this a few times a week now. Soon enough, the wives are back to themselves and the husbands are happier than ever. Works wonders. You'll be good as new in no time." I hoped he was right.

The downpour had turned to a drizzle sometime during the examination. As the doctor left, I stood on the front step and let the drops dampen me. I wanted to go across the street, walk through the front door to my own home, stretch out on the davenport I had chosen, and settle in for a long nap with Luna by my side. I might need the place if Henry ever got around to running off with Alice.

Lightning flashed with a roll of thunder trailing a few seconds behind it. The light in the Betsers' front bedroom switched on, reminding me that the house wasn't mine. If anyone needed drugs, it was Bitsy, that woman who talked in short sentences and tried to force her way into friendships with pretzel salad. She seemed to spend a lot of time in that room. Maybe she was unpacking all those boxes. Maybe she was hiding something. Or maybe the soul of the place was making her restless and she was packing to leave.

I pulled my arms across my body and rubbed at the rash. I had forgotten to tell the doctor about that, but maybe it was all part of this housewife syndrome, my body showing it was as unhappy as my mind. Henry would probably be glad that there was a way to fix me. If the drugs did their job, then maybe I'd be the wife he remembered, the one he had chosen to marry. Then maybe he'd forget all about Alice, and we could live happily ever after like we were supposed to.

CHAPTER SIXTEEN

The advertisements promised I would feel like myself again, but what if I didn't remember who that was anymore? Miltown was supposed to make me the wife my husband had been missing. Make me smile even on a rainy day. But a few days after starting it, I hadn't noticed a difference. Not yet, anyway.

I did feel a bit calmer, more relaxed. I had the energy to put together a Jell-O salad for our card game. I was sleeping a bit more at night, but only after going out to the living room and letting Luna curl up with me on the couch. But I still didn't look like the women in the magazines. I still didn't feel like the Lulu I wanted to be. Instead, I felt like I was suspended in one of my own gelatin salads, wobbling, yet held on display as life continued beyond my reach.

The doctor had said that it might take more than a few days for it to work as it was supposed to, for me to be the wife and mother my family needed. And I wondered: Did Mama ever think about any of that? Did she ever consider who Daddy needed her to be other than the woman who fried his chicken to a crisp and washed the manure from his coveralls? Did she lose sleep over not knowing how to comfort me the morning I found blood in my underpants and began to cry, certain that I was broken?

If over time Miltown made me myself again, I was curious to see who that person was, but while I waited, life continued on, including Nora's insistence on playing cards. I would've preferred to host the ladies at my house, to not be so far from Esther, but Nora said it was Bitsy's turn.

The lemon scent greeted us at the door, as if to announce the cleanliness we were about to enter into. The sun soaked the living room in light, a stark contrast to my own house, which faced the opposite direction and drowned in shadows after midday. Bitsy took advantage of being westward facing and filled her picture window with a jungle of plants. Philodendrons twisted and climbed alongside a spider plant whose foliage coiled like overgrown fingernails. I couldn't help but notice she should repot her mother-in-law's tongue, the leaves suffocating in their claustrophobic container, a mistake I had made when I had last attempted to nurture a houseplant.

Above the ugly davenport were mirrored shelves with various knickknacks all sitting at attention, the porcelain figurines holding the same smile and stare as their owner. But most annoying were the vacuum lines in the carpeting—expertly lined, perfectly parallel, running the full length of the living room floor.

As we settled around the kitchen table, I noticed the cleaning schedule stuck to the refrigerator. Apparently, Bitsy was one of them. I was the outlier.

Hatti placed her hand on top of mine and gave it a little squeeze, asking, "How are you?"

I should've left then. I could've said Esther and Wesley needed me, which they probably did. I could've left my salad and made a quick exit, but having been trained in politeness, I sat and hoped that Hatti's question would sound like usual small talk to the others.

"Fine," I said as I placed my other hand on top of hers and tried to change the focus from me. "How are *you* feeling? Has the baby been active?"

Unfortunately, Hatti wasn't ready to talk about herself yet. "You're okay? I mean, after the other night and all?"

"What do you mean?" Nora asked as she dealt the cards around the table.

"Oh, nothing." I pulled my hand out from underneath Hatti's and reached for my cards. "Whose lead is it?"

"But after the other night." Hatti really could be relentless, especially when it came to mothering. One time a baby bird had fallen out of its nest and Hatti was beside herself, watching out her window all day for the mother to return and take the baby back home. I wanted to explain that the mother bird couldn't simply lift a fallen child into a nest, not like we can, but Hatti couldn't hear that. She hadn't been raised on a farm, nor with the frequent reminder that death was a part of life. "When you passed out. Are you okay?"

Bitsy looked up from her cards, her eyes wide, as Nora asked, "You passed out?"

"Yes," I said, flashing a small smile, questioning how much I wanted to say to them. "After the work party. I guess I had a bit too much champagne." They didn't need to hear me complain about headaches and tiredness. Who among us didn't have those?

"Henry had to carry her into the house." Hatti dropped her voice, as if she was hiding her response from me.

"Lulu!" Nora scolded. She'd always been the eldest of our group, even though Bitsy was now the oldest—though I still wouldn't call her a part of our group. Nora made sure to invite her. They apparently spoke most days, either by phone or across the fence line, but that didn't mean she was one of us. "Tell me you called the doctor."

"Yes," I tried to reassure them. "He came the next day."

Nora placed her cards on the table. "And...?"

"He said I'm right as rain." They watched me, expecting me to say more—well, except for Bitsy, who kept her focus on her cards, shifting the same ones in her hand. She was such an odd bird, always present while also absent. Though in that moment, I preferred her indifference to the prodding of the other two. "Those were his actual words."

Nora wouldn't let it go. "But what does that mean?"

"He said that physically, I'm fine."

"But..." She shifted in her seat, and I knew that sign. She would soon need a cigarette, but I also knew she wouldn't take a smoke break until she got what she wanted from me. "Quit shittin' around, Lulu. What else did he say?"

"He called it hysteria. Said I have housewife syndrome."

Hatti's voice dripped with concern as she repeated, "Housewife syndrome?"

"Says it's nothing to be concerned about." I hoped that was true. Mama had told me the same about Daddy when he first saw the doctor. With Georgie, we knew from the start what possible nightmare lurked around the corner, yet he was the one who was still with us.

"And let me guess," Nora began as Bitsy sat and shuffled her cards. "He put you on Miltown?"

My surprise must have shown on my face. "How'd you know?"

"You know I know things." Nora took a cigarette from her case and tapped it on the table. She stuck it in her mouth, where it teeter-tottered on the edge of her lip. "You don't mind if I light this up in here, right?"

"Well..." Bitsy finally stopped shuffling her cards. "Gary doesn't—" But she never finished her sentence, as Nora puffed until the tip glowed.

"I know some gals who have used it," Nora said.

"Well, the ads are in all the magazines," Hatti said.

"Has it helped?" I asked as Bitsy got up from the table to fetch a bowl (from the forsythia luncheon set, two-and-a-quarter books) that Nora could use.

Nora laid a card on the table. "Some swear by it. If it does half of what the ads promise, I'm sold. But what can it do for your hair?"

I put my hand to my head. "Is it that bad?"

"Well, you know it's just us. It's not like you need your Sunday best, but it looks a bit"—she searched for a word—"flat. It's not doing your cowlick any favors. But what do I know? I'm lucky I have clothes on. Marjorie has been in quite the mood. Threw her oatmeal right off the high chair. And after I mopped the floors two days ago. That child, I swear she's going to be the death of me." She closed her eyes and took a breath. "So maybe I should see about getting myself some of those pills."

"Tell your doctor you're not happy, and that should do the trick," I told her.

"Happy?" Nora punctuated her question with a laugh.

"Yeah, he asked me if I was happy, and I didn't have an answer for him."

"I'll tell him about the oatmeal and ask him if putting up with that day in and day out would make him happy."

"Oh, now," Hatti began, "it's not that bad."

"Hatti Brooks," Nora warned, "don't go gushing about your kids right now. Yes, I love mine, but that doesn't make it easy."

The truth of the statement silenced the room, other than the nap timers that ticked toward the end of our game. I had set mine for earlier than theirs, knowing I needed to get back to Esther. She'd been fussing at the end of her naps. Hatti fingered her gold locket, and Bitsy continued to shuffle her cards as if it was her duty to keep them moving.

We went on playing, making it around the table before Nora spoke again. "It could be worse."

"What do you mean?" Hatti could rarely let a statement like that go unquestioned.

"We've all heard the stories." Nora tapped her Lucky Strike on the rim so that the ashes cascaded like snow into the bottom of the bowl. "Remember, we read that article. A couple of years back. I think in *Reader's Digest*."

"You *made* us read it!" Hatti apparently still hadn't forgiven Nora for that.

Bitsy continued to fidget with her cards as she asked, "What was it about?"

I remembered the article. It had fascinated and scared all of us. Bitsy looked across the table at me, her eyes settling on mine instead of my lips as I said, "It was the story of someone who had a lobotomy."

"They drilled holes into this poor woman's head to cure her malaise." Leave it to Nora to give a matter-of-fact recounting, to which Bitsy focused her eyes on her cards and began to run her hand over her bangs, pressing them into her forehead as if attempting to iron them into place.

"But"—Hatti tried to wave off the memories of the article—"that was fiction."

"Based on a true story," Nora reminded her.

"That poor soul." Hatti shifted in her chair. "I don't want to talk about this anymore."

"I'm just saying…" Nora exhaled another puff of nicotine haze before snuffing out the cigarette. "It could be worse, Lu."

Three of us nodded in agreement as the fourth continued to fuss with her bangs, petting them from forehead to eyebrow, stroke, after stroke, after stroke, as the timers ticked, ticked, ticked.

A few hands in, and Hatti and I both needed to use the powder room.

"It's down the hall and on the right," Bitsy said as if we didn't already know. We could walk blindfolded through any of these houses and still know exactly where to go.

I let the pregnant woman go first. Waiting my turn, I looked at the portraits that hung along both sides of the hall. They showed snapshots of younger years, when Gary's stomach wasn't quite so round. Apparently, he had been in the war, and it looked like Bitsy had a sister named Ellen, at least according to the writing across the top of a photo that had to have been taken a good twenty years ago. There were baby pictures of the boys, who I could not tell apart, and one of them standing in matching uniforms at what must've been the academy. I looked over the display of this family's moments and realized someone was missing: Katherine. I saw her eyes in those of Bitsy and Ellen in their younger years, but I couldn't find a single portrait of the girl herself.

As I looked over the photos and hoped Hatti would be done soon, I overheard Nora asking Bitsy about her cat that was apparently still missing. "Remind me what she looks like."

Bitsy's voice wasn't as loud as Nora's. I could barely make out what she said, which gave me hope that I misheard her. Gary had said the cat was "one of those tiger types." But I swore I heard Bitsy say, "Gray."

I thought of Luna. I didn't know where she went in the daytime, and I didn't need to know. Even if she was Bitsy's, she chose me for a reason. If anything, I was doing Bitsy a favor helping care for a cat that apparently she couldn't manage herself.

Hatti wasn't done yet, but I needed to use the bathroom. Ever since Wesley, I couldn't hold it like before, and especially not since Esther came along. I decided to use the bathroom in their master bedroom instead of asking her to hurry up.

As I opened the door, I couldn't believe my eyes. Perhaps Bitsy wasn't the perfect homemaker she seemed to be. Though the knickknacks and magazines were perfectly in place in the living room, piles of clothes lay strewn across every surface of the bedroom. And not only Gary's. Bitsy's nightgown was wadded up on the floor as if she had stepped out of it and not given it a second thought that morning. Her dressing gown had been tossed across a chair, and the dress I had seen her wear the day before was slung over the dresser.

After the state of the bedroom, I shouldn't have been so surprised to see the bathroom counter cluttered with bottles and clothes, even some dried-up washcloths. The roll of toilet paper wasn't even in the holder, but instead on the floor beside the toilet.

As I washed my hands, I couldn't help but notice the medicine cabinet hung open. Inside were the basics: Bayer, laxatives, a turned-over bottle of acetaminophen, and a curled-up tube of toothpaste. But there was also an amber prescription bottle.

I listened for a moment, making sure no one was coming to find me. When the coast seemed clear, I picked up the bottle, expecting to find Gary's name, maybe some blood pressure medication or something for gout. He seemed like the type of guy who would need both. The label was rather faded, as if fingers over time had worn away parts of the inscription, but I could still make out enough to see that the medication wasn't for Gary. It was for Bitsy. And the pills were tranquilizers—phenobarbital, to be precise. A prescription much stronger than my own.

The whole time Hatti and Nora had been asking about my diagnosis and the need for Miltown, Betsy had remained silent. She didn't share that she had her own prescription. She didn't share why she was taking the drug. She let the others ask me questions, put myself out there to be examined, but she remained silent.

By the time I left her bedroom, Hatti had returned to the kitchen, and I was alone in the hallway, staring at the door to the front bedroom. Sun and shadow peeked out from the space beneath the closed door. Both called to me. Both begged me to look behind another door to see what else Bitsy was hiding.

I lingered in the hallway, listening before I walked to the door. When it seemed safe, I put my hand on the doorknob. My fingers stiffened as I began to turn the cold knob. The hinges moaned only slightly as I pushed the door open. Thankfully, they didn't cry like the ones in the farmhouse, but I paused for a second, making sure no one had heard.

Through the slim opening, I could see piles of boxes and a desk against the far wall. Apparently, this room wasn't simply used for storage. I began to slink through the narrow opening, keeping an ear out for any indication that someone was coming. Not hearing a soul, I walked to the desk. Recipes clipped from magazines and loyalty stamps were scattered across the desktop. A calendar poked out from beneath them, along with a newspaper article.

I pulled it from beneath the mess and read the headline: Despondent Knollwood Wife Takes Own Life.

Despondent wife. Nora had said those words weeks ago.

This was the woman from Bitsy's neighborhood. She must've known her after all. I tried to read the article, to see if there was more information than what Nora shared with us, to see if maybe it told why the woman had done what she did or if she had left a note. I scoured the page, looking for any clue. My eyes trained on the words, all those brutal words—*loss, senseless, tragic, mad*. I was so engrossed that I didn't realize I was being watched.

"Mrs. Mayfield?" a small voice asked.

I gasped and turned to find Katherine standing behind me. Much like her mother, she remained silent. She clung to a doll, whose one eye blinked as the other remained wide open.

"Katherine!" I held the article behind my back, not ready to give it up just yet. "I didn't see you there." My head throbbed from the sudden jolt. The girl squeezed her doll, holding it with one arm tightly pressed against the neck. I rubbed at my own throat, which suddenly felt tense. "I was looking for the restroom," I said in the silence.

"I'll show you." She waited for me to follow, and I had no choice but to drop the article on the desk. She led me to the hallway and pointed to the bathroom.

"My mistake." The girl made no move to leave, so I decided to tell her, "Wesley's been wanting to play. How about I ask your mother if you can come over this afternoon?"

Katherine looked down at the doll. "She won't let me."

"Why not?"

She rubbed at the molded hair on top of the doll's head. "She says he gets me into trouble."

Then the girl went back into her bedroom, closed the door, and left me alone in the hallway to fume. Heat rose through my body. I couldn't believe this woman thought my son was a troublemaker, when it was her daughter who seemed to have a problem listening and staying where she was supposed to be.

I couldn't say any of that to Katherine, but I had it in my mind to tell her mother a thing or two. I straightened my dress, pulled back my shoulders, and ignored the spinning walls as I marched into the kitchen, where I found the three of them eating my salad.

"Well done, Queen," Nora said with a mouthful of gelatin that she nearly choked on when she looked at me and saw the anger on my face.

Before I could say anything, Hatti asked Bitsy, "So it looks like Gary's going to be working with Henry?"

"Possibly." Bitsy looked at her bowl, spooning up another bite as she said, "He was told it looks promising."

Promising. Wasn't that how Jack had also described Henry? The heat in my cheeks rose, and Nora shook her head in warning. But I didn't care. The words bubbled from my stomach to my throat. My brain rehearsed them before they exploded out of me: *How dare you call my son a troublemaker!*

"Bitsy, how—"

"Oh!" Bitsy's exclamation interrupted me, her fingers fishing something from her mouth. She held whatever it was between her thumb and forefinger.

"Is everything okay?" Hatti asked.

I squinted to see what she held, but part of me already knew. I could tell by Bitsy's wide eyes and clamped fingers.

"What is it?" Nora asked, leaning in for a closer look. "Oh, a hair. I hate it when that happens."

Embarrassment rushed through me, but vindication followed closely behind it. On one hand, how filthy was it that a hair had made it into my salad? But I knew whose hair Bitsy would believe it to be.

"How embarrassing! I'm so sorry."

"It happens," Hatti tried to comfort, but she didn't know that the mistake hadn't been improper cleaning.

With Bitsy still holding on to the hair, Nora reached across and took it from her. "Oh!" she exclaimed. "Gray. Well, that can't be Lulu's." She and Hatti laughed as Bitsy and I looked at each other. Bitsy had a few gray hairs of her own, especially along her temple. They were quite noticeable with her hair pulled back. But the difference between her hair and the one she had found was the length. And the species. What Nora hadn't noticed before she dropped the hair onto the floor was that the hair wasn't human. I had made the salad late at night, had made it while taking long moments to distract myself with a cuddle on the couch. No, the hair wasn't anyone's at the table.

It was feline.

I could feel Bitsy putting the puzzle together. Picture her searching her yard frantically. Her eyes landed sharp on me.

And I simply smiled.

CHAPTER SEVENTEEN

Marriage has ways of dismantling certain measures of privacy, whittling down the walls of modesty over the years. This was why Henry didn't even knock before he came into the bathroom as I settled into the tub. It was also why he didn't hesitate to unzip his pants and pee as I sat only a few feet away from him, blanketed beneath a barrier of bubbles.

"Don't wait up for me," he said. "I've got to get these blueprints done tonight. Jack wants to see them tomorrow."

"When's he going to make a decision?" I asked.

Henry zipped his pants and closed the lid, but he didn't bother flushing. Thankfully, Marian had trained him well in putting down the toilet seat, a habit Daddy and Georgie never seemed to pick up. I had been considering getting a new toilet rug and seat-cover set, perhaps the green one with the pink rose overlay. It would only cost one book, so I certainly had the stamps to do it, but I hadn't yet committed to making the decision. The one we had was still fine, even if I was growing tired of it.

"I don't know. Last December, he said by May, but here we are, almost August." Henry didn't wash his hands. He leaned against the vanity and looked at me as I sat naked beneath the bubbles. He didn't delight in the possibility, the potential peep show he had walked in on. Instead, he thought about work. "I had Alice do some asking around, trying to get information about what Jack's thinking about Gary, but he wouldn't let on."

He said her name with his wife sitting naked in front of him, a reality he didn't seem to notice. I wondered how he felt when he said her name. Did he say it out of habit, almost mechanically? Or did he feel a zing of pleasure when her name crossed his lips? If he did, he didn't let on. Instead, he ran his hands through his hair, pulling it back, revealing a widow's peak that had become even more defined.

"I've got to get these done even if it takes me all night." Henry didn't try to look beneath the bubbles. He didn't come run his finger along my arm, resting on the side of the tub. He didn't notice me at all. He turned his attention to the vanity, looking over the collection of compacts and bottles. Did her name echo in his thoughts, distracting him from seeing me?

"I can make you coffee," I offered.

"Nah. Don't get up. Enjoy your soak."

While marriage may have chipped away at certain aspects of privacy, our thoughts remained our own. While I could've asked about Alice and watched the focus of his eyes, the movement of his hands, the posture of his body to tell me what his words wouldn't, I decided to settle into the warmth of the bathwater. I put my head against the back of the tub, the water reaching farther up my neck, dampening the lowest roots of my hair. I closed my eyes and inhaled the scent of lavender until a rattle broke the silence. I opened my eyes, expecting to see Henry holding a baby toy, but instead he was shaking a pill bottle.

"You've been taking these?"

"Mmm-hmm."

"Every day?"

"Mmm-hmm."

He put the bottle down and turned to look at me.

"Do you think they're helping?"

The real question was: Did *he* think they were helping?

I didn't tell him how the pills made me feel, my senses more clouded than on a typical day, my thoughts no longer wandering because my mind was too dulled to think. I couldn't tell him then that I would rather walk through the world in discontent than to feel the numbness those pills offered. It took more effort for me to hear the joy in Wesley's laughter, more rocking for me to feel gratitude with Esther in my arms. The pills pushed me beyond the surface of myself, so I floated through my days, watching my life unfold on a shore too distant to reach.

But I couldn't turn the question back on him. And I also couldn't tell him how, a few times, I skipped taking them. On the days I most wanted to feel, I would happen to forget to pop one in the morning. So I sat up, stretched a smile across my face, and told him, "Absolutely."

Henry held my gaze and I held my grin. As we looked at each other, I wanted to crawl inside him, to peer out through those eyes of his, to see what he saw in that moment. What did the world look like through Henry Mayfield's eyes? What did I look like, stretched out in that tub beneath the cloud of bubbles? Could he see through them? Could he see through me?

I often wondered if we saw things in the same way—not in a figurative sense, but literally. Did he see colors the same way? What if blue to him was green to me? Or what if I saw colors he couldn't even imagine? Wouldn't that explain so much? We tasted foods differently. Heard sounds others didn't. Responded to our children, other people, emotions in vastly different ways. Maybe it was more than perception that caused that. Maybe at our core, the world existed in two very different realities.

"Good." He put the pill bottle back on the counter and left the bathroom, giving me the smallest gift of not forcing me to pull myself from that water.

I sat in the bath until its coolness began to rattle my teeth. I toweled off and twisted my hair into a turban. For another night, I would skip the rollers. I didn't have anyplace to be the next day, so no one to see. And my body was so tired that I ached for a good night's sleep, not one where I had to fight the pressure of those plastic cylinders to try to sleep.

As expected, I didn't find Henry already asleep in bed. It was empty, his side still made from when he got out of bed that morning. He always started the day that way, straightening the covers, pulling them firmly into place. I used to do that as well. I used to make the entire bed, but just like the rollers, I had stopped doing that over the last few months.

I decided to look for Luna, to take her some food before I

turned in. With Henry working late, I might not be able to let her in that night. I put on my robe and walked into the hall, but I only got a few steps before I heard his laugh, followed by another man's voice.

"I'm sorry. I didn't mean to come over and drink your bourbon," the man's voice carried down the hall. It wasn't a voice I knew well. I tried to think of who it could be. It had a tone I had heard before. I tried to place it. Conscious of my attire, I stood against the wall, not daring to take another step and risk being spotted.

"No, no, we should've done this sooner," the words slurred out of Henry's mouth, probably imperceptible to the other person, but I heard the change in cadence, the relaxing of his voice. The letting down of his guard. The laugh that came louder and more full-bodied than when he was completely sober. I could tell he'd had two, maybe even three drinks by then, not enough to be drunk, but definitely relaxed. And more than on a typical weeknight. "We haven't had much of a chance to get to know each other since you moved in."

"Well, I know it sounds silly. You know how the women can be, but it's pretty important to Bitsy." That voice belonged to Gary Betser, Bitsy's husband. Had she sent him across the street because of a hair she found in her salad? I slid along the wall, crouching to the floor, following the shadows of the hall to stay hidden as I leaned in to hear better. "It's hard to explain, but this cat, it means a lot to her."

"Sure."

"She just, I don't know, she has it in her mind that maybe your wife—"

"Lulu."

"Yeah, Lulu. Maybe she has seen the cat."

"I can't say she's mentioned any cat. I know she and Bitsy have become good friends."

"Huh. I've heard her talk about Laura?" His voice trailed off, in search of the right name.

"Nora."

"Yeah, that must be it. It's nice she's made a friend."

A friend, as if Nora was the only one who made room for her around the card table. The only one who baked her a pie to welcome her to the neighborhood. The only one to watch out for her daughter when the girl's mother wasn't paying attention. Apparently, Nora was the only one who mattered.

"Well, I'd appreciate it if you'd keep an eye out. I mean, if it was up to me, I'd just as soon let the cat go, but she's gone and gotten attached."

"Attached?"

"Yeah." As his voice dropped low, I crept along the floor to hear better, not realizing where I was in the hallway, that I had reached that spot that I knew to avoid in the quiet hours of the night when my only task was to make sure no one else woke up. Now that my focus was on the living room, I forgot to watch my step and I hit the spot that let out a creak beneath me.

The men stopped talking. I stopped breathing. And the early sounds of unrest began to drift from the nursery. I knew I should go to Esther, help her settle before it became impossible to get her back to sleep, but I wanted to hear what Gary was about to say about Bitsy and her cat.

I closed my eyes and prayed to the heavens to quiet Esther.

Just this once. Please, God, strike the child quiet. And He did. For a moment. Long enough for me to hear Gary say, "You see, a while back, well, she needed some help. She wasn't quite acting like herself."

"I'm sorry to hear that." Henry sounded more sober now.

"Yeah, if you had seen her before, you wouldn't recognize her. She's a different woman now. I suppose I first noticed it when she stopped cleaning. You wouldn't believe what a pigsty the house was. She couldn't manage it. She couldn't manage much of anything—not the boys, the cooking, none of it. She started making these awful frozen dinners that tasted like aluminum. No matter what, she was always so—"

Henry filled in the blank before Gary could. "Unhappy."

I could hear the fusses building, the precursor to a wail that would require attention. Esther just needed to hold on a few minutes longer.

"Yes," Gary's voice rose with relief. "No matter what."

"Mmm-hmm," Henry mumbled in agreement. "I don't understand it."

"Honest to God, I don't either. Anyway, this damn cat... For whatever reason, she's gotten attached. I mean, I couldn't care less what happens to it, but if you see it, give me a call, would ya?"

Esther's cries climbed to a crescendo. I needed to get to her, but then Henry said more. "The cat helped?"

"Well, sort of. I mean, we tried other things, you know, pills and such."

I leaned in to the limits of the hallway shadow, trying to hear these words over the building wails, wondering what "and such" meant.

"I mean, I don't know you folks or anything, but if your wife—"

"Lulu."

"Yeah, Lulu. If she's out of sorts, well, there's a guy—"

"Thank you, but we have a doctor."

"Right. Right. I'm sure you've got it under control, but if you change your mind, you let me know. I guess there's a reason they call them the fairer sex. I just didn't know they were so fragile."

If I hadn't taken Miltown that day, the hairs on my arms might have stood up when Gary uttered that word: *fragile*.

As Esther nursed herself back to sleep, I watched Gary walk back home. As he passed under the streetlight, I finally realized what he reminded me of. That wisp of hair on top fluttered just enough to bring to mind that fox that Daddy'd had to deal with. It was one of the few times I saw him take out his rifle. He perched and waited, and as dusk fell, we heard two shots ring out: the first for the strike and the second for good measure.

I'd watched as Daddy dug a hole and placed the fox inside it, the ember-and-ash fur fluttering in the last movements of air that would ever again touch that breathless fox. Each shovelful covered the animal with dirt, smothering the smoldering hues of sunset in the fox's coat.

"He was so pretty," I told Daddy as we walked back to the house.

"Yeah, but he was sly. And once one gets into the henhouse, they'll always come back for more."

CHAPTER EIGHTEEN

Summer days lingered long, delaying nightfall as if the heat and humidity made the setting sun as sluggish as the rest of us. What I needed to do would best be done wrapped in the cloak of night, but I couldn't wait. If I wanted answers, I needed to walk across the street in daylight.

Nora always said that having a schedule made things easier; you didn't have to think as much. The list told her what to do each day. "Easy peasy," she always said. While that may have been true, schedules also created predictability, a fact I would use to my advantage.

I had long since surrendered the cleaning schedule, and that day I decided to also give up taking Miltown. I didn't like the way it made me feel, even more tired and further removed than normal. Henry thought the drug was exactly what I needed. He seemed to think it was making me better. So I couldn't tell him that I didn't want to take it anymore. Sometimes secret-keeping is done for survival.

I kept another secret from Henry and all the others: I needed to get back into Bitsy's house, into that room, to see what she was hiding in there. To see if something in one of those boxes could explain what Gary had said to Henry. What he had offered him. What could happen to me. So while the sun rose toward midday, I waited for the wives on Twyckenham Court to head to the grocery store. Then I took the spare key that Emily had given me before she moved on to a different neighborhood. I walked across the street and I let myself in.

When I was a child, I slipped out of the house too many times to count, but this was the first time I had snuck into one. The house was eerie in its silence: the ugly couch waiting for someone to come rest on it, the butterfly wings on the kitchen wallpaper frozen, the stares and smiles in the photographs paused in time, watching me as I tip-toed down the hallway. I avoided the spot in the floor that creaked in our house—a habit, not a necessity. I felt the air thicken, my breathing turned shallow, as if the house was warning of an intruder. Perhaps I should've taken Miltown that morning, if for no other reason than to calm my nerves and racing heart.

The hinges let out a subtle moan as I opened the door. I didn't need to be quiet, but I still tiptoed as I brushed past boxes and walked to the desk. The sun spilled through the curtains as dust danced in the rays. I had left the article on top of the desk. When Katherine had surprised me, I hadn't had time to tuck it beneath the other papers. I expected to find it where I had left it, but it wasn't there.

I lifted stamps and recipes, Bitsy's calendar and address book. I moved aside her stationery and even looked under the desk lamp, but the article wasn't anywhere. I opened the top desk drawer and riffled through pens and pencils, old envelopes and half-used erasers, but still no article. I looked through each drawer but came up empty.

Littering the floor behind me as I searched were the stacks of boxes—watching, waiting, calling to me. When I couldn't find anything in the desk, I turned to see them. Each box had a name written on it: Gary, Jake, Larry, Ellen.

I pulled the Ellen box from the pile, lifted the lid, and found the article right on top.

"Ellen Craske took her life in her Knollwood home Monday afternoon," the first paragraph reported.

I scanned the article, searching for information, glancing over the words before I needed to get out of there. The article didn't mention that she had left a note or given an explanation for what she'd done, but near the end, it said, "She left behind her husband, William Craske; daughter, Katherine Craske, and sister, Elizabeth Betser."

Her daughter? My stomach dropped as I thought of the story Nora had told, that the woman's child had been in the house when she taped up the doors and turned on the gas. The story broke my heart when I thought of a nameless, faceless child, but now I could picture her and my heart shattered even more.

I dug deeper in the box, finding pictures of Katherine as a baby, the ones that had been missing from the Betsers' hallway. There she was with those wise eyes even as a newborn. I looked at that baby in her mother's arms, the mother with the same distant stare as her sister, the baby looking just like both of them. And then I heard a car door close.

I ran to the window and looked out. Nora was next door, taking groceries from her trunk, and Hatti was pulling into her own driveway. My time was up. I needed to get out of there before Bitsy came back. But I still wanted to know more. I put the lid on the box and put it back on the pile.

That's all I meant to do. If I had stopped at that, I would've made it, but then I saw the name on another box: Medical. And it called to me. I needed to know what was inside, but the box was at the bottom of the pile. I looked out the window and didn't see Bitsy, so I moved the boxes quickly, not wasting time with being orderly. Finally, I reached the one I wanted. I pulled off the lid to find a paper labeled Discharge Form. Bitsy's name was typed out on the first line. My eyes raced down the paper, sprinting to find answers.

Diagnosis: Depression
Medical Condition: Treatment-Resistant
Procedure: Lobotomy
Prognosis: Compliant Behavior

That day during cards as we had talked about the horror of the story we had read about a woman whose mind had been severed, we hadn't known that a woman like her was sitting among us. I thought of Bitsy's short sentences, her distant glares and vacant stares. My body shook with the realization of what had happened to her.

On the last line of that page, scrawled next to "legal consent," was Gary's name. He had given permission for them to alter his wife, but had he asked her first?

Another car door closed. I hoped it was Hatti, but when I looked out the window, I saw Bitsy and Katherine exiting their car in the driveway. I put the lid on the box and made it to the door as I heard the garage door open and Katherine ask about lunch. "In a minute, dear," was all Bitsy said.

I had to get out of there while she was in the kitchen putting away groceries, so I slipped back down the hallway, again avoiding the creaking spot just in case. I made it to the front door and pulled it open with a whisper. The sun burned my eyes as I stepped outside and began to pull the door closed, slowly, quietly. I took a deep breath for what felt like the first time in minutes. As the latch nearly caught, I began to turn to walk down the stairs, hoping to cross the street with no one noticing, hidden in the plain sight of daylight.

But the latch didn't catch.

The door pulled against me.

The knob slipped out of my hand.

And Bitsy said my name.

My heartbeat began to thrum in my ears and pulsate in my temples as sweat raced to the surface of my skin.

"Bitsy!" I said too loudly.

"What're you doing here?"

That was a fair question. And how was I going to answer it? Bile rose in my throat as I thought of what had been done to her. How had she felt before and after? Did she miss the person she was before? Did she remember who that even was?

Maybe Bitsy wasn't that unique. All of us are evolutions of ourselves, changing over time as the calendar moves forward. Who we are when we leave this world is not who we were when we entered. So when I looked at Bitsy and tried to figure out how to explain my presence on her front step, I wondered if I knew a bit of what she'd experienced. My mind might not have been altered by an outside interference, but was I the same person I had been before?

"I was stopping in—"

"To get your dish?" Bitsy said before I could think of an excuse.

"Yes." Thank God!

Her eyes squinted at me as my armpits began to feel damp and sticky. But she didn't make a move. She stood paused in time. That poor woman, I thought. Perhaps this was a side effect of the procedure.

"I was about to knock"—the words started before my mind had formulated a response—"when I noticed the door was ajar. I remember Emily saying she had problems with this door sometimes. It wouldn't latch quite right." I couldn't stop myself from talking. "You better have Gary take a look at that." Then my mind caught up. "Now that I think of it, perhaps that explains your missing cat." Yes! That was it! "Maybe she walked right out the front door."

The mention of the cat did the trick. Bitsy looked down at the ground, too focused on what she had lost to wonder why I was really there that day. But I wasn't thinking about Luna. I was wondering who this woman used to be.

And who I might become if Gary helped my husband find a cure for his latest problem: me.

CHAPTER NINETEEN

That night, I could taste sounds when I woke in the dark. The ticking clock burst boysenberries on my tongue, a dance of sweet and tart that was interrupted by the screech of Luna's paws on the glass door. I ran to open the door quickly, wanting to end that sound and the sensation of a radish snack and its peppery burn. But it was the hoot of an owl, its throaty tone reverberating through the air, that unsettled my taste buds with a metallic zing.

Luna ran to the couch, ready to nap. I thought I could rest with her, but through the window, I could still hear the owl crying, asking *who-who* into the night. *Who* was a very good question, I thought to myself as the cat settled into a crescent shape on my lap. *Who* was Ellen, and why had she been despondent? *Who* was Bitsy, and why had her husband done that to her? Would Henry do the same to me?

Luna shifted on my lap. She rolled onto her side and I began to rub beneath her chin, her favorite spot to be petted. I knew this because it would always make her purr the loudest. But that night, as the streetlight reflected shapes onto Mrs. Mayfield's mirrors on the living room wall, the rumbles of her purr filled my mouth with the taste of Pine-Sol.

Perhaps that's why I got up and cleaned the whole house. I couldn't explain the energy I felt, as if the Miltown haze had lifted and a surge of electricity ignited me to action. All I knew was that movement stopped the incongruity of sounds and tastes.

After I had cleaned the living and dining rooms, I stood in front of the wall oven and scrubbed at the burnt-on drippings. My nightgown swung with the movement, my bare feet cold on the checkered tile floor. I had meant to clean up the mess the day the peach pie bubbled over, but I had been tired. Then I forgot. Then Thursday came and went, and I didn't clean the oven as the schedule told me to.

But I couldn't take it anymore. I knew each time I turned on the oven, the mess was only cooking all over again, setting in even more. The grime wasn't coming off easily. It was as persistent as the grass stains on Wesley's dungarees. But I would tackle that task on laundry day. Shoot. I still hadn't gotten around to that yet this week, had I?

Next week I'd get back on schedule, I told myself.

Luckily, the Frigidaire Cycla-matic defrosted itself—Henry insisted on only the best—so I had one less task to complete on Fridays. That reminded me; I needed to check the drip pan to see if it should be emptied.

Halfway into the oven, I scrubbed until the sponge began to shred and my elbow cried for rest. I would need something stronger. A straight edge would do.

I scoured and sweated, my head inside that dark box. I didn't mean to think about Ellen and the story Nora had told us before we knew she was Bitsy's sister. But as my arm moved back and forth and my nightgown tickled my thighs, I couldn't help but think about her and what she had done.

Word from the bird—that's what Nora had said—the story goes that she put Katherine, that poor child, down for a nap one afternoon. She did it when the sun was still up, the birds were still chirping. It wasn't the darkness of the night. That's what I thought about: Why, when she did what she did, didn't she wait until the night? Katherine would still be tucked in just the same, but in the night, the silence and the sounds, the hum of the appliances, with no voices to interrupt those thoughts, that seemed like the time to do what she had done.

Well, Ellen chose the afternoon. I wondered if she'd waited for Katherine to fall asleep. Maybe the girl was good and obedient and had drifted off right away. But maybe she hadn't. And what if she would've snuck out to see what her mother was up to? How would Ellen have felt if she took Katherine with her?

Apparently, trusting she had gone to sleep, Ellen went into the kitchen. It seemed to be an old place with small rooms, each one with a door of its own, not like the newly built Greenwood Estates homes. Our homes favored a more open-concept approach where the living room spilled into the dining room, which opened to the kitchen. Henry told me they did it for flow and efficiency. Plus, with advancements in heating, homes no longer needed to be compartmentalized. Ductwork meant the entire house could be warmed evenly instead of needing a fireplace or stove to heat a single room at a time.

So, in the compartmentalized house, Ellen closed the kitchen door. Then she covered the cracks with plastic wrap. I wondered how well it stuck, if it clung to the doorframe like it did to the top of a Pyrex or Tupperware dish. Or, did she need to use tape to reinforce it? It probably would've been good to use tape as well, to really seal it off. After all, her child was just down the hall.

The hall... That reminded me: I needed to mention to Henry that the creak in front of Wesley's door was getting louder. He didn't seem to notice it, but I did, especially when I crept through the house at night.

The last few flakes of burnt butter and peach syrup clung to the bottom of the oven, forcing me to lean farther inside. Had Ellen leaned in that far? I imagined she probably had to sit on the floor. In a house that old, she wouldn't have a wall oven that she could stand in front of. Did she merely sit outside the open door? When her husband got home, did he find her collapsed onto the oven door or in a heap on the floor in front of it?

How confused he must have been to have gotten home and found the kitchen door closed, sealed off, plastic-wrapped as if to preserve his wife forevermore. They'd say she sealed it off so well, he couldn't even smell the gas when he walked into the house. And her child was still in her room, waiting for her mother.

What had gone through her mind in the moments leading up to that decision? Did she know when she put Katherine down for her nap? Surely she did. Did she linger with her? Did she sing her one last lullaby? Wesley favored "Over the Rainbow," though I never sang anything else often enough to know if he preferred it. The melancholy that lurked beneath the surface resonated with my soul.

Did that woman sing the same song? Did she kiss her child on her forehead one last time as her chest rose and fell with the deep inhalations of rest?

I still wondered if she had left a note. I tried to imagine what she would've written, how she would've explained what she had done. Did she write it on stationery with her name embossed along the top? Perhaps she found a scrap of paper and scribbled a quick message. Maybe she apologized. Maybe she justified. Maybe she simply said goodbye. Or maybe she didn't do any of that. Maybe she just opened that oven door, laid her head to rest on it, closed her eyes, and drifted off to sleep.

I didn't realize the moment when the final remnants of the pie lifted off. I kept scrubbing, kept moving the straight edge over the oven surface as I thought of notes and decisions, cleaning schedules and pie, and if bluebirds fly above the rainbow, why, oh why, can't I?

CHAPTER TWENTY

The next day, I kept thinking about Ellen—a woman I had never met, but somehow I felt as if she was now a part of me. I tried to play dominoes with Wesley and sing lullabies to Esther, but I couldn't concentrate. At naptime, I downed a few aspirin and told myself to rest, but then the phone rang.

"Mrs. Mayfield?" That voice. That cheer. The faint whistle of each *s*. She called enough that I knew her voice by now, the way she elongated *may*, nearly adding an extra syllable to it.

"Hello, Alice." I attempted to imitate her whistle.

"Henry wanted me to let you know that he has invited Mr. Ellis over for dinner tonight." Not tonight. "He apologizes that he can't call for himself, but he wants to make sure dinner and drinks will be ready at six?"

She ended the last sentence as a question, but that was only out of courtesy. We both knew she wasn't asking on behalf of Henry; she was telling me the arrangements that had been made and that my afternoon would now be spent prepping for this dinner. A nap would not be possible.

"Yes, of course," I told her, though I wanted to say, "What the hell is he thinking?" She and I didn't have that sort of relationship. Instead, I had to pretend as if I had everything under control, that as Henry's wife, my days were spent anticipating his needs and I was happy to oblige, because if I didn't, someone like her was waiting and willing. Maybe she believed my performance, but I didn't.

"Mr. Ellis is hoping for one of your famous salads," she told me before disconnecting.

I slammed the phone onto the cradle. If only I hadn't stayed up all night, then maybe I could do this. If my head didn't constantly throb. If my hands didn't ache. If I could be like the rest of them, then I could do it all and smile, too.

I poured myself a drink and second-guessed my decision to not take Miltown that morning. No, I didn't need that fog on top of everything else. What I needed was to figure out how to pull off this dinner for Henry and his promotion. For us, he would say.

Even still, anger burned in my chest. I couldn't believe Henry hadn't called me himself. He hadn't asked if it was possible. He assumed I could put it all together, and he asked the office girl to inform me. But why would he question if it was possible? His mother would be able to pull off a last-minute dinner party, but he seemed to forget that we didn't have help like she did.

My mother would've been able to do the same, though without help. She had a way of always having extra food on hand for those helping in the fields during planting and harvesting.

Somehow there always seemed to be enough fried chicken, mashed potatoes, and corn bread. She always had fruit on hand for fresh-squeezed lemonade—her special elixir that quenched even the most extreme of thirsts.

But I wasn't like either one of them. I didn't have extra hands to prepare a meal, nor did I know how to stock root cellars and make servings stretch. So I did the only thing I knew how to do. I checked the pantry and the freezer.

By the time I settled on the menu, I knew even a quick set would not get the Jell-O in shape by dessert, so I needed to improvise. The last thing I wanted was another flop like when I'd tried to make the welcome dish for the Betsers. I had mandarin oranges, pineapple, and cottage cheese on hand to make an orange gelatin salad and, thankfully, enough cream that I could whip up. If I needed this to be done quickly, I would have to use the freezer, which just so happened to be where I found the main course.

My mother knew how to be resourceful, and apparently, I did as well. Henry had left me with little choice. Plus, if I had learned anything in my time in Greenwood Estates, it was that these people would eat about anything you put in front of them. That night I would test that theory with the three beef TV dinners I had stowed away in the freezer. Surely if I hid the packages and meticulously plated the food, no one would know the difference.

At six o'clock, I met Jack and Henry at the door with a Tom Collins and a smile. Henry's eyes sparkle when he saw me in the magnolia-leaf green pencil dress—his favorite color on me. I had even put on the pearl necklace and earrings he gave me on our first anniversary.

"Thank you," Henry whispered in my ear after he pecked my cheek.

I wanted to tell him "you owe me," but I would save that for later. He had no idea what it took for me to pull together this evening, get the kids situated, and zip myself into that dress before they arrived. But when I saw that sparkle, I knew he was thinking about me and not her.

The kitchen timer dinged right on schedule. I had already plated the food, but I needed the appearance that what I was about to serve had been home-cooked.

"It smells wonderful," Jack said. He was either kind or a good liar.

"Thank you," I replied. "Tonight's menu is tender slices of beef roast with rich gravy, little browned potatoes, corn O'Brien sautéed in butter, and garden-fresh peas with a pat of creamy butter on top." I had memorized the description on the packaging. Thankfully, Henry didn't question where the "garden-fresh peas" came from, since we did not, in fact, have a garden.

"Sounds wonderful," Jack said. "It's been a while since I've had a home-cooked meal. I'm looking forward to it."

Little did he know, he still wasn't having one. I flashed a smile and looked downward, attempting to be demure. "I'm sorry Mrs. Ellis couldn't join us tonight."

"Yes, well…" Jack took a sip of his drink before continuing. "She's off getting her nerves in order." Then he turned to Henry and elbowed him. "You know how women can be."

The doorbell rang, saving Henry from having to respond.

I wanted to ask Jack what he meant, but of course I wouldn't. Instead, I went into the kitchen to get the dessert from the freezer so it had a chance to thaw. As I was about to carry the plates of food into the dining room, Henry came into the kitchen.

"We need another plate."

"What?"

"Someone else is joining us."

I looked from Henry to the three plates on the kitchen counter.

"I thought it was only going to be the three of us. That's all I prepared for."

"I know. I did, too. But Gary just stopped over. Jack saw him and asked him to stay."

My mind raced, wondering why Gary—the man who had lobotomized his wife—had stopped by. Did Henry know what Gary had done? Did Gary know what I had done? Surely he didn't know that I had snooped around their house. I had tried to be so careful, putting everything back where I had found it. Bitsy hadn't seemed to suspect anything. Or so I thought. I lowered my voice. "I don't understand. Isn't all of this about the promotion?"

Henry closed his eyes and shook his head. "Yes, I'm trying to figure out where Jack is. I thought this might help, but I didn't plan on Gary."

"Why did he come over?" I hesitated to ask. Henry looked toward the living room, not answering me. "Couldn't he see the car in the driveway? Surely he figured we had company."

"He wanted to give me something." Thank God he wasn't there to tell Henry about me. But then he continued, "Something he mentioned the other night. It's nothing."

I scratched at the rash on my arm and tried to stop the room from spinning. "He had to come now?" I asked.

"Geez, Lulu, I don't know. Just find a way to make it work." He pointed at the plates, walked into the living room, and left me alone in the kitchen as my heart felt like it was about to beat out of my chest.

As much as I wanted to tell Henry to get Gary out of our house immediately, I took a deep breath. I couldn't say anything while Jack was there. Henry needed this promotion. He had worked so hard for it, and I couldn't mess this up for him even though the fox stood in our living room.

So I cut, sliced, and scooped, repositioning and reproportioning the food to look like four full servings. They all ate it as if they enjoyed it, while I wished that Luna was under the table so I could give her my pot roast.

"You're a peach, Lulu," Jack said as he wiped a glob of gravy from the corner of his mouth and sat back in his chair. Peach. If only I'd had time to make a peach pie. It had been months since I had made one. My mouth began to water from the thought of it. "Can't wait to see what you've cooked up for dessert."

"You should try my wife's cooking," Gary felt the need to share as I reached by him to clear his plate. He went on about all the amazing dishes she concocted, and I couldn't help but notice that he had practically licked his plate clean.

"I'm sorry," I began. And I probably should've stopped with that, but it was nearly seven o'clock, and while it was still a few hours from my typical bedtime, I was tired. I had spent the last few hours sprinting around that house, making everything right for this evening. And then here came Gary, interrupting it all. My eyes felt heavy. My legs hurt. My hands ached. All I wanted was to get out of this bullet bra, draw a bath, and sink within it, but instead, I needed to clear the table and get the dessert ready. So I suppose I was too tired to know what I was saying or to even realize I was saying it aloud. I didn't stop with that apology. I said the rest softly: "You felt you had to eat this instead of the meal your wife had prepared for you."

"Lulu!" Henry scolded, and that was when I realized I had said it out loud for all to hear. We both looked at each other in surprise. I stood beside Gary, suspended in the moment like a bit of fruit cocktail in one of my salads. I didn't know if I should apologize or cry, but before I could do either, Jack began to laugh.

"Not only can she cook," he cackled, "but she can razz, too."

Using his approval as a chance to leave, I did a little curtsy and excused myself to the kitchen, where I discovered that my shortcut perhaps hadn't worked as planned. The salad had deflated since I had pulled it from the freezer. As I began scooping it out, I realized the consistency wasn't typical. Instead of bouncy and springy, it was sticky and soupy. With each spoonful, it plopped into the bowls, a mess of electric-orange liquid and chunks of cottage cheese. But what could I do? It was all I had other than Twinkies, and I was pretty sure Henry wouldn't approve of those cylinder sponge cakes serving as the final course. Plus, I was too tired to whip up something new. And nearly too irritated to care. So I scooped the orange mess into bowls, spooned a dollop of whipped cream on top, and served it as if it was meant to look like a bowl of sunshine vomit.

To his credit, Jack ate the entire bowl, while Henry choked

down half of it and Gary ate only the whipped cream. I'll confess I didn't even try it. I left the men to their shoptalk as I loaded the Mobile Maid.

I stood at the kitchen sink, sipping a cup of Sanka as I looked out the window. I didn't look into the backyard. I wasn't even checking to see if Luna was there yet. Instead, I watched a moth that had gotten stuck in a spiderweb. The web had been there for a few months now, evidence of the fact that I hadn't washed the windows in quite some time. When I'd first spotted the spider, I considered getting a broom and removing it from the window, but the more I watched it, the more I didn't know if I wanted to destroy what it had built.

That night, a moth had landed in the web. First, its feet stuck, but it could pull them off, one at a time, only for each one to get stuck all over again. If the feet had been the only things to get trapped, perhaps it could've made it out. I had seen that happen before. But this time, the moth made a critical error. In its struggle to loosen its footing, it moved to the side so that one of its wings came into contact with the web. It began to try to move its body sideways. It no longer worried about its feet in the same way. Instead, all focus and panic went to unsticking its wing. Without that, it would never break free.

And it didn't. The spider sat to the side, feeling the moth's struggle vibrate its silken web. But it didn't move. It didn't react. It waited until the struggle ended and the moth quieted.

I felt Gary's presence behind me before I heard him.

"I brought you a few dishes," he said when my attention was

on the spider. When I startled, he didn't apologize. He walked up beside me and placed the dishes in the sink, his bowl still full of the orange disaster. He stood so close that I could smell his English Leather cologne, the mossy fragrance so strong that my sinuses ached.

"Thank you," I said as I stepped to the side to give him room. He slid in my direction and turned on the faucet. With my back against the cabinets, and thanks to the Mobile Maid, I had little room to move.

"That was quite a meal," he said as he reached for the towel that I had left wadded up on the counter beside me. I slinked into the corner of the cabinets, feeling the countertop push into me. I attempted to take a drink of coffee, but my hands shook.

Suddenly hearing the silence of the house, I asked, "Where are Mr. Ellis and Henry?"

"Henry's walking Jack out."

"Oh, well, I should go say goodbye." I made a move to step around him, but he wouldn't let me pass.

"Begging your pardon, Mrs. Mayfield." He ran his finger through a trail of water on the counter. "I can't help but wonder if there's something you need to tell me."

"No." The word shook out of my throat as I feared that they knew I had been in their house. I thought I had put the papers back into the boxes. I tried to think back to what the room looked like when I left it, but I had been too concerned about Bitsy and Katherine in the kitchen to take a close look on my way out the door.

He drew his index finger through the water and then dried it. "Hmm," he said as he tossed the towel onto the counter. "I don't think I have to tell you that stray cats don't last long."

I breathed a sigh of relief. He didn't know I had been in their house. He was only talking about the cat that—if he was observant enough—he might even be able to see outside the window right at that moment.

"Yes, I hope Bitsy finds her cat soon. We've all been looking for her."

"You know, I've never been much of a cat person myself, but one thing I have to give them credit for is the way they sniff out a rat among us." He smiled at me, revealing crooked teeth the same color as his yellow Formica countertop. "I know it sounds silly, but my wife is about in hysterics over this thing. And one thing you should know about me is I do not appreciate hysterics. In fact, I'll do just about anything to make sure my family, my neighborhood, my life, remains calm." He stood still for what felt like minutes. Perhaps in reality it was only a few seconds. Had Henry walked into the kitchen at that moment, he might not have noticed anything out of the ordinary. He would have seen a pause in a conversation between neighbors as a spider outside the window wrapped up its prey.

As I stood cornered in my own kitchen, the hairs on my arms rose. I refused to look away from him, so in those silent seconds that stretched for what felt like hours, I looked through his glasses and into his insipid eyes and begged my body to not tremble.

"Good night, Mrs. Mayfield," he said as he finally moved away from me. "I'll see myself out."

I held myself together until I heard the front door close. Then my body trembled, releasing the energy it had bound up when he had me cornered. He needed a calm life. Didn't we all? And look at Bitsy. *Hysterical* was not a word I would use to describe her. But maybe she had been. Maybe that's how he justified doing what he did to her.

The couple bites of dinner I had choked down threatened to come back up. I needed something else to focus on, so I grabbed the dish towel and scrubbed the counter dry, counting down the time to when I could escape into a bath and feel clean again.

CHAPTER TWENTY-ONE

"I'm going to bed," Henry announced from the living room as I stood shaking at the sink. He didn't even bother coming into the kitchen. He didn't thank me, nor apologize for the late notice. He didn't reprimand me for the aluminum-flavored food and the regurgitated-looking dessert. He didn't say he loved me. He didn't ask if I was okay. Instead, he began to shuffle off to our bedroom.

"I'm sorry." As soon as it came out of my mouth, I knew I shouldn't have said that to Gary, especially not in front of Jack. Henry stopped, but he didn't turn to look at me. He nodded, but then kept walking. "Henry!" I called, careful to not risk waking the kids.

This time he turned toward me. His eyes were rimmed with shadows, the bags beneath them heavy with exhaustion. He rubbed at his temples before asking, in a tone of equal parts annoyance and exhaustion, "What, Lulu?"

He didn't acknowledge my apology. He didn't look at me and see that I was as tired as he was. He didn't seem to consider what it had taken for me to serve his guests that evening. The meal may not have been my best, but what did he expect on such short notice? And he didn't know that his new friend had cornered me in my own kitchen.

I crossed my arms over my chest. I could've said a lot of things. I could've told him that I didn't like the way Gary made me feel. I could've confessed that I did know where their cat was and that I had snooped in their house. I could've told him the truth I had found in that room. But explaining all that seemed too complicated at that moment, so instead I said, "You're welcome."

Henry lifted his gaze to meet mine. He pursed his lips and shook his head as he squinted at me. In truth, he paused for a split second, but that time stretched longer, deeper, expanding the interval between the clock's ticks to what felt like an eternity.

We had never been the type of couple who fought. We usually got along. Sometimes we might have had disagreements, but we resolved them quickly, quietly. We weren't like Nora and Dennis, who could sometimes be heard outside their home, especially on spring days if they had the windows open.

Henry and I didn't raise our voices to each other. We might give a look or a remark. When I'd said I wanted a house in the country, he explained how a neighborhood better suited us. When he'd wanted to wear loafers to the office, I told him to stick with the derbys. When I'd said I might like a job at the local paper, he said I had too much to do around the house.

We disagreed, but we didn't fight. But that night, it seemed like maybe we should've fought. Perhaps we should've raised our voices. Maybe I should've told him that I didn't appreciate having to host on such short notice. And then maybe he would've told me why he had even invited Jack over like that. Then I could've told him that I didn't trust Gary and I thought it was a mistake to let him stay for dinner.

Maybe I'd go even further. Maybe I would tell him how I never wanted that dishwasher, the thing he thought I needed, and I couldn't stand the sight of it. I wanted to scream at it every time I stubbed my toe or caught my apron on it. Maybe I would tell him how I was beginning to hate the walls of our house, how day after day it felt like they inched closer together. How my skin felt too tight, hot, inflamed, and not my own. How the sun made my eyes burn, so much so that I wondered if closing them forever would be such a bad thing. That I couldn't even look at my oven without seeing her and how she'd lain her head to rest on the door and closed her eyes for the last time.

But we didn't say any of that to each other. Instead, that epoch of a split second, along with any attempt at a conversation, ended with his words, "Don't be so dramatic."

With that, he went to bed and I waited. What else could I do? If I retorted, it would be proof of the pill's failure. So, on wobbly legs, I stood in the kitchen and watched the spider in the window methodically swaddle the moth in its web before it dragged the wrapped meal out of sight and waited for its next victim.

When I knew Henry was asleep, I tiptoed into our room to get my nightgown. I listened to Henry's rhythmic breathing, knowing what his sleep sounded like, listening for the staccato of his inhales and exhales. I had listened to those sounds every night for the last five years. Even before that, if we were being honest, if we ever confessed to those nights we spent together before we were married. That was in the time when I still slept, when I found comfort in his arms, when I found solace in those breaths, as if in his presence, all was well.

I fumbled through the darkness, the streetlights offering the only amount of light in the room. The shadows shifted across the walls as a car drove by, casting a light across Henry's face. He moved his head from one side to the other, repositioning so that his back was to the window. I paused, quieting my own breathing until I was certain he was asleep again.

Then I walked into the bathroom and carefully closed the door. As the light flicked on, the pill bottle caught my eye. Those damn pills. I wanted to toss them at the mirror, let it shatter as they spilled out.

I reached behind to unzip my dress. Some nights Henry would help me with that. Or he had. Before he would lock himself away in his office and I started taking baths shortly after dinner. When we used to go to bed together, he used to unzip my dress for me. Some nights that simple gesture was all it took to light the spark between us. Some nights my dress would fall to the floor, followed by my slip and stockings. They would lay crumpled on the floor as we made our way to the bed. Some nights, I left them all in a pile so in the morning they acted as a monument to our lovemaking.

No such monument had existed for a while now, not since before Esther.

I stretched to reach behind me, having gotten accustomed to

unzipping myself. As my dress fell to the floor, the tub caught my eye in the mirror. I wanted to draw a bath and sink beneath the suds, but Esther began to fuss. I knew Henry would tell me to let her be, to stop spoiling her, to stop giving in to her every need. But wasn't that what a parent should do, even if ours hadn't?

I put on my nightgown and tiptoed my way back out into our room. I needed to get to Esther, but in the darkness of the room, I caught my toe on the chair Marian had insisted we have. Her father had gifted it to her mother on their wedding day. It was beautiful, but its toile de Jouy print did not match the rest of the decor in our room.

"It'll be fine," she'd said with a dismissive wave before adding, "It'll add a little class to the room."

Henry always laid his suit jacket across the chair overnight before returning it to the hanger the next morning. A man of constant routine. He claimed it was so the jacket could air out before the next wearing, but part of me always wondered if he put his jacket there as justification for his mother's insistence of the chair.

My toe throbbed, but I stifled my discomfort. I plopped into the chair, which emitted a screech. Of course the chair squeaked as if it held a built-in alarm, should anyone dare to use it for the purpose it had been created. Henry stirred in his sleep, his snoring stopping for a moment. I squeezed my toe, hoping the hurt would quickly fade. I took a deep breath and rested a hand on the breast pocket of Henry's coat, feeling a rectangle tucked within it. I assumed he had forgotten to remove his handkerchief, and I figured I'd do him a favor and remove it before it was forgotten. But when I reached into the pocket, I didn't feel a cotton square. Instead, I discovered a folded-up piece of paper.

I needed to get to Esther, but first I wanted to see what this was. Perhaps it was something from work, a note about a project. Maybe it was a message from Alice or, worse, a love letter.

A small voice dreaded what I would find and questioned if I should look, but the louder voice told me to keep going. *Open it. Read it.* Coaxing me to know.

Struggling to read the writing in the dark, I held the paper upward, stretching into a faint glow of light just enough so my eyes, which had grown accustomed to the darkness, could make out the scrawled message. I didn't recognize the handwriting, nor the phone number and certainly not the name: Dr. Ruthledge.

I folded up the paper and dropped it on Henry's suit jacket before I made my way to Esther's room. I took her from her crib and pulled my breast from my nightgown. I felt her latch before I could even sit in the rocking chair.

Dr. Ruthledge. My mind repeated the name. Perhaps he was one of the firm's clients. Maybe those blueprints Henry had spent so much time working on each night were for him. Maybe he was one of those fussy types who kept requesting change orders, never satisfied with the renderings. I wondered if I should hate the doctor for being so demanding and delaying Henry's promotion.

In the darkness of the room, as I rocked in silence, I thought about the dinner, the failure that it was, and I hoped that Jack could be forgiving. I didn't care what Gary thought. He shouldn't have been there anyway. And why was he there again? Oh, yes. Henry had said Gary wanted to give him something. It concerned what they had talked about the other night.

I thought back to that night when I had tiptoed into the hallway and overheard what Gary had said about his wife. I didn't know what Nora saw in her. She was exactly the type of person Nora should be calling me about, to tell me about how that odd lady next door wouldn't stop going on about her missing cat.

I tried not to think about how Gary had approached me in the kitchen. What kind of a man does that to a woman? I could see the dirt beneath his nail as he slid his finger across the counter. I could see the liver spots that dotted his temple, smell his onion breath, feel the yoke he wielded.

If he made me feel that way, how did Bitsy feel?

What had Gary promised Henry the night he spoke of his wife's unhappiness? I thought of how distant Henry had been. The looks he had been giving me. The paper in his breast pocket.

And I stopped rocking.

Night had settled over Greenwood hours ago. No one else looked to be awake on all of Twyckenham Court. Even Bitsy's house remained fully dark. I looked at that window and wondered what other secrets lay tucked away in those boxes, like the one that revealed her lobotomy. That was how Gary had calmed her.

I wanted so badly for Dr. Ruthledge to be the persnickety client, but in the wee hours of the night, the truth dawned on me: My husband thought I was the same as Bitsy. And the fox in the henhouse wanted to show him how to turn me into the happy housewife I should've been.

CHAPTER TWENTY-TWO

I felt antsy, in need of something, so I went to the kitchen for a glass of milk. Luna waited at the sliding door for me. She didn't paw frantically, as she had when we first met. She seemed to know by now that I would come for her. I let her in. But I still couldn't settle. Instead, I paced and she walked figure eights around my legs, her fur soft against my skin, her purr calling to me to relax. Sit down. Rest.

But how could I rest? Not then. I needed to know what Henry was planning, why he needed that doctor's number, what he must really think of me.

So I made a plan. I'd be the housewife he expected me to be. I'd start sleeping in rollers, wearing my pearls, keeping the house. I'd put on my face each day, every day, so that my rouged cheeks would beam when he walked in the door every evening after work. I'd take those damn pills and I'd forget about how they made me feel, because no one was going to do to me what Gary had done to Bitsy. He had made her a different person, but I would choose to change myself.

I told Luna my plan. She seemed to approve. She also insisted that she come with me when Esther stirred. Luna followed me down the hall to the nursery, where she nuzzled onto my lap, burrowing beneath the baby blanket.

Determined and depleted, apparently I dozed off, resting longer than I realized. My consciousness elsewhere, I didn't hear Henry open the door the next morning as the sun began to infiltrate the gap in the curtains.

I don't know what woke me first, if it was Henry calling my name or Luna extending her claws into my thigh as if anchoring herself to hold on. This wasn't the way to start my new plan. I should've been up and dressed, with medicine digesting, eggs frying, and the cat released back into the wild.

Shoot! The cat.

At first I thought Henry hadn't noticed. I thought the baby blanket covered her enough that perhaps Henry hadn't caught sight of her. Maybe I could convince him to leave, and then I could sneak Luna out without him ever noticing.

"I'm sorry," I whispered. "I lost track of time. I'll start the coffee in—"

"What's going on?" His voice rose so that Luna jolted, pushing her back against the swaddle and her claws deeper into my legs.

"Shhh—" I told him, hoping to call his attention away from the cat. "Don't wake the baby."

Henry walked toward me. "Lulu," was all he could say. His voice sounded different. It caught in his throat, not on his tongue like the moments when the stutter tried to reassert itself. He had gotten good at maneuvering it, hiding it, pausing to collect himself before forcing a repetitive sound from his mouth. "Oh God. Lulu."

Luna jumped from my lap. There was no hiding her. With what Gary had said to him, surely Henry would know who she was. Surely I'd have to walk her across the street and return her to Bitsy. And then I'd be alone in the middle of the night once more. I expected him to reach for her, but instead he let the cat run out the door.

The swaddle had loosened with Luna's movement. I brought Esther to my chest, hoping Henry wouldn't wake her. I couldn't believe we had slept so long, so fully.

But why was Henry still saying my name? Why had tears begun to pool in his eyes?

He reached for the baby. How long had it been since he had held her? Not that he held Wesley much at all, but now that I thought of it, I didn't know when I had seen him hold his daughter.

"Shhh…" I warned. "She's sleeping."

"No, Lulu."

He took the bundle from my arms.

"Gentle!" I warned. How had he forgotten?

I watched him unwrap the blanket, hold it in the air, and drop it to the floor.

"Henry! The baby!" I called. I tried to reach for her. I expected to hear a thud as she hit the floor along with the blanket.

But there was silence.

Always the silence.

So much silence since…

Henry knelt on the floor in front of me. I tried to push him away. I tried to find her. Why wasn't she crying? Why didn't I hear her? See her? Where was she?

"Lulu," Henry whispered. The morning light peeked through the curtains and lit the tears that streamed down his cheeks. I had never seen him cry before. He didn't cry quietly, not like me, but I suppose he hadn't had to.

I tried to stand, to push him away, to find our daughter, but Henry held me in the chair. He pressed his body against mine, his face so close that I could feel his breath across my cheeks. His tongue tied, but he forced out the syllables, his voice rising with urgency, "L-L-L-Lulu, don't you remember? She's gone."

CHAPTER TWENTY-THREE

I looked at the blanket, my tears blurring the pink heap on the floor, but I could see clearly enough to know that Esther wasn't there.

Hadn't she been?

My mind struggled to ask this question, not wanting to know the answer, not wanting to believe what my eyes saw, what Henry said.

As he ran to make a phone call, I knelt on the floor, my knees creaking with the motion. I hadn't knelt in years, not since before the polio, when we used to go to the Lutheran church every Sunday morning. The creak of my knees reminded me of the sound of the wooden kneelers groaning and shifting with the weight of the congregants as they got into position to humble themselves before their god.

My baby.

This was the only prayer I could mutter on the bedroom floor.

My baby.

I didn't speak a request, only a name, because the request was too real to me, so real it didn't need to be stated, because any god worth worshipping would know what I needed: my little girl in my arms, ready to start her day as I thought she had for weeks now.

Nora wasn't there to hear my cries like she did the morning I needed a clean sock. Now, with empty arms, I needed so much more. But she wasn't there when I needed her. No one was.

What did I expect? When had anyone been there when I needed them most? When I fell out of the tree at age five, the tractor was too loud for Daddy to hear me calling for him. When the hornets stung me, Mama was with Georgie and wouldn't let me get close, in case the polio attached to me, too. And in those late nights when sleep wouldn't come and I had to decide if I was leaving for college or staying to help Mama keep the farm, Daddy had already passed, having taken his last breath years before.

But this time I wasn't fully alone.

"Mama?" The little voice came from behind me, full of sleep and confusion.

"Wesley!" I wiped the tears and snot from my face, trying to pull myself together for him.

"Why're you in here?" he asked. "Taking pictures again?"

The boy was so brilliant. Of course! My camera! It could prove that Esther had been there, that I hadn't been hallucinating her entire existence.

"Wesley! Run and get Mama's camera."

"But I'm not allowed to touch it."

"You are now! Please, I need the photos that are in it. Run fast!"

I could hear Henry on the phone. I couldn't make out the

words, but I could hear the intonations of his voice. If I could get the film developed, that would prove Esther had been alive.

"I got it!" Wesley's voice reached me before he came back to the nursery.

"Hurry!"

I knew the sound of Wesley running, even though he wasn't supposed to do it in the house. But I didn't hear that familiar, fast padding. Instead, I heard a different, whirring, straining sound.

As Wesley rounded the doorframe and walked into the nursery, he pulled at the film that hung loose from the open camera.

"I don't see pictures, Mama. Where are they?"

There in his hands was the film that was meant to save me, exposed to light and smudged with fingerprints.

"Wesley, no!" I yelled. He looked at me, frightened. I ran toward him, reaching for the camera, wanting to wind the film back in and hope against all odds that those photos hadn't been lost forever. But in my hurry, in the rise of my voice, Wesley had startled. The camera fell from his little fingers and bounced onto the floor, the door coming off its hinges and the lens shattering with the fall.

Once again, I melted to the floor and began to sob, but this time I didn't cry quietly. Wesley walked toward me. I had been a fool to think I was alone. Of course I had him, but a four-year-old can only offer so much comfort. Even still, he tried. He tried to be the one to rub away the hurt. He put his arm around my shoulders, leaned his head against mine, and said, "I'm sorry, Mama. What were the pictures?"

I tried to calm my sobs enough to reply. I took a few deep breaths and said, "Of Esther."

Wesley sat down beside me. "It's okay," he said. "I'm sad she died, too." Then, as I knelt on his sister's floor, he reached for my hand, turned it palm up, and began to recite his own variation: "With a circle and a pat and a heart on top of that, I give all my love to you, yes, I do."

What had I become? How had this even happened? What did this mean if I had spent weeks living in a delusion that my daughter had lived when even a four-year-old knew better?

With Henry calling for help—quite possibly that Dr. Ruthledge—I did the only thing I knew to do. I kissed Wesley on the top of his head as he sat on the floor, fumbling with the camera.

"I'll fix it. I promise," he said.

He meant it, but what I knew was there was no fixing any of this. I kept hold of the empty blanket as I walked to the front door and stepped outside. Luna met me on the step and meowed a greeting to me. When I began to run, she didn't hesitate. She trotted alongside me as the blanket waved, a pink flag whipping in the race to escape.

I hurried down the street barefoot, the morning light making my nightgown more sheer than I'd realized. I should've grabbed my housecoat. I should've planned ahead. I should've done so much. Hidden more. Trusted less. Known I'd never really be one of them.

My nightgown clung to my chest as my breasts bounced with each step. Cars drove by, but I paid them no attention. I didn't look through the windows to see which neighbors were watching me race down the Twyckenham Court sidewalk in my nightgown. I didn't wave hello and pretend all was well.

Soon enough, phones would ring throughout Greenwood, housewives starting their day with the latest neighborhood news, the reports of Mrs. Mayfield in her sheer nightgown, scurrying half-naked down the sidewalk as a cat she had stolen from poor, sweet Bitsy Betser weaved in and out of her feet with every step.

What they wouldn't know to report was what her husband was about to do to her.

Looking back, I should've gone for the car. That would've given me a real escape, a real chance to flee, but in my haste, I fled to the place that felt safe.

I could hear Henry calling for me, but I ran on. I crossed into the grass still damp with dew. Luna took off ahead of me as if she knew where to go, as if she agreed that this was the place to hide. Of course, we were both wrong.

As I hid among the tentacle branches, the willow's roots pushed into my feet, reminding me that parts of it existed in unseen places. I had no plan, only momentum moving me forward, making me believe that if I kept moving, I could get away. Like Georgie when we were kids and he would close his eyes to block out unwanted things like the monsters under his bed, the call to do chores, the need to take more medicine. I couldn't squeeze my eyes shut just then. I had to keep my feet moving over all those roots. But if I didn't look back, if I didn't notice Henry, if I pretended like he hadn't just driven his car onto the grass and flung the door open to chase after me, then it wasn't really happening. This was only a childhood game, and I could get away.

"Lulu!"

He called for me. His voice heavy—not with anger, but with panic. If he was concerned, then why was he doing this to me?

I didn't answer him. I didn't respond when Gary began calling for me as well. They were too close behind me, so I ran toward the weeping willow, its tired branches sagging and shadowing the ground beneath so that grass refused to grow. I reached for the trunk, running my fingers across its rough bark, this time not out of curiosity, but out of a need for it to protect me, to show me the way.

I grabbed the lowest limb and tried to pull myself up. My feet scraped across the bark as their voices grew louder.

"Lulu!"

Henry called from behind me. I didn't want him to say that name anymore. Who was that person he called for? He called as if I were a child. Why couldn't he stop and simply let me be?

I tried again to scale the tree, to pull myself upward, to get within the branches and let it hide me from the one trying to capture me. If only I had listened to Wesley all those times he'd asked me to climb with him. Then I would've known the hand and foot holds. I would've known where to grab, how to pull and shift my weight so that I could escape the ground.

But Henry probably would've figured it out as well. After all, he had been a boy at one point, and climbing seemed to be something they innately knew how to do. I wondered if Henry had ever climbed, if his mother ever let him. It seemed like something rougher, dirtier, grittier than she would allow her son to do. She had raised him to be proper. Yet how well did that parenting work out? He'd still grown up to make mistakes. He'd married me, after all.

I reached and fumbled, trying to grab on to something as my

breathing quickened from the strain. Blood trickled down my arm as the bark scratched my skin with every attempt. My feet were raw, but I wouldn't feel that until later, as I sat alone on a bed with a sterile white sheet. Tears blurred my vision, but I wouldn't stop. I couldn't.

Until I had no choice.

I cried to God to give me grace in that moment, but all I got was an arm around me that pulled me away from the tree.

He was so strong. I admired that back at school, as I'd watch him play basketball or we'd sneak away for a swim or he'd pull me in close and wrap himself around me. I'd admired his strength then. I found comfort in it. I didn't fear it until that day.

"Lulu." He spoke directly into my ear, his voice calm, measured, no longer panicked. "Lulu." He kept saying it again and again with a rhythm the same as my breath.

I pulled away from him. I demanded he let go of me. I called to Luna to claw Henry, but she didn't help either.

Henry continued to hold me, repeating my name.

I wanted to hear the birds waking up for the day. They should've been doing it at that time, but I couldn't hear them. I couldn't hear their morning songs while he spoke into my ear.

I closed my eyes, wanting to disappear but knowing that I wouldn't. By then, I knew grace wasn't coming for me, so I thought I would ask for something, a little something, to see if he would accommodate me in some way.

"Shhh."

"What?" he asked.

"Shut up. For a minute. Just shut up."

"But—"

I shushed again until he listened. As he quieted down, I heard their songs. I opened my eyes and looked at the tree stretching across the cul-de-sac island. The sun was beginning to peek through the branches, the orange warming the green leaves and twisted branches. For a minute, he was quiet and I could hear the songs, the calls of the birds, more varieties than I could identify, echoing through the tree as they woke to another day.

I saw a finch flit from one branch to another, calling to his partner. I couldn't see the other bird, but the one chirping seemed to know where she was. He sang to her, his chest puffed out. I wondered what he was saying. I liked to think he was singing her a song, telling the story of the beauty of another sunrise, another day. Maybe that's not what he was saying at all. Maybe he was calling to her. Maybe he was searching for her, saying her name again and again, demanding she listen, demanding she do what he thought was best for her. I would never know what that finch said, and isn't that really the disappointment of being human? We think we know so much. We think we are the superior species, and yet there is so much we don't know. Like the songs of birds. We hear the tune, but we don't know the words. We only know what we want to hear.

As I listened, Henry spoke again. "Lulu!" He pressed around me like a straitjacket, suppressing any movement of my arms. I flailed my legs, trying to break free, but I kicked the tree. A jolt of pain radiated through my ankle, up my leg, and burst out of me in a scream.

"Stop it!" Henry's whiskers pressed into me, a million pinpricks pushing into my cheek.

"Don't touch me!" I tried to break free, but he wouldn't let go and I began to shudder at his touch, wondering if he had also touched Alice with those hands. "Get off me! I don't want your hands on me, not after they've touched her."

Henry didn't let go, but I felt the pressure loosen as he tried to make sense of what I'd said. "Who?" he asked. "Esther?"

"No!" The word escaped from deep inside. "Alice. Don't pretend. I know you're having an affair."

"Don't be ridiculous!" His words hissed in my ear, but he still wouldn't let go. "Why would you—"

"The way you looked at her, the hours—"

"Lulu," his voice dropped, too choked by emotion for the syllables to hold together. "Don't you know?" I could feel his body shaking against mine. "It's you. It's only ever been you." For a moment I could hear the birds chirp again. Then Henry said, "How could you doubt that?"

I stopped pushing against him and let him hold me as the depth of my madness sank in. There was no baby and no affair. What else had I imagined?

"You have to calm down," he said, measuring his voice. "They are watching."

As the morning sun rose higher and cast beams through the willow's reaching branches, I looked around. We weren't alone anymore. It wasn't just me, Henry, Gary, Luna, and a few birds. It was the whole street of neighbors, including the ones I called friends. Nora stood and stared, her hand gripped over her mouth. Hatti waddled behind her and cried. Everyone was there, including Bitsy, who walked toward us. She didn't look at me. She bent down to the ground and picked up Luna as I let Henry hold me.

"Bitsy!" My syllables came out broken, choked with regret.

The wind rustled the leaves so their shadows fluttered across our faces. She looked straight at me. Her hazel eyes—a ring of gold glowing from around the pupil—pierced through me.

As I stood bound by Henry's hold and Bitsy's gaze, Gary asked, "Can I help?"

"No!" My shout scared Luna, who scratched Bitsy.

Henry tightened his grip around me again.

"Let's get her in the car," Gary said. As he walked toward me, I leaned back into Henry and kicked my legs, warning Gary to stay away.

"Lulu! Please! We're trying to help," Henry said.

"How?" I asked as I continued to squirm in his grip, trying to break free. "Like he helped her?"

"Honestly—" Henry began.

"You know what he did." My throat burned from the screams and the sobs, but I had to say more. I had to speak up for myself. I had to let all of them know what Gary had done and what he thought Henry should do to me. As I watched Bitsy nurse the scratches that seeped blood on her forearm, Nora began to walk toward us. I thought maybe she was coming to talk to Henry, to convince him to let me go. But instead, she put her arm around Bitsy.

"Don't you see it?" I shouted. "Don't you know? He gave her a lobotomy."

I swear that the birds and the breeze both quieted for a moment. No one spoke. No sound was made except for one. It started low and rose. "Oh, Lulu," Gary chuckled to himself. "You really are crazy."

"But—" I tried to say, but both Nora and Henry called my

name, begging me to stop. "Come on!" I cried. "Don't you see it? Nora, the article. You remember. Doesn't it make sense?"

"Lulu, please," she pleaded with only those two words, too wrecked to say more.

Gary stepped closer. "Do you think they will believe you?" His auburn hair fluttered in the breeze. "I mean, look at you." He ran his fingers over Esther's blanket.

Henry began to speak. "Now, Gary—"

"No, no, you should also know what she did. She stole my wife's cat, broke into our house—and then the way she was with Katherine."

Henry's grip loosened. "What do you mean?"

"The way she took her without permission, encouraged her to go against her mother's rules." He prowled around us and began to speak louder so the audience could hear him. "You certainly have paid special attention to Katherine. I don't know, maybe you saw her as a replacement for the one you lost."

"No!" I shouted. "Look at you! You send away your sons. No wonder Bitsy clings to her even though she's not yours!" I looked around him to see Nora and Hatti trying to make sense of all that was happening. "She's Ellen's!" I called. "Her sister's. The suicide—"

Bitsy held up her hand. The woman looked so small that day, so confused, so alone despite her husband standing beside her. She clung to the cat. Gary put his arm around her, and I saw her flinch. I saw the way her body stiffened in his presence. Then she spoke. "Katherine's *my* daughter."

"Bitsy—" I tried to say something, but the world spun and the haze of my mind began to blur my thoughts. I tripped over words. "Of course she is." I was so tired. "I didn't mean—" I couldn't even string together an entire sentence.

Then the breeze blew again, lifting Bitsy's bangs from her forehead. That's when I did something I knew better than to do: I hoped. I believed that Mother Nature had heard my prayers and she was on my side, about to show us all the scars of what he had done to her. Why else did Bitsy plaster those bangs into place, if not to hide the evidence of her procedure?

But as the hair lifted off her forehead, I could see that it was as clear and porcelain as the rest of her face. There were no silvery seams stitched into her temples, no signs of a lobotomy. Only a sad, frightened, broken woman standing in her nightgown, reflecting myself back to me.

That's when I stopped fighting and I let Henry carry me to the car. As we drove away, I didn't look at any of the neighbors. I didn't even see if Wesley was standing outside our house, waving to his parents as they drove off. I wadded up the blanket and wrapped my empty arms around myself, needing to feel something but no longer trusting that anything was real.

Part Two
THE MIRROR

"I felt myself melting into the shadows like the negative of a person I'd never seen before in my life."

—Sylvia Plath, *The Bell Jar*

CHAPTER TWENTY-FOUR

All those weeks, I had focused on the strange woman across the street, but I had missed the mad wife in the mirror.

CHAPTER TWENTY-FIVE

Trust can come and go. It can be earned and lost. Losing trust in others can sting, a fact I knew well. But losing trust in yourself can pierce like a wolf's bite and shred to pieces any semblance of self, all belief in reality, any understanding of truth. While I had been watching out the window, piecing together the puzzle of the new neighbor, the wolf had sunk its teeth into me. And that morning, it threatened to devour me.

As we pulled out of the neighborhood, I twisted the blanket on my lap. "You have to believe me." My voice shook with urgency. Henry hadn't spoken a word since he had gotten in the car. When he didn't respond, I scooted across the seat and reached for him. "Please, Henry." He kept his eyes on the road. "You can't trust Gary."

"This isn't about him." He said it so quietly and measured. I wished my voice could match his.

"But he's lying." Under different circumstances, I would've

kept my voice calm, but there was no time for politeness. He needed to understand. He needed to believe me. "I've never trusted that guy. The way he's tried to finagle his way into your job. That night in our house, after dinner, the way he cornered me in the kitchen—"

Henry's eyebrows scrunched together as he finally turned toward me. There was that look. I knew what he thought—that this was another lie or a delusion, more proof of my hysteria. I had never told him about it because what was there to tell? On the surface, Gary had come in to thank me for dinner and say goodbye. How could I get Henry to understand how I'd felt like a trapped animal? Instead of explaining, I kept going. "And Katherine? I was just trying to help. She's a sweet girl who seemed sad. But look at him. Look what he did to his wife."

"He didn't do anything."

"Yes, he did! You have to believe me." By now I was sitting in the middle of the seat, holding on to Henry's arm with both hands, trying to shake him into understanding. "I saw the discharge paper. It said she had a lobotomy."

"When did you see that? When you broke into their house?"

"Please, Henry, believe me. I know what I saw."

Without hesitation, Henry mumbled the last words we would speak to each other on the drive that day: "Like how you saw Esther?"

His words pierced my heart like shards of glass, splintered daggers of a truth I couldn't yet come to terms with. If I focused on Gary or Bitsy or how Henry wasn't listening to me, then I didn't have to reckon with why that blanket on my lap was empty and always had been.

We didn't speak for the rest of the drive. Any words I had would only solidify his belief that I was nothing more than the hysterical housewife, another woman lost to the epidemic of nerves mixed with boredom and madness.

But what other conclusion could he come to if in fact he and Wesley were right? For weeks, I had been caring for a baby, hearing her cry, holding her to my breast to feed, but she had never existed? Had I imagined the pregnancy as well?

No. I knew that much was true. I knew that I had carried her, that my stomach had stretched and my feet had disappeared. But as I looked back, as I tried to remember where my reality broke from theirs, the last moment I knew to be true was when the labor started, when Wesley brought me a glass of water in the living room, and he told me he'd be the best big brother he could be.

And what did I recall beyond that? The car ride home, the bundle on my lap, and the Betsers moving in across the street.

We rode in silence. I didn't ask where we were going. I recognized the route even though it had been more than a decade since I had last been there, and only a couple of times at that. But I knew the place before we turned into the driveway, the leggy pines crowding one another, pointing to the sky, a claustrophobic path carved out beneath them as they shifted and creaked in the passing breeze.

The sanatorium loomed over the landscape, a stone structure jutting from the earth, the windows always darkened no matter the time of day. Mama had shushed me when I said the place scared me the first time we arrived to visit Georgie back when it was a hospital for polio patients. Three stories of stacked bricks and white columns… It had more detail than any building I had ever seen.

As we drove down the pine-shrouded drive, I couldn't help but feel as though I was coming home, but not to one I wanted to return to. After all these years, that moment a decade ago that forever changed our family was coming to haunt me again.

They put me in a room of my own. I don't know if that was standard care. I didn't ask. I didn't talk to anyone. It wasn't exactly a summer camp where we got to know our fellow inmates. Henry told me not to call them that, but wasn't that what we were? Were any of us there because we chose to be? When Georgie had been there, he was placed there in the hope of avoiding permanent paralysis. It had partially worked. But it hadn't prevented his leg from withering. I hadn't contracted anything contagious, and yet there I was, in a room, on a bed with white sheets as rough as sandpaper.

"I'll be back soon," Henry told me.

Soon. He used that vague word. The one I would say to Wesley when he wanted something, and I didn't want to say no but I also didn't want to do it right that moment. It was the perfect word to stall, divert, hope he forgot.

Henry squeezed my hand but didn't look me in the eye.

In the quiet, a shiver tickled its way up my spine. I hoped Henry had packed me a sweater. I didn't know what he had put in the bag while I was on the bedroom floor sobbing as our son attempted to comfort his mother.

"Remember," Henry said. I waited for him to say more. I thought he was starting a memory, about to reminisce about something, but there was no story to unfold. It was a command, a directive, a plea. "Lulu, remember."

There was a lot I remembered, but there were some things I'd rather keep buried in the recesses of my mind, the crevices of my body, instead of letting them intrude into the forefront of my reality.

But I couldn't tell him that. I needed to do as Mama used to say and be sweet. Because if I didn't, they might sever my brain, too.

So I looked away from the blanket. I smiled and nodded as if agreeing to obey.

He stood to leave and said, "Rest and get better."

He said it as if it was as simple as that, as if a little nap would fix it all. As if this was a passing fever and tomorrow I'd be right as rain. My empty arms and aching bones knew I needed help, but what I also needed was a husband who believed me. And a reality I could trust.

CHAPTER TWENTY-SIX

That place didn't have a soul, but it had eyes. Everywhere you went, someone was watching. Sometimes it was a nurse, but more often it was a fellow inmate. We all watched one another, seeing if we were like them. Judging and comparing, hoping against all odds that we weren't as bad as the others. That we were the exception, the one who didn't belong.

And I didn't. I still knew that to be true, even if I doubted so much else.

That first morning, I felt feverish, dizzy, out of sorts—but who wouldn't in a place like that? The nurse who woke me informed me that I needed to shower before I did anything. I thought that would be a good thing. I didn't know she was going to watch me. She stood in the threshold of the shower room and watched as the faucet spit ice water onto my body. I kept my arms close to me and turned my back to her as much as I could, but she still saw more of my nakedness than my husband had over the last two months.

I hurried to clean myself, rinsing out the shampoo before it had a chance to fully lather. I ran the bar of soap over my ribs, my sunken stomach, my deflated breasts. They no longer dripped with milk, having already given up, having known before my mind caught on that they weren't necessary. In that moment, I wanted to slip beneath the waters of a tub, but I would settle for washing down the drain with the shampoo bubbles.

After she watched me get dressed, the nurse took me to the cafeteria. We walked past a woman who sat at the entry, rocking, mumbling, drooling, whispering. She spoke quickly, but to herself, as if she were the only one who would listen.

The nurse grabbed me a tray of food and then told me, "I'll be back to get you for your appointment with the doctor." Then she left me alone in a room full of eyes.

I tried to choke down a few bites of what I thought was oatmeal, but my stomach refused to accept more. The combination of food less palatable than those damn TV dinners and smells more noxious than a manure-filled barn in the heat of the summer took any bit of appetite I had. So I sipped on coffee, hoping it could help with my headache, since the buzzing lights in that place seemed to make it throb even more.

I looked around at the others. Worse than the food were the sounds, moans, and the sights of those who no longer looked human, especially the woman by the door. She looked at every person who walked in, but her eyes were blank, her stare beyond us, her body nothing more than a shell pretending at being human though it seemed her soul had left it years ago.

I wanted to plug my ears, close my eyes, wish myself to another time and place, but then I would be just like her, sitting, rocking, moaning to no one other than herself. I needed to get out of there. I needed to get home. I wondered where Wesley was right then. And then I feared that he might know where his mother was and what she had become.

What would he think of me? How would he look at me? Would he see me in the same way I saw the woman by the door?

You're not her, I told myself. *And you're not Bitsy either.*

Had she been in a place like this? Maybe when I got back to Greenwood, we could swap stories over spades of the sights we saw. I could tell her about the woman who stripped off her top every time she got hot. Or the man who pounded his head into the metal food tray when he saw his own reflection. Or the woman about my age who cowered in the dark corner of the cafeteria, hoping the shadows would hide her shiner of a black eye.

I knew they were watching me, too. I saw some of their heads turn when the nurse came back for me.

"Are we ready?" she asked when she returned with a smile. Her eyes seemed too kind for that place. I couldn't help but wonder why she said *we*, but then I thought maybe she knew. Maybe she had heard. Maybe she thought Esther was still with me.

As we walked out of the cafeteria, she paused in front of the woman at the door. I looked her over and quickly realized she wasn't as old as I had first believed. Her pale skin looked smooth—flawless, nearly—with no signs of wrinkles. Had we been sitting around playing cards together, we might have asked her what cold cream she used.

"Don't tell the doctor," the nurse said with a wink as she handed the woman a lollipop. The woman scrambled to unwrap it and pop it into her mouth as quickly as possible. Her rocking slowed as she savored her treat.

I couldn't help myself. As we walked away, I had to ask. "What's wrong with her?"

"Oh, she's better now," the nurse said.

"Better?"

"You should've seen her before the lobotomy."

My knees felt weak and my legs nearly gave out when she said that word. I muttered, "I didn't see a scar."

"They don't all have scars, not when we go through the eye socket." The words zinged through me, and the hallway began to spin. She said it so matter-of-factly. "I tell you, when it works, you could be right next to someone and have no idea they had one."

Perhaps you could even live alongside someone, share a game of cards or even a meal, and not know what had happened to them. At least that was when it worked. I was too afraid to ask what happened when it didn't.

CHAPTER TWENTY-SEVEN

The shadows looked different in that place. They seemed to reach at contrasting angles, crawl across the walls in patterns different from in our Greenwood home. They seemed ever present, shifting as the hours changed but always looming, like the buzz of the overhead lights.

The lights that hummed loudest were in Dr. Ruthledge's office. Perhaps that was on purpose, a way to keep his patients talking so they could drown out that electric thrum.

"Please sit," the short doctor said to me that morning. The room wasn't the doctor's office I had expected. There was no exam table. There was a couch, where I sat, with an armchair across from it. As he took his seat, I could see his bald spot. I wondered if he knew it was there since it was in a spot that a man like him probably didn't even know about. At least, he didn't try to hide it with a sweep of hair across his shiny scalp.

"I've already spoken to Mr. Mayfield." Of course he had.

While I was locked away in a room, they had talked about me as if I were a child. "He's very concerned about you. As we all are. But let's see how we can help you. What is it that you'd like?"

"Please, I'd just like to go home."

"We'd all like that for you, but we can't do that, not yet. You understand why, right?"

"Yes."

"Good. But I'd like to hear you say it. Why is it that your husband brought you here?"

"I haven't been feeling well," I said as I watched the plant behind him, a fern like the ones that grew in the woods behind our home. "For weeks now, I haven't been feeling well. I've had headaches nearly every day. My hands and legs have hurt. I've been exhausted."

"Yes, well, that's pretty common after an event like you experienced. But I'm not asking how you're feeling. I am asking why you're here."

I shifted on the couch and crossed my ankles. "That's what I'm getting at. I've been so tired that I can barely get out of bed. I haven't felt like myself."

The doctor looked at the notepad on his lap as he continued to write. "Yes"—his voice sounded impatient—"and how long has this been going on?"

I paused for a moment and tried to count. It had been weeks. It had started back when I got home, though even during the pregnancy I suppose I had my moments.

"Maybe a few months?"

"Yes"—he kept his focus on the paper—"so, as I previously

stated, since the event." He emphasized both syllables and landed hard on the final letter.

I had never thought of Esther's birth as an event, but I knew that's what he meant. He wanted me to say it, didn't he? He wanted me to confess. He wanted me to tell him that I knew what I had done wrong, to prove that I was aware. I didn't want to say it. I didn't want to admit that Esther had never come home. That Esther had never cried out for me in the night. That she had never even taken a breath. That my body had failed at the one job it was supposed to do: grow, protect, and birth her into life.

"So let me ask again, Mrs. Mayfield." He used his middle finger to push the glasses up the bridge of his nose, his weasel eyes squinting at me as he repeated himself. "Why is it that your husband brought you here?"

I felt a cool breeze blow across my arms. I gathered them around myself and wished I had brought her blanket with me. I closed my eyes. As my fingers rubbed the rash on the backs of my arms, I tried to imagine that they were feeling the satin edging of her blanket. I took a deep breath. I apologized to Esther, afraid that if I said the words aloud, I would be releasing her.

But I had no choice. I saw the lollipop lady and all the others around that place. I knew Bitsy. I was not going to become like any of them, so I took a deep breath and I said, "Because of my baby."

"What about your baby?"

I looked him in his beady eyes. I knew who he was in that moment. He had one task: to get my admission. He didn't care how much it hurt me. He needed me to do my job so we could do his. So I said the words he wanted me to say.

"My baby's dead."

"Have you always believed that?"

I should've cried. I should've mourned. Maybe that's what my body had been doing, mourning the loss of my girl. But I couldn't give him that satisfaction. And if I melted then, what would that mean for my prognosis? So I played at being the good girl, the one who followed instructions, the one who did what was expected of her, and I said, "No." *Forgive me, Esther.*

For the next few minutes, I continued playing the part as he explained that grief can do strange things to us, especially to mothers. To women. I kept quiet and nodded as he monologued, but I watched the plant. The fronds in front drooped and pointed to the floor, but the ones in the back reached toward the sunlight that peeked through the window. I wondered where the plant had come from. Had it been plucked from the forest floor, potted, and placed inside this asylum, only to reach for the freedom it once had?

"We're going to start psychoanalysis, try some drug therapy, and go from there," he said.

"Miltown?" I asked.

"No. It's fine for some, but clearly it isn't strong enough for you. I've got something else in mind." I looked at him, a sob about to escape me. "And if we need more, well, we'll cross that bridge when we get to it."

"Please, Doctor, I don't want a lobotomy."

He closed the file in his lap and crossed his hands over it. "Let's not get into specifics just yet, Mrs. Mayfield."

Let's not get into specifics.

Those words pinned me to the couch as if a lead weight had

landed on my chest, wrapped around my arms, and held my feet to the floor. I wanted to scream. Cry. Flee. But I needed to remain stoic, save the tears for the dark hours when I knew I'd be awake, when I would hear her cries whether she existed or not. For now, I needed to look him in the eyes and appear as normal as I could. For now, I needed to smile the smile he wanted from me so he could save me. I just hoped that when he got around to it, there would still be someone worth saving.

CHAPTER TWENTY-EIGHT

That night, through blurred vision and a tranquilizer haze, I sat alone in my room and fiddled with a thread on Esther's blanket. I tried not to listen to the sounds outside my door, the footsteps and the carts wheeling by, the cries and the shouts, the collective sigh of surrendered people.

I wished for a distraction—a radio to drown out the sounds, Luna to comfort me, Wesley to tell me a story about his day. I sat on the bed, the chill cutting through my feet, making me long for my slippers. My eyes begged to close, my body ached for escape, but I couldn't settle enough to sleep. As the night hours ticked away, I clung to the cotton blanket, stroking the white rabbit emblazoned onto the fabric. It reminded me of another rabbit.

When I was about ten years old, one of our spring kittens had uncovered a rabbit nest and injured one of the babies before I could get to it. The mother moved the others elsewhere, but left that one behind. Mama told me that rabbits sometimes have to leave the suffering to save the others. It seemed to me that sometimes humans did the opposite, abandoning the healthy for the hurt.

I wouldn't let go of that baby bunny. I carried it around, insisting she was sleeping. I remembered holding that little one, keeping the cat away, running to Daddy to show him what I'd found, begging him to let me bring the little one inside, to care for her and bring her back to health.

"Oh, Lucy." That's what he said, with a sigh and with the first syllable of my name drawn out, not the name Henry had given me, but the one Daddy had chosen for me, named after his *nonna*. "My little light." That's what he'd say some days, but on that day, he sighed my name and told me that nature belonged outside. Then he took that little sleeping bunny from me and placed her gingerly into his coveralls pouch. "I'll find her a new home," he told me.

I remember now. I remember how he promised me that. I kissed the little baby on the white stripe across her forehead and then I let her rest in Daddy's pocket. When I asked him at dinner that night where she was, he said she'd gone on home.

I imagined her home, a house underground, similar to ours, but sized for a rabbit family. I imagined the reunion, the happiness her mother and siblings must've felt when she hopped into the house and they all welcomed her back.

But now I knew differently. Now I understood that she hadn't been sleeping. My rescue came too late, and her home was a world well beyond our farm.

Despite my efforts, love, and hope, she didn't survive.

I tugged on the thread of the blanket as I thought over the last weeks, how I had heard Esther cry. How I had sat in her room and rocked her. How I had taken out my breasts and nursed her. If I closed my eyes, I could feel her. If I inhaled, I could smell her. If I listened, I knew she would call to me.

I kept pulling until the blanket's smooth edging began to detach. And I kept going. I kept pulling so that it came apart, just like me. My hands ached, my joints stiffened as I demanded they keep going, keep tugging, keep tearing apart the thing that had lied to me.

A nest of pink formed on the floor, the satin tickling my bare toes as the asbestos tile cooled my feet. I should've brought those slippers, though I hadn't even been the one to pack my suitcase. I could ask Henry to bring them for me. But that would require planning; that would mean realizing that I would need to stay there longer than I wanted to.

I needed to get out of there. I needed to get back to Wesley. I needed to be in my home, the one with the squeaky hallway, the obnoxious dishwasher, and the back patio with my only companion, Luna.

Here, bars blocked the windows. I don't remember them being there when we visited Georgie. Maybe they were. But they weren't necessary then. Those patients were not at risk of opening the windows and choosing the ending of their stories. At that time, most were bedridden. Some in iron lungs. Most clinging to life and hoping for healing.

Now the patients might've seen healing in a different way. A dangerous one. One that required restrictions, confinements, bars to keep them physically safe when mental soundness wasn't an option.

The more my fingers felt that familiar fabric, the more the memories came. Not the false ones. Not the delusions. But the reality of how that blanket—that silly piece of material that had cost a book of green stamps—had always been empty, how it had never held Esther. How I had never held her.

I thought I had. My arms tried to tell me that they knew her, but now my mind told me otherwise.

I dropped the blanket onto the pile of satin binding, creating a mound of tangled nothingness on the frigid sanatorium floor. I left it there as I lay down, tucked my legs into myself, and closed my eyes. But I didn't rest. I remembered.

CHAPTER TWENTY-NINE

Sometimes forgetting is a mercy, and recalling is a pain too deep to bear. But that's what Henry asked me to do.

I remember the labor, how it started sooner than we expected, with more intensity than with Wesley. I had been told that second births go faster than firsts because my body knew what to do. I trusted that was true.

We'd rushed to the hospital, thinking we would meet our baby quickly, just as the doctor had said. But labor lingered. It slowed and stalled. They moved me. Drugged me. Let me get some rest.

When had I ever been able to sleep? But in that moment, I did. And maybe I shouldn't have. Maybe if I had been awake, I would've known something was wrong. I would've called for the doctor so he could help. But instead, I rested like they told me to.

I woke from the dampness between my legs, the fluid that

had burst from me. I thought that was a sign. She would be here soon! The nurses hurried, rushed, called the doctor, who suited up, who requested more help, who told me to push. Now.

Immediately.

With all the effort I had!

I tried.

But I was still so tired.

The nurse, the one with the kind eyes, the ones the color of the sea, she told me I could do it. She squeezed my hand and smiled, but I saw the fear behind her ocean eyes.

"That's it," she told me. "Your baby's almost here. That's it. Just one more."

I gave them one more. I felt the release, the relief.

And I heard the silence.

I saw the hurry.

The nurse let go of my hand. She rushed across the room with the others before she ran out and called for more help.

Where was the baby? Why were there no cries?

I saw the nurse's tears before the doctor came beside me and said, "I'm sorry, Mrs. Mayfield. We did all we could, but she didn't make it."

She didn't make it? My baby didn't make it? What did he mean? What was he saying? That wasn't how it was supposed to work. She was our baby, the completion of our family, the dream we'd been dreaming, the life that would complete us.

"What happened?" I asked.

"We think maybe it was the umbilical cord. It was wrapped around her chest. Maybe it contributed—"

Maybe. All the doctor could tell me was *maybe.* I needed more than that. I needed certainty. But how could that have been true? The cord that had connected us, nourished her, brought her life, had also taken it from her? It didn't make sense.

I went home two days later, cradling the blanket that had been meant to warm and comfort her, but that would remain empty and useless to everyone but me. To me, it was the thread I needed to cling to when I needed a mercy to get me through.

CHAPTER THIRTY

A week or so after I'd arrived at the sanatorium, a rash like a mask appeared on both cheeks and across the bridge of my nose, so red and distinct that I doubted any amount of makeup would conceal it. Not that I had a need for makeup. Though, had I known Henry would be joining us for our daily session, I might have put on some lipstick if I had any.

Thanks to the regular schedule of tranquilizers each day, my mind operated in a haze, so when I first saw Henry standing in the waiting room, I didn't believe he was real. I nearly ran to him. After all, that was the longest we had been apart since we had gotten married, but then I remembered that he had listened to Gary. He had phoned the doctor. He had put me in the car. He had driven me and left me alone in that asylum.

"Lulu—" he said as he walked toward me. He didn't tell me I looked good. He never was the type to lie. But he did peck me on the cheek, kissing me closer to my jawline to avoid the rash. "How are you?"

I hadn't showered in days; I didn't need those eyes on me. I had barely eaten, and from the way my shirt dress billowed around me, I had already lost weight. Thankfully, the doctor ushered us into his office before I had to reply.

During our sessions so far, Dr. Ruthledge had asked so many questions, requiring me to talk until he seemed satisfied, but the words sometimes struggled to find their way through the mist of my mind, no matter how much I screamed to myself from the inside to wake up, sit up, and say what he needed to hear. I tried to be the patient he wanted me to be, to play the game he set for me. If I won, I went home. If I failed, well, I didn't want to think about that.

He thought he was fixing me, but if that were true, why did I still feel the way I did? Just as the cold cut through, provoking an unrelenting shiver, so did the exhaustion, burrowing into my joints so that they ached. My head pounded. My eyes preferred darkness. I struggled to get out of bed. But what did I even have to get out of bed for? I didn't need to fry any eggs, didn't need to get Wesley's day started, didn't need to dust or vacuum, nor put together any sandwiches or roasts or gelatin salads. So why bother? The only reason was to prove to them that I was better. Complacent. On my way to going home.

"Lulu," the doctor said to me the day he changed the game. Here I thought we'd been playing along with each other, not knowing he was about to rewrite the rules. "It's come to my attention that you still aren't eating."

I knew Henry was looking at me, but I kept my eyes on

the doctor. Of course I wasn't eating. The food looked worse than that sunshine vomit I'd made for the dinner party. The problem was, if I skipped a meal, they wrote it up. If I went to the cafeteria but didn't eat, they wrote it up. If I ate and was sick to my stomach, they wrote it up. Every action or inaction was used against me.

I sat up a bit straighter so that the leather couch squeaked. "With all due respect, Doctor," I said through a smile, "I do eat."

"Not much."

He did have a point. "I suppose I haven't had much of an appetite."

"Yes, and that's what concerns me," he said, right before he presented me with a new plan, something more than talk and tranquilizers.

"I know you want to get home and we've made progress, but I think there's a way we can get you healthier sooner. Mr. Mayfield and I have already discussed this." There they went again, talking behind my back. Henry reached for my hand when the doctor said his name. I both missed and hated his touch in that moment, a tornado of feelings I couldn't think about right then, not when the doctor continued, saying, "I'd like to try something different."

I remember this moment. I remember exactly what I was looking at when he told me what he had in mind. The fern behind him drooped more than usual, and a frond was beginning to brown. I wanted to get up and pluck it off, give the plant a drink, help it get better. I stayed glued to the couch, not letting myself move because I knew the doctor wouldn't want that; that's not why we were there. He paused before he told me what he wanted to do. He paused because he wanted my undivided attention, but he wanted me to give it to him without him having to ask first. And I did. I looked at him.

"I think it's time we try—" And I swear the clock stopped ticking, the time between seconds elongating once again, giving my heart time to quicken as my mind tried to think of a way to escape, a way to not let them poke at my brain until I became quiet, content, carefully sculpted into the happy housewife I should've been. I wanted to scream, to run, maybe vomit or fight, but that couch, those drugs, and Henry's chapped hand held me in place as the weight of how they wanted to alter me held me motionless until time moved forward again and the doctor uttered the words "electroconvulsive therapy."

My heart stuttered. The words echoed in my mind, their meaning unfolding slowly, like a distant thunderclap. The doctor continued to talk, but I didn't hear most of what he said. I made eye contact, nodded, fidgeted with a button on the couch, and finally stammered, "No."

He hadn't suggested the procedure I most feared, so while relief attempted to wash over me, I still feared the tide that was building.

"ECT, for short. We've had good results with it." He spoke as if I hadn't said a word. This man who had asked me to talk during our sessions apparently knew how to hear, but he didn't know how to listen.

"No," I said again.

And he continued, "I think you're an ideal candidate."

I wondered if I screamed if that would make him listen, but I figured all he would hear was further justification for this treatment. While I shouted inside myself, I sat silent in the room and tried not to drown in the wave of fear as Dr. Ruthledge did his due diligence and explained the possible side effects: temporary headache, muscle aches, nausea, dental pain, disorientation, loss of memory…

"Loss of memory?" Henry asked.

"Yes, some patients have reported memory lapses."

Henry had asked me to remember. He thought that was what I had needed. Even Dr. Ruthledge had been asking me to do the same during our sessions, but now there was a possibility of forgetting.

I wanted to ask what it meant, what exactly it was, what it felt like. But then again, did I really want to know? Instead, ignoring the doctor, I turned to Henry and asked, "This is what you want?" Henry let go of my hand. Even though I hadn't welcomed his touch, rescinding it hurt even more. But he didn't speak. If the doctor was going to make me talk, if I had no choice in the matter, well, he shouldn't be able to remain silent either. He needed to speak up for himself. His voice needed to proclaim what exactly he wanted to do to his wife. I shifted on the couch again, angling toward him as I asked, "Henry?"

"Dr. Ruthledge says it's our best option."

Out of my periphery, I saw the clouds roll heavy across the sky as the plant withered without anyone else even noticing. We all sat in silence, and I stared at the side of Henry's face until he finally turned toward me.

Those eyes of his that I used to get lost in looked so tired, with creases beginning to chisel starbursts alongside them. I looked at that boy who had been my first in so many ways. I stared into the deep wells of our shared existence, and I said to him, "Gary probably told himself the same thing."

Henry's eyes closed, the creases beside them deepened, and a single tear escaped. But I didn't want to see his tears. Instead, I stared at the plant as Dr. Ruthledge talked about the success they had seen in ECT patients. I thought of the woman in the cafeteria, and I wondered: Would this earn me a lollipop, too?

CHAPTER THIRTY-ONE

They came for me the next morning when I should have been going to breakfast. I hadn't decided yet if I was going to the cafeteria, but it didn't matter. They had other plans for me. I knew that when two orderlies arrived at my door with the nurse.

"Good morning, Mrs. Mayfield." That's what the nurse said to me. She spoke as if everything was normal. She greeted me like it was a typical morning, like we were two acquaintances—neighbors, perhaps, as if she were about to ask to borrow a cup of sugar.

"Please come with us."

I knew I had agreed to the therapy, but did I really have a choice?

I pulled my legs to my chest and began scooting back on my mattress. I had nowhere to hide. No place to run. I moved backward until the wall stopped me. I wrapped my arms around my legs, cowering in a ball as a chill gripped my entire body.

"Please, Mrs. Mayfield. It will be easier if you come on your own." One of the orderlies made a move to step in front of the nurse, but she stopped him.

I remember the time I took Wesley to the doctor, when he needed an immunization. He had trusted me that morning, gone along as a good boy, held his mother's hand, and smiled at the doctor. But when he heard the word *shot*, his trust in me left him. He begged me not to. He didn't want that pain. I knew it was for the best. He didn't realize the protection that shot would give him. He began to plead, shake, cry. When that didn't work, he jumped from the exam table. The doctor stood in front of the door, blocking any exit, so Wesley darted beneath a chair. I reached down and pulled him out, my strength greater than his. He flailed in my arms, kicked his legs, screamed his disapproval, but I picked him up and held him down.

It was for his own good, I had told myself.

It's for her own good, they told themselves.

I didn't want to be Wesley then. I had no escape, nowhere to hide, no spot that would protect me from the strength of those orderlies, who would simply grab me like I was a toddler.

So I listened. I stood up. I followed the nurse down the hall.

"I haven't had breakfast this morning," I told her, hoping to delay their plans by reminding her of my physical needs.

"That's for the best."

Dr. Ruthledge was already in the room when we walked in, along with a few other nurses. The room was small, with an exam table in the middle.

"Good morning, Mrs. Mayfield." Why did everyone act as if this was typical? "This will only take a few minutes, and then you'll feel much better."

How did he know that? Had he felt this for himself? And perhaps I would feel better in a few minutes, but what would I feel like before that?

"Please take off your rings," the nurse said to me.

"My rings?"

"Yes, all metal objects," Dr. Ruthledge explained.

I looked at the diamond solitaire and the plain silver band beneath it. Since the day Henry had placed them on my finger in the church in front of our friends and family, I had never removed them—not when doing dishes, not when taking a bath, not even when my fingers swelled during pregnancy.

"Please," the nurse said in my hesitation.

My hand shook as I gave them to her.

"It's okay," she said to me, her eyes full of the same kindness as the nurse at Esther's delivery. "Everybody gets scared. But you don't need to be."

I wanted to believe her. I wanted to trust her just as I had trusted that other nurse, the one who had cheered me on, held my hand, encouraged me to keep going. But look how that had ended.

They made me lie down on the table. They didn't use straps. They didn't fasten me in place, but they stood around me, the orderlies watching, waiting in case they needed to grab me like I had Wesley. Poor Wesley. Where was he just then? Was he still asleep? Probably not. Henry's mother probably had him on a schedule. And who knows what she was making him eat for breakfast.

The nurse who had taken my rings smeared a thick grease onto my temples so that my forehead cooled beneath the damp, sticky gel. Of all the people, in that moment, I thought of Bitsy, those dimples, the distant stare, the short staccato sentences, her severed mind.

You aren't her.

There, laid out on the metal table, I heard the voice, not through sound waves moving into my ears, but through a knowing reverberation in my core.

You aren't her.

I knew that to be true. We were very different people whose lives happened to intersect on Twyckenham Court. I wasn't her. She wasn't me. And yet laid out on that table, I thought we seemed more alike than we were different.

I know noises happened around the room, but my world grew quiet. I escaped inside myself as they busied themselves around me. I closed my eyes and fled to the tree of my childhood. I saw the leaves blowing in the wind, heard the creek trickling beneath me, felt the rough bark on my hands. I began humming to myself, bringing Wesley's favorite song to mind as I lay still, in air so cold it seeped through my skin and gathered in my bones.

"Open up," Dr. Ruthledge said to me, like he was a dentist about to examine my teeth. Instead, he placed a rubber bit into my mouth. I felt like a horse on Daddy's farm. "It's so you don't hurt yourself."

I wasn't sure how I could hurt any worse than I had over these last few months.

I bit down, my teeth sinking into the rubber, the taste bitter and stale like a balloon that had long since lost its air. I told myself to think of that tree, to imagine myself sitting in its branches once more. I thought of squirrels and ladybugs, crows that cawed overhead, and happy little bluebirds that flew across the painted sky.

And then it happened in a flash. A jolt moved through my body. Tightened my muscles. Arched my back. Twitched my mind until I felt nothing. Knew nothing. Recalled little of the monotony of that place, as if with a flip of a switch, Dr. Ruthledge lit the embers that melted those days so they forged together into an indistinguishable mass of time.

But what I wanted was for that treatment to burn the memories of the last year to ashes that would scatter in an instant, too elusive to rebuild. Too scorched to try.

CHAPTER THIRTY-TWO

I had once wanted to belong. When I woke the next morning and a fog had settled thick over my mind, I desired nothing more than to be left alone, to disappear, to melt into the walls and slip away. I longed to be invisible, to evaporate like Esther.

While some newer memories faded and others blurred together, I remembered more than I wanted to. I could still hear the silence of the delivery room. If the memory hadn't been burned away yet, I doubted that it would disappear. But one thing I knew for sure: I did not want to be shocked again.

Dr. Ruthledge seemed pleased with my progress, even though I told him I still felt unwell, but by then I knew he only heard what he wanted to. I knew that complaining wouldn't get me any closer to going home, so I swallowed my malaise and it sat like a boulder in my stomach. I stayed in my room and kept the shade drawn, preferring to rest in the shadows, hoping that they would welcome me soon.

Shortly after they'd shocked me, Nora visited sometime in the afternoon. I was asleep when she arrived. The tranquilizers they prescribed were much stronger than Miltown, pulling me into sleep even when I didn't want to rest, a problem different from what I'd had before. I felt her presence before I opened my eyes. The only person I wanted to see was Esther or maybe Ellen, Bitsy's sister, a stranger to me who now felt like a sympathetic spirit, a parallel soul, separated by life but bound by despondency.

When I woke she was there, sitting at the table by my still-full lunch tray, holding the empty blanket, stitching together the binding I had torn off.

"Hey, Lu." She spoke in a voice I barely recognized. Instead of billowing and filling the room, it was low, quiet, reserved. A cigarette dangled from her lips as her hands moved along the blanket. "Hope you don't mind. I had a sewing kit on me, and I thought I'd fix this while you rested."

Suddenly, I felt self-conscious. I wished for makeup or a mirror to check my hair. I worried how she would judge my appearance, but she kept her focus on the blanket. I shifted in my bed, trying to sit up despite my spinning head—a side effect of the drugs. I knew to take it slowly, to work my way toward sitting. I propped myself up, resting my head on my hand, and said, "You don't need to do that."

"It's no bother." Nora's hands moved rhythmically along the seam. I didn't stop her. I let her continue working, continue stitching together what I had torn apart. Surely she knew it was no longer needed, but she kept going and I let her. I wondered how many times she had seen me holding it. What must she have thought? "It's kept me busy while I waited. It won't take me long. It'll be good to have this fixed."

She paused after that last sentence, as if hearing the words that had already left her mouth. Would it be good? Had that blanket ever been good? And would fixing it only make her friend mad all over again?

"It'll come in handy for you, with as cold as it is in here." She shivered to get her point across, and we both accepted the justification. She paused to tap her cigarette on the food tray, the ashes spilling onto the pile of pale, peppery corn. "I assumed you weren't eating this?" I shook my head no. "I mean, as delicious as this looks. I always have preferred my corn mushy and with extra juice." She chuckled and then went on, "I'd say it's a shame to waste this, but it looks like waste itself."

I couldn't help myself. I let out a small laugh, something I hadn't done in my time there. I had missed her so much. I couldn't believe she was sitting in my room, visiting me in that place. I wondered for a moment if she was really there, if she really sat at that table. Could I believe what I saw? I could hear her speak and smell her burning cigarette. I could feel her there with me, as if something lost had been found. And I decided that even if she wasn't in that room with me, I wanted to believe that she was there.

"Did you see this Jell-O square?" She nodded toward a block of red gelatin. "I can't believe they would serve such rubbish, as if they don't know that they have royalty in their midst. Perhaps you should show them that you're the Queen of Molded Foods."

I smiled at the thought, but I didn't want to show them anything. I didn't feel like getting off the bed, and I was tired of pretending. Where had that gotten me? I tried to show the doctor I was capable, better, improving. And yet they'd still shocked me.

"How's Wesley?" I asked, trying to distract myself from what they had done to me.

"Fine. He's a good kid. The other day he and James found a beetle on the ground. Do you know what my kid tried to do? Kill it. That little booger had his foot in the air, ready to stomp down on it, when Wesley pushed him out of the way."

"He pushed him?"

"Yeah, but James deserved it. That beetle hadn't done anything wrong."

"Still." I shifted on the bed to sit up a bit more. "Wesley shouldn't have pushed him."

"Lu, do you hear me? He's a good kid. You should be proud."

She was right; he was a good kid. And I missed him so much. I began to ache all over, in my arms and my chest. I wanted to hold him, to feel his curls and count his freckles. To hear that giggle and the way he said *L* words. I ran my finger over my palm, reciting in my mind our little rhyme to each other.

Nora pushed the needle through the blanket, pricking her finger on the other side. She went quiet for a moment to concentrate on backstitching.

"How's Hatti?" I asked.

Nora told me she'd had the baby and that her little girl hadn't been like the others. "She has the four-letter word: colic." A word that could make any mother shudder. No amount of rocking or shushing or gripe water would fix that. Only time and patience and earplugs could get you through it. "I told her it's only for a season. I didn't say it's one of the longest seasons of your life." We both moaned with memories. For a moment, things felt normal, as if we were sitting together in one of our kitchens, talking like friends do. But then she asked, "Do you have scissors?"

Reality returned when I told her, "They don't let us have things like that here."

"Shit, Lulu." Nora pursed her lips, as if remembering where we were. Then she held the thread to her mouth and used her teeth to break it. She held the blanket out in front of her and ran her hand along the edge as she checked her work. The rabbit stared at me, smiling as if he remembered everything. I wanted to tell her to keep the blanket, to take it home with her, throw it away, give it away, burn it. I didn't care.

But I did. I knew that as much as I wanted to, I couldn't let go of it. Not yet. Not ever.

"Listen, there's a reason I came today," she said as she draped the blanket across my lap. Then she took another puff of her cigarette, inhaling deeply before letting it go. "I had to tell you I'm sorry."

Pity was not what I'd expected to get from her. "You don't have to—"

"Yes, I do." Her hand shook as she held the cigarette to her painted lips and took a long drag. "You weren't well. I should've seen that."

Maybe she should've. Maybe if she would've asked more questions, taken more notice, then reality would've shattered its way in sooner. And what if it would've? What would these past couple of months have been like? As much as everyone believed my mind to have been broken, maybe those weeks of delusion had given me the gift of time.

"Can I have that?" I held out my hand.

"You don't smoke."

"Yeah, well, it seems I've been doing a lot of things I don't usually do. Maybe it can help."

Nora sat down on the bed beside me. As I took a puff of her cigarette, she rested her head on my shoulder and told me, "I've missed you."

The combination of the nicotine and the warmth of her body beside me intoxicated me so that I let my guard down. Ever since they started me on those drugs, and especially since they had shocked me, I had begun to question my memory. If I had been wrong about Esther, perhaps I had been wrong about other things, too.

"Things have been getting fuzzy, and sometimes I'm not sure I can trust myself." I dug my hands into the blanket, but Nora reached for me and grabbed hold. "I need to know things. There's no one else I can ask. Can you help me remember?"

"Absolutely," she said as she squeezed my hand.

"Did I overstep with Katherine?"

"Oh, I don't know. I'm not sure what happened. I know Bitsy was upset the time she couldn't find her on your back patio and when you took her to the cul-de-sac."

"She followed us," I told her. At least, I thought that's what happened.

"Bitsy's protective. With the boys away and all Katherine's been through, she likes to keep a close eye on her."

"Because she's her sister's." Nora nodded her confirmation. I had remembered that right. "But what about Katherine's father?"

"I don't know details. Bitsy said he wasn't fit to take care of a child, so she was going to do everything she could to give the girl a fresh start and a family."

"Everything?"

"Yes. Even a lobotomy."

"How do you know?"

"She told me." Of course she did. After all, Nora was the miner of secrets. She had a way of unearthing even the most closely guarded gems. I wished she had learned the truth sooner. That morning in the cul-de-sac, Gary had used my insanity to cover for what he had done to his wife. He had denied that he had lobotomized her. But he had.

Then she continued, "It was after her sister died. Apparently, it runs in the family. Bitsy was upset about her sister and wanted to take care of Katherine but couldn't manage it. That's when Gary sent the boys away to school, and off she went to have her operation. Grief does strange things to us." Nora took another drag and exhaled a curl of smoke. "I lost one, too, you know?"

"What?" I wondered if I had heard her right. "I didn't know."

"Yeah, well, we didn't really talk about it. It was my first. Thankfully, it happened before the baby shower. I can't imagine what it would've been like if I had to look at all of that stuff after—"

She looked at me and I knew the pain she feared, because it was in my house, mostly contained within one room, but there nonetheless, tucked behind a door, calling in the middle of the night, the place where my mind had broken open.

"Oh, Lu. I'm sorry."

"There's one more thing. Do you think Henry had an affair?"

Nora flinched at the thought. "Henry? No. Never. He's a good one, Lu."

"Then why did he put me here?"

"I love you, but you needed help." Nora reached for the blanket and said the sharpest words anyone had ever said to me: "You thought this was your baby." As much as the words pierced, they were true. She reached for my chin, turned my head toward her, and whispered the words I heard before they'd flipped the switch and shook me. "You're not her. And if you don't want to become her, then get your shit together, because you're the only one who can save yourself."

CHAPTER THIRTY-THREE

Sometimes saving ourselves starts with a seemingly simple act. For me, it meant showering the next morning before Henry and I met with Dr. Ruthledge to discuss the results of my shock treatment. I choked down some breakfast, combed my hair, and put on the best dress I had available. But I didn't swallow the tranquilizers; I needed to stay alert. I wanted them all to see that the treatment had worked. I was cured. I could go home. I wouldn't be another Bitsy.

Henry met me outside Dr. Ruthledge's office. He reached for me, seeming as nervous as the first time he dared to hold my hand back in college. "You look good," he told me.

I couldn't help but see how tired he looked, the redness in his eyes and the draw of his cheeks.

"How's Wesley?" I needed to know.

"Good. Been spending a lot of time with James. Oh, and he lost his first tooth."

Oh. That was how he said it, like it was something typical, usual, a common occurrence. He had lost his first tooth, and I hadn't been there for it. I tried to imagine what he would look like with a gap, and what he would look like when the permanent tooth poked through the same spot that had previously held his perfect little baby tooth.

"Shoot!" Henry said. He ran his hand through his hair, pulling it backward, exposing the first silver strands. "Wesley drew you a picture. I left it in the car." He nodded toward the window, where the sun sparkled off his frost-blue sedan.

"Maybe we can go for a walk and get it," I offered.

In that moment, those chocolate eyes of his softened to the sweetness I had hungered for. He rubbed my hand, fumbling with my fingers, rubbing my palm. "Yeah?" he asked. "You'd be up for a walk?"

"I think some sunshine could do us good."

His smile both warmed and broke me. I wanted nothing more than to do everyday things like go on walks with my husband, but his enthusiasm showed that something like that had not been typical for a couple like us.

"Maybe," I began as I stroked his hand and stepped closer to him, "we should go now."

"Now?" Henry tried to look around me to see into the doctor's office.

"It's okay," I told him. Then I went even further. "I'm okay. Can't you see it?"

"Well, you do seem like you're feeling better."

"I am, so what do you say we just go home?"

Standing in the mental hospital, begging my husband to

take me home, I thought back to those two college kids. My reluctance to accept his proposal was not because I didn't love him or because I didn't think he loved me; it was more a question of if he would continue to love me when he saw beneath the surface.

"I want you to come home," he said. I wanted to run out of there before he changed his mind. "But we need to talk to the doctor."

"No, we don't. Look at me. I'm good."

Henry paused and I saw it in his eyes. I knew he wanted to take me home; he wanted life to be back to normal. "I don't know—" he stammered, as if trying to convince himself, but before he could, the nurse called us in.

"I have good news," Dr. Ruthledge began. He sat with his hands folded. He didn't need to look at any paperwork. He crossed one leg over the other and leaned back in his chair, and for a moment, I allowed myself to feel hopeful. Apparently, no amount of treatment could stop me from being a fool.

"The first session was a success," the doctor began.

Henry squeezed my hand and smiled. They both seemed relieved, happy with the report, but I had caught a word that my husband hadn't. "The *first* session?"

"Why, yes. I know it was only a couple days ago, but we're pleased with what we see, so we're going to move forward, keep going, and after a regimen of, oh, perhaps five to ten more, we believe you'll be ready to go home."

Five to ten? I looked at Henry, expecting to see the same

confusion on his face, but instead he continued to smile and nod along with the doctor. Apparently, he wasn't going to speak up, so I had to. "Five to ten?"

"Yes, as is often the case, for best results we need to conduct multiple sessions—"

"You said one. It would just be one."

Henry whispered my name and then attempted to tell me to "calm down." I pulled my hand away from his and scooted to the edge of the couch. "We'll get through this," he tried to reassure me. "Together." But his wasn't the body that they wanted to charge repeatedly as if it were a dead car battery that needed a jump to work again.

"One!" I told the doctor. "It was supposed to be one and then I'd go home."

Henry tried to intervene, but Dr. Ruthledge held up his hand, believing he could placate me. "Mrs. Mayfield, you may have thought you heard me say that, but I didn't specify how many sessions we'd need. Often we need to see how the first one goes before we have an idea of what the regimen should be. Given your case, we need to do more for best results."

My cheeks burned so that the rash prickled my face. I wanted to scratch at it, but I ignored it. Sensing I would get nowhere with the doctor, I turned to Henry. "Please," I softened my voice, careful to not sound too desperate. "Take me home. You can see for yourself that I'm better."

Henry clasped his hands together, but his fingers fidgeted, as if betraying his attempt at a calm resolve. As his eyes began to moisten, I prayed he would recall our early days together, when his mother had still hoped he would find someone else but he knew he wanted only me. I wanted him to remember the vow he'd made to me, the promise, the pledge to love and care for me. Now was the moment I needed him most.

But before he could answer, the doctor said, "We all want to do what's in your best interest." I refused to look at him. Instead, I kept my focus on Henry, pleading without words. "I know you're feeling better, and that's what we want to hear, but do you understand this is for your own good?"

With that, Henry dropped his gaze and I knew.

"Please," I muttered, forcing the word past the emotion tangling in my throat.

"L-l-l-l—" He stopped. He couldn't even say my name. He kept looking down as a tear dropped onto his wool pants.

I slouched into the couch. I looked past the fern and out the window. It was a sunny day. I'd had so much hope for it. I really had thought we could go for a walk, listen to the birds, act like ordinary people.

"I want you to get home to your son just as much as you do, but we can't rush this," the doctor pressed. And then apparently the man couldn't simply shut up. He had to keep going. "Let's not forget the serious nature of what brought you here."

How dare he bring up Esther. Did he really think either of us could forget her?

I stared out that window and at the blue car that shimmered in the sun, the car with the keys tucked into the visor because we lived in a neighborhood safe enough to make that possible, and sometimes when Henry went elsewhere, he was so in the habit of tucking them behind the shade that he didn't think to do otherwise. *God, please let this be one of those days.*

I sat up a bit straighter and took a deep breath, Nora's words turning over in my mind: *Save yourself.*

Then I looked the doctor in the eyes and said, "I understand. But I hope you won't mind if I use the restroom."

Mama sometimes called me obstinate, said I got my stubbornness from my father's family. Like the time she baked a rhubarb pie and had the audacity to add strawberries. She knew rhubarb was my favorite. Mama would tell me it was such a bitter choice, but that's exactly why I preferred it to the heavy sweetness of any other pie. The one time Mama put strawberries in with it, I refused to even taste the pie. She called me obstinate, not as a compliment, but out of frustration. But what she had meant as an insult might be exactly what I needed to save myself.

"Oh, not at all," the doctor said as he granted me permission to go to the bathroom. "That'll give Mr. Mayfield and me a chance to talk a bit more in your absence."

I flashed him a smile and stood to leave. I didn't look at Henry. I didn't give his hand a squeeze nor his leg a pat before walking away from him. I didn't pick up my pace until I made it to the staircase. I didn't start running until I got outside. That's the thing about showing improvement: A place like that gives you more leniency, so no one thought a thing about me walking right out the front entrance.

I opened the car door and slammed it shut behind me, as if the harder I closed it, the more difficult it would be for someone to open it and pull me out. I needed to find the keys and get out of there. I looked up at the doctor's office window to see if they were looking for me, but I didn't notice anyone. Of course, they didn't know yet that they had let me get away.

Before I reached for the visor, a piece of paper caught my eye. On the seat beside me was the picture Wesley had drawn. It consisted of three stick figures, all with crooked, crescent smiles. I was the only one wearing any sort of clothing, a pink skirt that reminded me of Esther's blanket.

The blanket! In my haste, I hadn't bothered going back to my room to grab the one material possession in all the world that I most wanted. But I couldn't risk it. I hoped she would forgive me. If my time there had taught me anything, it was that the blanket had been empty, but her presence had been real. It still was. And I didn't need a piece of cloth to feel her.

But I knew. I knew in my bones that I wouldn't forgive myself if I left her behind.

So I looked up at the window. No one was watching. I opened the car door carefully, quietly, as if I feared they would hear the squeal of the door springs through the office window. I walked as quickly and casually as possible, though my feet begged me to run. I couldn't look suspicious, I told myself. And as a small part of my mind told me to forget about the blanket and get back to the car, my heart informed the rest of me that it wasn't possible to leave without her.

I forced myself to take the front steps one at a time and to open the door like a tranquilized patient should. And when the nurse with the kind eyes greeted me in the front hall, I smiled.

"Hello, Mrs. Mayfield," she said. "You're looking well today."

Apparently, escaping looked good on me.

I forced the words *thank you* out of me as calmly as possible, while my heart throbbed so forcefully that I was afraid she would hear the drumming for herself.

I strolled to the staircase, and once she was out of sight, I hurried up both flights of stairs, holding on to the banister, pulling myself upward. I rushed into my room and grabbed the blanket, peeking into the hallway before starting back to the car. A few patients milled around in the halls, but none of them seemed to care what I was doing. After all, in a place like that, your only focus is yourself.

I had made it back to the stairwell and down the first flight of stairs when I heard Henry's voice. I loved that voice; its depth and familiarity were reminders of home. But in that moment, it wasn't the safe haven I wanted it to be. I tucked myself against the wall, listening. He was looking for me, wondering what was taking me so long. As Dr. Ruthledge's secretary said she would go to the ladies' room and check on me, I started my descent down that final flight of stairs.

The kind nurse was still in the front entryway.

"Taking a walk, Mrs. Mayfield?" she asked.

I took a deep breath and put on a smile before I said, "Yes, it's so lovely out."

"Well—" She paused for a moment, and I considered pushing past her before Henry realized I wasn't in the bathroom, but then she let out a sneeze.

"Bless you," I said, as I walked to the door and opened it.

"Thank you. And enjoy your walk."

"I will."

I forced myself to walk instead of run, and I slammed that car door shut when I got back inside. Time ticked and I needed to go, so I placed the blanket on the seat beside me and I reached for the visor, again praying that Henry was as predictable as I had thought him to be. I tilted the shade and the keys fell into my lap, a prayer finally answered while so many others had died in silence.

As I pulled out of the parking spot, I looked at the office window again, but still no one was watching. I didn't squeal tires or speed out. I rolled down the window and let the breeze blow my hair as I drove down the tree-shrouded drive. I had a nearly full tank of gas and miles to go before I could rest. Like those cries in the night, home had been calling and it was time I paid it a visit.

CHAPTER THIRTY-FOUR

The road home can be a long and winding drive, a labyrinth of memories and mistakes. I hadn't been to the old house in longer than I liked to admit, but of course I still knew the way. I both hurried and dawdled, at first watching my rearview mirror for Henry or the doctor, but the closer I got to home, the slower I went. At one point, I pulled off the road and sat in the tall grass of the ditch, watching clouds roll overhead until dusk arrived. You see, the house was both a beacon and a burden, calling me back, but I was no longer the person I had been, just like it was not the house I had left.

The house had always looked old, but now it lurched on its foundation, tilted as though it wanted to lie down and rest. Mama's rosebushes had gotten leggy, and the rose of Sharons climbed so high they nearly blocked the second-story windows. The glow of the porch light revealed wood that poked bare from the paint chips that had long since peeled away. *Daddy never would've*, I began to think to myself, but then I stopped. Daddy had been gone close to a decade, leaving his wife to manage it all.

I felt like a stranger standing on the front porch, hoping to be let in. I knocked on the screen door, which hung crooked on its hinges, threatening to fall with each tap. When had the place become so decrepit? While I waited, the porch light flickered, and a jolt raced through me as the stale taste of rubber lay thick on my tongue, that memory too singed to be forgotten.

As I considered knocking again, the inside door creaked open and a voice I knew well said, "Lucy?"

I had been so strong that day. I had showered and gotten dressed. I had been hopeful with Henry and sat up straight beside him in the doctor's office. Regardless of how my body ached and the rash across my cheeks itched, I had put on the brave face. And then, when I needed to, I ran.

But now, standing on that porch as the gray-washed planks that my grandfather had cut, sanded, and nailed into place bowed beneath the weight of my slender body, I had no more strength to give. In the place where I had learned to dam up my tears, the barricade broke and I sobbed.

"Mama!" Georgie's crutches clacked on the wooden floor as he moved away from the door and called for our mother.

Through a veil of tears, I saw something I had never seen before: my mother running toward me.

"Lucy? Lucy!" She kept saying my name. Each time, it echoed through me, reminding me of who I had been, as if calling me back to myself as I came home. She pushed the screen door open so hard I thought for sure it would come loose of its hinges once and for all. "Get in here!"

I walked into the house so full of memories and smells. I swore I picked up hints of cinnamon and nutmeg, as if she had pulled a peach pie from the oven only moments ago. I walked into the warm glow of the living room, and Mama stood in front of me. I didn't know what she knew. I hadn't phoned her, but I didn't know if Henry had said something. Did she know I had lost my mind? Did she know I had been tucked away in a mental hospital? Did she know I was on the lam? I was afraid to look her in the eyes, because I thought my eyes would tell the story I would rather keep hidden.

"Let me look at you," she said.

I was so glad she didn't ask how I was, because I didn't have an answer, but I wondered what she saw. There were moments with Wesley when I'd look at him and see him differently. He was always growing and changing, but sometimes it would take time for me to realize that, and then one day I'd catch sight of him in an ordinary moment, maybe as he ran into the kitchen and begged to lick the beaters, and I'd see him differently than I had a minute ago. A lot of moments had happened between the last time my mother had seen me and that evening when I escaped the sanatorium and come to stand on her front porch. What did she see? Had I changed?

She had. She was so much smaller than I remembered. Her wrinkles pressed in deeper, the lines beside her lips and eyes showed her years and heartache. But her determination stood.

I straightened my dress and wiped at the persistent tears. That's when she looked at me, clear as day. And that's when her voice changed, her breath caught in her throat.

"Dear God."

I must've looked worse than I realized.

As she brought her hand to her mouth as if to stop her astonishment from escaping, I lowered my eyes and my guard, and I confessed, "They say I've gone mad."

"No. No!" She moved toward me. Taking my chin in her hand, she turned my head from side to side. "Oh, child. You look just like him."

I always had. I wondered sometimes if Mama wished I looked more like her. If I had been a small version of her, would she have paid me more attention? But I'd gotten Daddy's almond eyes and apple cheeks.

"Have they seen this?" she asked.

"Seen what?"

"The wolf's got you, too."

Perhaps I wasn't the only one who had gone mad. I looked at Georgie, who shrugged.

"Mama," I said, "you're not making any sense."

"The rash. Have they seen it? And what else? Look at you, how tired you are. What are you feeling? Aches, pains, sore arms, legs, hands?"

She had never known me as well as she did that moment. For once, she could read my mind. I didn't need to speak. She saw the answer in my eyes, and she saw the signs of it all spelled out so clearly in the butterfly rash across my face.

"It's not madness. It's lupus," she said. "Just like him."

CHAPTER THIRTY-FIVE

In all my life, no one had used that word with me. Daddy had *a sickness*, that's what they'd called it, but that was all they said of it. *He's having a bad day. A better one. It's got him good right now.* What did any of this mean? If this was lupus, if this was what had taken Daddy, what would it do to me?

Mama ushered me into the kitchen and sat me down at the table. Then she placed a piece of peach pie in front of me as steam still stretched and curled from it.

"I'm not very hungry," I told her.

"Yes, you are. Look at you, all skin and bones. You'll feel better with something warm in your belly. Now, eat up."

As I took my first bite, Mama began to warm milk on the stove, sprinkling in some cinnamon. I had been so proud of myself and how I had replicated my mother's recipe, but as the first bite woke my taste buds, I realized I hadn't gotten the measurements right. The flavors were similar, but not balanced quite the same. Hers held a depth of richness that mine lacked. Or maybe it was that hers unlocked a sense of time and place that permeated beyond my taste buds.

So much was the same as when I had lived there. The grandfather clock that Nonna's parents had given them as a wedding gift still stood in the front hall. Her cast-iron skillet sat on the back-right burner, and the fry pan with the copper cover (two-and-a-quarter books) hung above the range. I reached under the table and felt my initials that I had carved years ago. I wondered if Mama had ever found them.

Something had been added to the mantel since I had last visited. Over the years, I'd given her framed photos that she displayed there: our wedding and theirs, an updated photo of Wesley every year, one of him shortly after birth when he looked like a pruned-up newborn version of my father. But there was one I didn't recognize. I got up and walked over to get a closer look. There, staring back at me, was a family portrait I hadn't seen before, but I remembered it well. It was taken the last time I had seen Mama and Georgie, the day of Wesley's birthday.

It was our first family portrait. Henry held Wesley, who had just turned four. My cheeks were full, my legs still spindly, poking out of my egg-shaped body. My dress acted like a tent, billowing outward but not able to hide the pregnant belly beneath it. I ran my hand across the only photo we would ever have that was proof that Esther had existed. In all the ones to come, she'd forever be invisible to everyone but me.

"Where'd you get this picture?" I asked.

Mama turned off the water and reached for a hand towel. "Henry."

"But how—"

"He dropped it by one day when he came to tell us how you were."

"But how did he get it?"

With the kitchen clean, Mama took a seat at the table. "I don't know. Something about some broken film and this was the only picture on it. He thought I might want a copy, so he brought it for me."

I didn't like to think of that morning on the floor of Esther's bedroom as I clung to an empty blanket and Wesley tried to comfort me. But that was where the picture had come from, the roll that I thought would prove Esther had come home.

"He's a good one," Mama said. "Like your father."

She may have been right, but I still didn't know what he would do with me once he found me. And I didn't want to think about it.

I brought the picture to the table and sat down, still looking at my pregnant self. What I wouldn't have given to be able to go back to that moment before all this happened—before her birth, the delusions, the mental hospital, the therapy that shook me.

"If he's so good, then why'd he send me there?" A shiver ran up my spine. "Mama, if you knew—"

"Stop." She said it to her cup of coffee, not looking me in the eye. "He's doing what he can." I watched her hold her mug, her fingers stroking the porcelain. When had my mother's hands gotten so old, so bound by wrinkles, her knuckles knotted?

"Do you know what they did?" I asked.

"Henry told me some. Said they were doing what was best."

I swear I could taste rubber again. I took a sip of milk, hoping it would drown out the flavor that haunted my taste buds. I swallowed hard and then pleaded, "Don't make me go back there."

The grandfather clock's chime reverberated through the silence as I waited for my mother to reply. I had to know if she would let me stay or if she would send me back. After the final toll thrummed, Mama took a sip of her coffee, patted her lips with her napkin, and said, "If they aren't capable enough to diagnose you, they aren't worthy of going back to." I wanted to leap across the table and kiss her. But then she continued, "I'll call Henry—"

"Mama—"

"Stop." She slammed her mug down so that coffee sloshed up the sides and a few drops landed on the table. "He's your husband. And he loves you. I'll call him. We'll talk. For tonight, I'll make up your bed and you'll stay here. The rest can wait till the sun comes up."

CHAPTER THIRTY-SIX

The night returned to me and so did the voices in the darkness. At first I hoped they were Esther's beckoning or Daddy calling me down for a piece of midnight pie. In truth, the cries in the night were screech owls calling me outside, their whinnies wavering through the single-pane windows.

If I were still locked away, I would have had no choice except to will myself to return to sleep and pray the drugs would make that possible. But here, I could decide what to do, so I reached for the afghan that Mama had left at the foot of my bed and I wrapped it around my shoulders. I walked down the creaking steps and through the kitchen, still remembering the path in the darkness. The fall air cut through the openings of the blanket's granny-square pattern as I walked out of the house and onto the porch, where moths dizzied themselves around the flickering light.

My feet had once been calloused and conditioned enough to

be numb to the jagged pokes of the gravel, but they had softened over the years. I considered going back for shoes, but I wanted to keep moving forward. I walked across the grass and through unsuspecting spiderwebs that pulled across my cheeks and caught in my eyelashes. I kept going until I reached the rooted soil beneath my tree.

Instead of the buzz of appliances and overhead lights, I listened to the soft hum of the final cicadas who were still too stubborn to wind down for the season. The calls of coyotes in the distance used to send me running back inside. Now I sat still, less fearful of those distant predators than I was of the screams of fellow inmates that had bellowed through the hallways and tormented me each night.

"Luuuuu-cyyyyyy, come in from the dark." That's how Mama used to call me in at night, as dusk turned to twilight and Daddy's day in the field had come to an end. On the nights when I lingered long enough that the dew dampened my feet, I counted it as a win, as if I had drunk the fullness of the day and gotten a taste of the impending night as well. But I knew after the second singsong call of "Luuuuu-cyyyyyy," my time was done.

Mama had tried to call me in from the dark for all those years. What she didn't know was that some summer nights while the others slept, I would sneak outside and gather fireflies. One time I placed them in a mason jar. I thought myself so clever; I had created a lantern out of nature! I had caught a dozen or so and placed them inside the glass jar, twisting the lid on tightly. I held it in front of me as I walked through the grass and back onto the porch. I sat it on the railing and watched them until my eyes became heavy.

In the morning, I ran downstairs and onto the porch, ignoring my mother's calls for me to eat breakfast. "Such a petulant child," she told Daddy as I pulled open the door and ran to the jar that no longer glowed.

My small hands, still soft with baby fat, shook the jar, demanding the fireflies gathered on the bottom to wake. When they didn't, I thought for a moment before realizing the solution. They, like me, preferred darkness. So I took them beneath the porch, into the shadows, hoping to trick them into thinking it was nighttime. I shook the jar again, willing them to wake and shine and be the light they had been the previous night.

But they couldn't wake, because they had suffocated in the stale air I had contained them in.

After breakfast, I sprinkled them under the peach trees. *To dust, you shall return.* I repeated the line I had heard the reverend say.

Mama had taught me that darkness was not to be trusted. I believed her for a long time, but as those tranquilizers released my mind, I felt at home again when those hours of *dormiveglia* returned. It was when my thoughts felt most real. Of course, I couldn't tell them, because they wouldn't understand. Especially not Henry.

In Dr. Ruthledge's office, Henry had promised that we'd get through this together, but what was together? We had vowed "in sickness and health, till death do us part." I wanted to believe that he meant it. Each visit could be evidence that he had chosen me and he continued to, but that didn't mean he knew what was best.

Together does not mean sameness. He didn't know—wouldn't know—what it felt like inside my body and mind. He would never understand existing in a body that fought itself. He would never know the urgency to live as the clock ticked louder, faster, time suddenly having a different quality to it. He wouldn't know what it was to be the light caught in a jar, watching the lid turn and tighten, each breath one closer to the final, last suffocating one.

CHAPTER THIRTY-SEVEN

I rested among the nocturnal until the first rays of a new day cut through the twilight hours. Soon enough, Henry found me under my tree. He sat down beside me before he spoke. "I'm glad you're okay." He stopped and ran his hands over his whiskers. From the looks of things, he hadn't shaved that morning nor slept that night. "I wish you wouldn't have left like that. I was so worried."

I didn't speak. Maybe that's how I had gotten there to begin with: I hadn't said anything. Or at least I hadn't said enough. What if I'd spoken up for myself more? What if I'd better explained how I was feeling, that something wasn't right—would that have changed things? Maybe I wouldn't have been sent to that place, been shocked, missed out on weeks of Wesley's life.

But shouldn't he have noticed even if I didn't say anything? Mama had. But he had been so busy at work, trying for that promotion that no longer seemed important. At least not to me.

"How are you feeling? Are you hurt, tired, hungry?" I wondered if he wanted to know if I had seen visions of Esther. "Did you know your father had lupus?" he asked. I shook my head no. "I can't…I can't make any sense of this. I've been thinking about it ever since—" He didn't finish that thought. "How did we get here?" That was a good question. And one neither of us had an answer to.

An acorn plopped onto the ground beside me. I took it in my hand and ran my finger over the smooth and rough textures, the combination of barriers meant to protect the seed, the potential for a new tree.

I didn't know how any of this had become who we were, but I did know one thing for sure: "I'm not going back."

"Lulu—"

"No!" I threw the acorn into the distance so it bounced along the ground and toward a squirrel that foraged at the edge of the woods. "That doctor's an idiot."

Henry and I had never been the type to fight, but perhaps we would become that couple. Or maybe the answer would be that we would become the type to live apart. Maybe he would have to go back to Greenwood without me. Surely Mama would take me in. She had been Georgie's caretaker. Perhaps now she would also be mine. All I knew in that moment was that if he thought he could take me back there, I would no longer remain silent. I wouldn't smile. I wouldn't be complacent.

I kept watching the squirrel at the edge of the woods, her anxious tail twitching as she held the acorn in her paws. She looked around, not trusting her surroundings, keeping an escape route in mind if a threat got too close. I knew those woods better than Henry. The path had probably changed over the years, but I could find my way through the forest if I needed to.

"You're right," he said. I couldn't believe what I'd heard, but I knew better than to get too hopeful.

"You agree?"

Henry searched my face, finally noticing my rash. "How could they have been so wrong? And then to do what he did. I'm sorry." He dropped his face into his hand, covering his eyes as if he couldn't look at me any longer. "I'm so sorry."

And he should have been. He hadn't listened to me. He hadn't seen me, not until that moment and only after Mama had figured it out. We sat together in the growing shade as the sun rose higher in the sky. How long had that tree stood there? How much had it seen? How many seasons had come and gone as it stood rooted in that one place, growing and dropping leaves, rebirthing and releasing year after year after year? How many times had the first beams of sunshine illuminated its languid branches and shimmered its dancing leaves, casting wavering shapes that shifted with the changing hours? I used to resist the dark places, but now I knew that the fullness of life includes all of it: the light, the dark, and the shadows that creep between.

The truth was, Henry had missed things. He could've been more attentive. But he hadn't caused my visions. He hadn't given me this disease. And he hadn't given me a lobotomy either.

"Well." I decided I wasn't going to be Nora. I wasn't going to yell or fight. And I also wasn't going to flee. But I wasn't ready to comfort him yet. "What did you expect when you took advice from Gary?"

"What are you talking about?"

"I saw the note," I told him, but he looked at me, confused and uncertain of what I meant. "I found it in your suit jacket. The doctor, he was Bitsy's. The one who lobotomized her."

"You heard what Gary said. She wasn't lobotomized."

"And you believed him?"

Henry shrugged. "I don't know." Then his voice dropped low as he said, "I don't know what to believe anymore." That made two of us.

"Well, he lied."

"Lulu, you can't accuse—"

"I'm not. It's the truth. Nora told me when she visited." He still looked uncertain. "Bitsy told her. I'm not making it up."

Henry ran his hand through his hair. "Well, he didn't give me Ruthledge's name. My mother did. He's the husband of someone in her women's club." Of course Marian had been behind all this. "We thought he could help. If we had known—" How many things would we change if only we'd had the benefit of knowing? "But you don't need to worry about Gary anyways. They're moving."

"What?" Apparently, the restless soul of the place had gotten to the Betsers, too. "So he didn't get your job?"

"No. They're moving closer to the boys, for a fresh start."

"I thought that's what Greenwood was. So does that mean you got the job?" He nodded. "Congratulations." If we had been ordinary, news like that would've meant a celebration and special dinner. But instead of joy, we sat broken in the dirt. I did decide to give him a little gift, a bit of levity. "You got the job even after the bowl of Jell-O vomit?"

He flinched as I said it. Maybe it was too soon to joke about that evening. There were certainly moments that would never be funny, but cottage cheese floating in a pond of orange cream wasn't one of them. I laughed first, and then Henry joined in.

After a moment he said, "I'm sorry for all of it. That dinner, the late notice, Gary. You were right to serve me that dessert." He forced a chuckle that quickly faded. "The past few months, all of it, it was too much. I should've seen it."

He was right. It had all been too much. And there was no guarantee that it wouldn't continue to be.

Then he asked a question I did not expect: "What do you want?"

I turned toward my husband, those brown eyes of his looking too similar to my own, showing too much defeat. Absent of assurance, he seemed so afraid. But what he seemed to fear most was me.

The tears began to gather, but before they could shroud my vision, I said to him with the utmost honesty, "I want her."

As that last word caught his ear, I saw his body react, shudder, as if a current had rattled him deep inside. He scooted close to me, and I opened the blanket to him. He put an arm around me and rested his cheek on my head so that soon enough his tears began to dampen my hair. As his body shook, I remembered something I had forgotten: Esther wasn't only mine. She was his, too. We never talked about it. We never spoke of her. We never discussed the loss. I suppose we had our own ways of coping, of retreating from a reality we couldn't face. But what would've happened if we would've retreated together?

As the tree roots pushed against us and the breeze blew cool, we held on to each other. And I felt it. For the first time in a long time, I felt something outside myself. I felt the pain in my bottom, the goose shivers across my arms, the cosmos above, the arm around me, the heave of his shoulders as we sat and watched and cried and finally mourned together.

As morning moved toward noon, I asked, "Do you know what I really want?"

When I arrived the day before, I had looked around at the peach trees, the barn, the house lurching on its foundation. It looked the same and yet so different. It had been the picture fully developed in my mind as to what home looked like, but my eyes had adjusted to Greenwood Estates, to the carefully appointed houses with the freshly poured concrete and warm streetlamps, the self-defrosting Frigidaire and even the Mobile Maid. The picture of home had changed over the years, but really it wasn't about any sort of house or structure—it was more than that. It was Henry and Wesley, Nora across the street, Hatti and her optimism. It was a place of hope and hauntings. And it was where I wanted to be.

As we held on to each other, I told him, "I want you to take me home."

"Are you sure?"

I reached for a leaf that had landed on the ground beside me. I picked it up and began feeling it, the variations of the sides, one smooth and the other with roughness, as if it held a braille message of some sort. Maybe some answer to the mysteries of the seasons, if only I knew the language. Maybe it could tell me the future or even the past. But I couldn't decode it. All I could do was try to trust.

With Mama's blanket still wrapped around us both, I leaned my head against my husband's shoulder and said, "Absolutely."

EPILOGUE

The wolf got me, that's what Mama had said, and I should've recalled from high school Latin that's what *lupus* translated to. It did get me. It followed me home and took up residence with me, and as much as Henry would attempt to wrestle it into submission, it would become a pet constantly by my side, but one you could never tame, nor fully trust.

Coming home reminded me of the day we left the hospital with Wesley. The staff let us walk right out and take the little person with us as if we knew what we were doing. He began to fuss in the car. His face turned red as he arched his back and clenched his tiny hands. He wailed so that his eyes scrunched shut and his mouth opened so that I could see all his naked, pink gums, devoid of any teeth. Henry had asked me if he was okay and I had shrugged. What did I know about babies? He was so small and seemed so delicate. I feared he was far more fragile than he was.

Henry thought the same of me the day we sat in Dr. Collins's office and received the official diagnosis, the day he brought me home from Mama's, the day he found me rocking an empty blanket. I had to learn that babies were more resilient than they appeared. Over time, Henry would come to learn the same of me.

Life resumed. Henry started his new job. Wesley's tooth began to grow in. Hatti and her baby survived colic. The Betsers sold their house. New neighbors moved in to a place that no longer had a hold on my imagination because I knew my home.

Cortisone shots replaced tranquilizer pills, and while I flinched as the needle pierced my skin, I accepted it better than the haze that those capsules had given me, the grogginess that persisted, the inescapable sleep that felt less like slumber and more like an absence from the world. Free from those drugs, I began to feel and hear and see again.

We hosted the annual New Year's Eve party a few months after I came home. Henry said we didn't need to have it that year, but I wanted to, so we did. But this time, I had help, as Nora, Hatti, and others all contributed dishes and drinks so the table—and guests—overflowed.

I spent the New Year's Eve party as both hostess and photographer, using my new camera, a welcome-home gift. I treated myself to the one from the store instead of the one from the loyalty catalog. I found other uses for all those stamps.

During the party, I snapped pictures and advanced the film, searching for the next photo as the guests mingled and the perfection salad jiggled as the centerpiece. I couldn't wait to have the film developed. I dropped it off to be processed just days after the party, but it took time and patience. Once the prints were ready, I barely made it back to my car before I opened the envelope and began to flip through the photos. The combination of colors mixed together to reveal images, to remind me of days past, a treasure trove of printed memories.

The developer had put the prints in opposite order. As I flipped through them, I saw the party in reverse. The New Year's cheers and kisses, before the conversations that came as the alcohol took effect, before the guests entered and the women revealed their outfits. I would look more closely at all of them later.

I didn't examine every detail in that moment because what I looked for in that package wasn't any images of the party. Instead, I searched for the first photo I took. Wesley thought the first one was of him. He smiled proudly, holding his truck (one book), showing off his treasure. His eyes squinted as the sun shone upon them.

But what he didn't know was that before I woke him that day, I had loaded the film into the camera, wound it to the starting point, and snapped a different photo. After Henry had left for work, I took the blanket from the hatbox on the top shelf of our walk-in closet and draped it over the rocking chair that sat in our guest room. I wound the camera, looked through the viewfinder, clicked the button, and advanced the film.

My newspaper editor always said to be mindful of the film. It was limited, finite, not without end. For important images, taking multiple would better ensure capturing the moment. But don't be excessive. Be discerning.

I took only one photo. It was all I needed.

It may have looked like a nursery awaiting an arrival, a rocking chair sitting in the corner, a baby blanket positioned and ready to swaddle. But it wasn't a story of arrival. It was one of departure.

Henry asked me to remember. I did. And I always will, every day for the rest of my life. Every birthday of hers that comes and goes, I will remember. Every Christmas we celebrate without her, every milestone Wesley reaches that she won't, every child her age who grows taller, goes to school, graduates, goes on with life, will remind me of how she didn't get that chance. I will always remember because I have always carried her deep inside me. Even when she wasn't in my arms, she was in my heart, calling to my soul, granting my mind a mercy for the moment I needed to heal just a bit before the dawn broke, the haze cleared, and I had to face the truth in the daylight.

An illusion may have been lifted the day the empty blanket fell to the floor, but in the shadow moments of the night, she calls to me again. I am no longer haunted by it. Instead, I embrace those moments because they belong to only us. No one else needs to know about them. No one needs to know about those times when she is with me, when we are together, when we step into those liminal moments of *dormiveglia* that pull us into each other's presence across space and time, and what some may even consider sanity.

Life is a continual process of letting go, but this I choose to hold on to. This I will never surrender, because I remember. Always and forever, I remember.

AUTHOR'S NOTE

Warning: This author's note may contain spoilers, so it is recommended that you read this after finishing the book.

Do you believe in ghosts? This idea haunted me—both figuratively and, at times, quite literally—as I wrote this book. Stories are shaped by the echoes of those who came before us, the histories we inherit, the truths we carry, and the mysteries we may never fully understand. We, too, leave our own imprints, lingering in the lives of those who follow. In that way, every story is transcendent, tethered to the past and reverberating into the future.

As I reflect on the process of bringing Lulu's story to life, I can't help but sense the hauntings and musings of multiple ghosts—some more metaphorical than others. Some lurked in the dark shadows, much like those who comforted Lulu. Others seemed to sit beside me in my office, as real and present as Brontë, the golden retriever at my feet. I set out to write a novel about the silencing of women's voices, about medical misdiagnoses and the dangerous consequences of being dismissed. In the end, it was the ghosts who whispered the truth.

The Ghosts of Female Storytellers
This book would not exist without the stories that have gone before it. In college, I was introduced to the short story "The Yellow Wallpaper" by Charlotte Perkins Gilman. I believe that the mark of a good story is that it stays with you long after you've read it. If that's the case, then this story—a collection of journal entries of a woman locked away in a mansion as part of rest therapy for her "nervous" condition—is a masterpiece. As vividly as if the scene played out in a movie, I can still visualize the final moments as the narrator chooses her freedom and her fate as she creeps across her husband and into the wallpaper.

Then there is *The Bell Jar* by Sylvia Plath. I spent hours meandering through wooded trails, listening to Maggie Gyllenhaal (the perfect choice!) narrate Esther Greenwood's story. Then I dusted off my physical copy and began highlighting and annotating, knowing I wanted to pay homage, not just to Plath's honest and perhaps semi-autobiographical novel, but to her life too. I turned my attention to *The Journals of Sylvia Plath* to better understand her and get a peek into her journey through depression.

I drew direct inspiration from her fiction and her life in ways that felt inevitable—Lulu's daughter carries the name Esther, and the neighborhood itself became Greenwood, both quiet nods to Plath's main character. And in one of the novel's most haunting reflections, Ellen's fate follows the path Sylvia herself once walked.

As I began writing with Gilman's and Plath's work in mind, another literary icon revealed herself to me: Flannery O'Connor. An important, raw, and sardonic Southern writer, O'Connor herself was diagnosed with lupus (the same disease that took her father) when she was twenty-seven years old. Despite the incurable disease that was hard to diagnose and treat, she continued writing and completed two novels and more than two dozen short stories. She died far too young at the age of thirty-nine.

And then there's one of my favorite modern storytellers: Billie Eilish. Her song "What Was I Made For?" became an anthem for this novel. I listened on repeat to the haunting lyrics, the ethereal melody, the diaphanous voice. Eilish's music played on a constant loop during writing sessions so that by the end of 2024, I was a top 1 percent fan according to my Spotify Wrapped statistics.

The Ghosts of the Everywoman

While those famous women provided a form of inspiration, it was coming to learn about hysteria as a medical diagnosis that ignited the idea for this book. If you've read my previous books, you'll know that I like to explore the everywoman in a historical context. In *The Last Carolina Girl*, an ordinary teen named Leah is simply trying to find a safe home to live her life, but she must fight for her future in an era of forced sterilization. In *The Girls We Sent Away*, girl-next-door Lorraine wants to graduate from high school and become an astronaut, but society has other plans for her when she becomes pregnant out of wedlock. These stories explore seemingly typical women who are living normal lives until they come up against an actual practice within our nation's past.

Which brings us to Lulu, a suburban housewife, who lives out the ghost story of the women whose mental and physical health suffered when their voices and experiences were silenced instead of being heard and understood.

Until 1980, hysteria was a psychological diagnosis, but at first, it was classified as a physical condition. The ancient Egyptians and Greeks referred to it as the "wandering womb" where they believed that if a woman was "out of sorts," it was because her uterus was migrating within her body, and the cure was to coax it back into the right position. In truth, the catch-all diagnosis was often dismissive of women and meant conditions such as depression, anxiety, postpartum depression and psychosis, lupus, rheumatoid arthritis, multiple sclerosis, and more went undiagnosed.

According to *Unwell Women: Misdiagnosis and Myth in a Man-Made World* by Elinor Cleghorn (a primary source for *The Mad Wife*):

> "When women confessed to their doctors that they were always on the brink of crying, or got so angry it scared them, they were diagnosed with 'housewife's syndrome.' If their skin broke out in hives and rashes, it was called 'housewife's blight.' The numbing tiredness that 'took so many women to the doctors in the 1950s' was labeled 'housewife's fatigue.' Many suffered in silence or turned to tranquilizers to blot out the 'strange, dissatisfied voice...within them.' It felt less painful that way" (264–5).

Symptoms of lupus can include pain, rashes, hair loss, fatigue, brain fog, and memory problems. It can also include unusual symptoms such as smelling colors and tasting sounds, at least according to one woman who struggled for years to receive an accurate diagnosis. And, important to Lulu's story, lupus can even cause insomnia, delusions, and hallucinations. It also increases the risk of pregnancy complications, including premature birth, miscarriage, and stillbirth.

When a blanket diagnosis is all a woman like Lulu receives, she cannot get the medical care and help she needs. Instead, her experience might be ignored, and the treatment to quiet her could be tragic. In Lulu's era, doctors treated patients with mild tranquilizers such as Miltown, psychoanalysis, psychiatric hospital stays, electroconvulsion therapy, or, like Bitsy, lobotomy.

A procedure that severs the connection between the prefrontal cortex, lobotomy mainly took place in the 1940s and into the 1950s. It's estimated that between forty thousand and fifty thousand people were lobotomized in the United States, with the majority performed on women. Justification for the procedure included emotional tension, depression, obsessive compulsions, anxiety, hypochondriasis, psychosis, and psychosomatic disorders.

In 1952, Dr. Walter Freeman, the creator of the transorbital lobotomy (which went through the eye socket instead of the temple), took the practice on the road with Operation Ice Pick. For two weeks, he drove around Virginia as part of a state-sponsored initiative. He performed 228 lobotomies out of his van, which he named the Lobotomobile.

According to Cleghorn, "In the 1950s, the lobotomy was championed as another of those revolutionary cures that didn't just treat the symptoms of a disease but ripped it out right at the roots. In reality, the lobotomy was medically sanctioned silencing, to stop women from voicing how, and where, and why it hurt" (*Unwell*, 256).

This ten-minute procedure could leave patients docile and perhaps even happy. But some were left in a vegetative or incapacitated state. Others died.

Between the time of the ancient Greeks and the eighties, hysteria was a catch-all diagnosis that could be a synonym for being overemotional or out of sorts. Or it could be a distraction from finding the root cause.

Now we know that diseases can present differently in men and women. For example, women's heart attack symptoms are not always the same as men's. While some differences were recognized before, research on them was limited because women were often excluded from clinical trials. This changed significantly after the National Institutes of Health Revitalization Act was signed into law in 1993, mandating the inclusion of women in NIH-funded studies.

Even still, women are fighting every day to be heard, to get answers to what they have been experiencing. Their pain sometimes goes ignored.

> "In the absence of a clinical sign that could be observed and interpreted by a doctor, a woman's pain was presumed to exist only in her head. In the 1950s, pain was not a clinical sign. Pain felt by a woman with undiagnosed lupus was nothing more than a subjective sensation. Pain couldn't be visualized on an x-ray; pain didn't sediment in a test tube" (*Unwell*, 252).

In my own life, I know too many everywomen who have walked a long and frustrating road to finding an accurate diagnosis for the symptoms that have not shown up in test tubes. These women have endured sometimes for years and sometimes while being told that the pain is psychosomatic. Because when the pain is as elusive as a ghost, some seem to speculate that maybe it doesn't exist at all. And when that is the belief, women go on suffering in silence as they fight to be heard.

And I wonder if one of those women was Isabel.

The Ghost in the Room Where It Happened
Lulu's story wasn't an easy one to tell. It was an immersive experience that I cannot fully articulate. I felt as though I had been invited in to peer through this woman's eyes as she revealed her story to me. But sometimes Lulu liked to hide in the shadows, and despite my looming deadline, she would sometimes be coy and elusive.

To help coax her out, I spent a week as a writer-in-residence at Weymouth Center for the Arts and Humanities in Southern Pines, North Carolina. When I applied for the stay, I had visions of silence and solitude with seven days of immersion and complete focus on my manuscript. I hoped the intentional time would encourage Lulu to help me add more layers and depth to this manuscript. What I couldn't have predicted was that inspiration would come from another source: a woman named Isabel, who perhaps had her own encounter with hysteria.

While there is a lot about Isabel's life that I do not know, what I have pieced together from information that has since been passed on to me is that Isabel and her husband lived at

Weymouth for a time in the mid-1940s. She held a degree from Smith and had a child, but her story took a tragic turn after moving into the Boyd house at Weymouth. A newspaper article called her "despondent," and the story goes that she perhaps went "mad" or "hysterical" before she took her life in that house, in the room right next to where I stayed.

But here's the thing: Isabel sometimes liked to whisper in the dark.

You see, my first night there, I was in bed watching a movie (*Before Sunrise*, which I'm happy to report is still amazing and a master class in dialogue) when my closet door opened. I assumed I hadn't latched it tightly. After all, it is an old house with settled doorframes. So I got out of bed, latched the door, moved something in front of it, and finished my movie. A few nights later, I had a hard time sleeping and heard a lot of creaking floors and closing doors. I assumed it was the other writer-in-residence and tried my best to get back to sleep. Another night, I thought I heard music playing, but I figured my brain was simply trying to find patterns in my white noise.

But then I started hearing about the ghost stories of the place: the apparitions people have seen over the years, the music people have heard playing at all hours of the night, the doors that open and close on their own, the shifted rugs, the footsteps on the balcony, the beds that move in the night. Yeah, that's the one that got me!

In the daylight, I am a logical person. I can rationalize that I didn't latch the door tightly. I'm sure the floor and door creaks were from the other writer. I know that music was simply my imagination, but I didn't turn off the white noise to verify. As logical as I can be in the daylight, the nighttime made me question what I really believe. Do I really think ghosts are real? I do know that I regret watching all those scary movies over the years.

I don't know if Isabel was really there with me, hoping I'd transcribe some of her experience into Lulu's story. What I do know is that I felt a renewed sense of purpose to tell this story and to give voice to those who have been voiceless. I hope this story will make Isabel proud, seen, and heard.

Lulu's story may be one of fiction, but the act of writing it made her quite real to me, because in truth she is an amalgamation of too many women's stories. Women like Isabel. Women like the ones I read about and researched. Women like the ones I know in my own life. Women all around us who have had to creep through their own shadow seasons.

Through this process, Lulu and Isabel taught me something important and perhaps timely: Sometimes it takes darkness to show us what we really believe and who we really are. For that, I am eternally grateful. And my hope moving forward is that we may all have the eyes to see the silent suffering in front of us, the ears to hear their cries, and the empathy to take their hand and let them know that they are not alone, because we are all ghosts of this mysterious realm called life.

READ ON FOR ANOTHER SEARING NOVEL FROM BESTSELLING AUTHOR MEAGAN CHURCH.

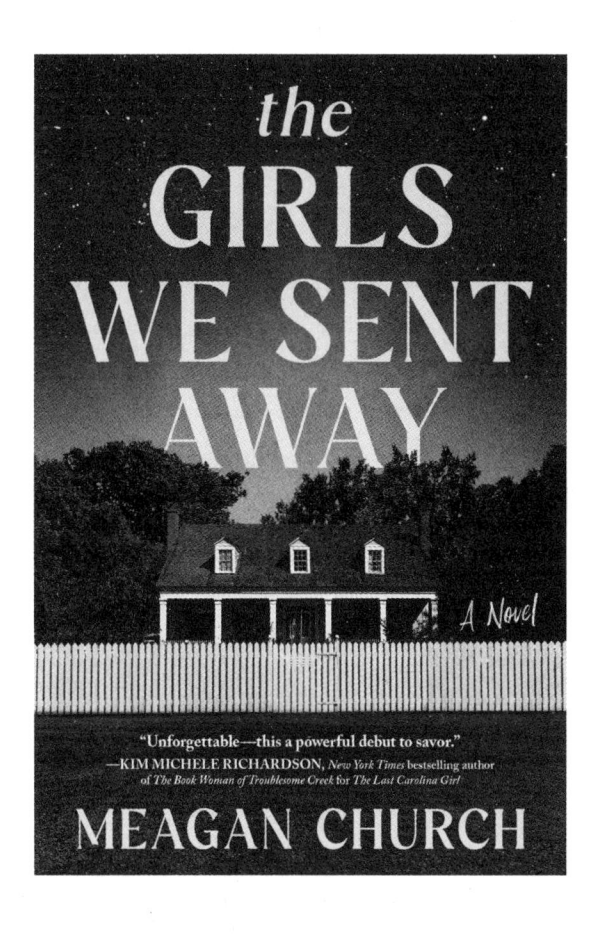

PROLOGUE

Drowning doesn't look like you think it should. And according to little Barbara Ann Walters, it doesn't *feel* like you think it should either. It's not an obvious splashing and yelling and causing a commotion. The young girl wished it was because then maybe someone would have noticed her. Instead, the Sunnymede pool members went on with their conversations, sunbathing, and lifeguard ogling as the four-year-old bounced from pool bottom to surface and back again.

It was the summer of 1964 in a typical, midcentury suburban neighborhood where a portion of North Carolina's green canopy had been cleared in the name of development. Whether from an aerial perspective or a street view, Sunnymede offered plenty of symmetry, order, comfort. Houses perfectly balanced. Trees precisely pruned. Lawns meticulously manicured. Inhabitants properly prim, for the most part. And a cautionary tale, if not.

On that particular late-summer afternoon, as Barbara Ann struggled in the middle of the pool, the Sunnymede Sisters gossiped in their gaggle. This group of middle-aged women who had spent years bonding over plasticware parties, rummage sales, and ambrosia salad spent weekday afternoons chatting in the shade, careful to steer clear of both the water and the sun. All donned the unspoken uniform of oversized sunglasses, hats, and muumuus, creating an orderly display of belonging.

On the other side of the pool, the adolescent boys—all in similar swim trunks, all with the same crew cut, all hell-bent on testing boundaries and ignoring the teenage lifeguard—jumped, pushed, and roughhoused into the deep end, too absorbed in their own antics to see anything else.

Including the girl who was about to give up.

Surrounded by a community of people, Barbara Ann sank to the bottom and bobbed back to the water's surface with only enough time to gasp for a small bit of air before sinking again. Her toes pointed like a ballerina's, arched and reaching, before pushing off the pool bottom as soon as they touched it. In the midst of silent panic, she almost looked as graceful as the dancer on her music box. Her arms flapped like wings, fighting to fly her out of her predicament as her eyes pleaded for help in a way her voice had no time to.

As she would rise a few inches above the waterline, the child tried to search for her father. He lounged only a few feet from the water's edge, but her plight prevented her from finding him, focusing on him, calling to him, the man who was supposed to save her.

In truth, the father didn't know what was happening with his daughter. He was too busy watching the bathing suit strap hang off the young lifeguard's shoulder. No one else noticed anything out of the ordinary either. No one noticed her bobbing. Sinking. Struggling. Drowning in plain sight.

READING GROUP GUIDE

1. This is a story about remembering. The first and final words of the book are "remember." At one point, Lulu says, "Sometimes forgetting is a mercy, and recalling is a pain too deep to bear." What do you think she meant by that? And how does remembering play such an essential part in Lulu's story?

2. Lulu feels most at home in nature and on her childhood farm. How does that rural upbringing contrast with the postwar suburban life she lives?

3. Why do you think Lulu becomes the Queen of Molded Food and a customer loyalty stamp collector?

4. From the moment Lulu first sees Bitsy from across the street, she seems to not like her. Why do you think that is? How does that affect their relationship?

5. We have moments of Lulu remembering throughout the book—her father's passing, Georgie's polio, her mother's seeming indifference. How did that past affect who she is in the present? How is this a story of generational impact?

6. How did you react when the blanket hit the floor and the truth of Esther is revealed?

7. This book is broken into two parts: the window and the mirror. What do those titles symbolize?

8. Lulu and Bitsy are both known by their nicknames. We learn Bitsy's real name is Elizabeth when Lulu finds it on the medical form. Late in the book, we discover that Lulu's real name is Lucy, which means "light." What is the significance of these nicknames?

9. This is a story of how medical misdiagnoses sometimes silence women's suffering. While only Lulu and Bitsy have official diagnoses in the book, discuss how all four of the women—Lulu, Bitsy, Nora, and Hatti—were all silenced.

10. The 1950s can sometimes be idealized and romanticized as a golden era of boom, stability, and contentment. How does this story paint a different picture of that time period?

11. Near the end, Lulu says, "I used to resist the dark places, but now I knew that the fullness of life includes all of it: the light, the dark, and the shadows that creep between." What roles do lightness, darkness, and shadows play in Lulu's story?

12. In the last paragraph, Lulu says, "Life is a continual process of letting go, but this I choose to hold on to." What do you choose to hold on to?

A CONVERSATION WITH THE AUTHOR

As with your other books, this is an emotional read with difficult themes. What was it like to for you to write this?

Honestly, it wasn't always easy, and I shed a lot of tears writing this book. There are lines that still get me—even after countless rounds of revisions. There are obviously emotional moments, but one detail that broke me was when she returned to her childhood home and she saw something she had never seen before: her mother running toward her. Most of her life, Lulu had felt neglected by her mother, but that reaction showed how much her mother loved her; she just wasn't always able to express it in the ways Lulu most wanted.

In my author's note, I discuss the ghost of Isabel that I encountered while writing this. So as difficult and emotional as the process was at times, I also felt a drive to tell this story on behalf of women who haven't had the voice to tell their own stories.

Your work is known for being character driven rather than plot driven. How did you approach pacing and tension in a narrative centered on internal struggle?

A reader once asked if I am a character-driven or theme-driven writer. I hadn't thought of it in those terms because we typically think character versus plot. But when she asked that, I realized that the initial ideas for all of my books begin with a theme. Then I move to character. And last of all I figure out how to work plot into the mix.

All of my books are character studies, and honestly, I'd leave them at that if I could, but my editor prefers that plot gets blended in there for the reader. With this one especially, I knew we needed a very close perspective to pull off the reveal. And I also knew that as much as I would like to linger in Lulu's interiority, the reader needed external action to move the story forward.

While I am not a plotter, I did more story structure work before beginning to write than I did on my previous two books. The timing of foreshadowing and reveals had to be planned to get the story to work. I still did not create a detailed outline, but I did have a framework to guide the writing process to make sure the story stayed focused and properly paced.

Which character in this book was the most challenging to write, and why?

Lulu. Hands down. At times, she was generous with her story. At other times, not so much. She did not seem to be motivated by my external deadline. Sometimes I had to be patient. Other times I had to keep pushing and pulling.

With that being said, Bitsy also needed some coaxing. The first few drafts were Lulu's drafts. With it being her story, it was essential that I gave her the most time and attention. But once her story was in place, I needed to revise with consideration to Bitsy. She may not have been the main character, but she still needed to be developed. While she did act as a mirror for Lulu, she needed to stand on her own as a character.

There is no defined city or state in this book. Why is that?

From the start, I made the intentional decision to not name the exact setting. This story is a representation of suburbia, not a specific region within the United States. I took inspiration from the television show *The Wonder Years* and left the setting simply as suburban America.

Was there a chapter or scene that was a favorite of yours to write?

I have two answers for this. My first one is chapter six when the idea of dormiveglia is first mentioned. That chapter came out whole and complete in the very first draft, which is not typical. It underwent very few changes over the course of multiple rounds of revisions. And it is still one of my favorites to read. I came across the term *dormiveglia* years ago, and I jotted it down, sensing it would make an appearance in some story, some day. As Lulu's story began to emerge, I knew that it belonged to her because she was a woman who lived most of her life in that in-between, liminal space.

The second is the scene late in the book when Lulu has returned to her childhood home and she remembers the fireflies she caught in a jar. She compares that moment to her own circumstances, saying, "He wouldn't know what it was to be the light caught in a jar, watching the lid turn and tighten, each breath one closer to the final, last suffocating one." I remember exactly where I was when that scene came to me. I truly got chills. I was sitting in the North Carolina Literary Hall of Fame during my writing residency at Weymouth Center for the Arts and Humanities. I was surrounded by portraits and ghosts of literary giants. That scene wove together the beauty of nature with Lulu's harsh reality, while paying homage to *The Bell Jar*. I couldn't type that scene fast enough.

What authors inspire you?

While writing *The Mad Wife*, I turned to incredible authors of the past, including Sylvia Plath, Charlotte Perkins Gilman, Flannery O'Connor, and Kate Chopin. I also read *The Woman They Could Not Silence* by Kate Moore. She writes nonfiction in such an immersive, compelling way. Perhaps the biggest surprise read for me this year was *Sipsworth* by Simon Van Booy. It's such a sweet and simple story, and full of richness and depth. There's my perennial favorite modern author, Elizabeth Strout. Right now, I'm slow reading my all-time favorite book *Crossing to Safety* by Wallace Stegner. I read only a couple of pages each night, a little bedtime treat to myself. Then there are my author friends whose stories I cannot get enough of: Joy Callaway, Terah Shelton Harris, and Kelly Mustian.

What advice would you give to an aspiring author?

Write. The only requirement to call yourself a writer is to have written. Life will try to get in the way. The kids will always need something. Your dog will probably want to go for a walk. Your work will require your presence. Social media will demand your attention. But start somewhere. Even if you can only carve out fifteen minutes, you can still get words down. They may be few and require a lot of revisions, but they're a start. And if you've written a book but you're waiting on an agent, editor, or readers, keep writing. Keep putting your fingers on the keyboard, the pen to the paper, and move forward. Writing takes practice, trial and error, and lots and lots of patience and perseverance.

What do you hope readers will take away from this novel beyond the historical details and story?

Empathy. Studies show that readers who spend time reading literary fiction are more empathetic in their real lives. This is called Theory of Mind—the ability to attribute beliefs, intents, desires, emotions, and knowledge to oneself and others. According to this theory, fiction readers often develop greater empathy in real life because they are accustomed to inhabiting the minds of characters from diverse backgrounds.

My books all follow seemingly typical women who find themselves up against a difficult moment in our nation's past. My hope is that these stories and others like them can shed light on women's experiences throughout our history, so we can do better, be kinder, give grace, and extend empathy.

ACKNOWLEDGMENTS

This is the final chapter I will write of *The Mad Wife*. And it is the hardest. There are so many who have made this story possible. I am humbled. Grateful. Thankful. And fearful that I will forget someone. Please forgive me if I do.

First of all, thank you, Dear Reader. We authors spend so much time creating these stories, living in these worlds within our imagination, and never knowing if they will find an audience. Thank you for choosing to spend hours escaping the world around you to immerse yourself in Lulu's story. I am grateful.

A dream of mine was to see my book on a bookstore shelf. That dream came true in 2023, and I am grateful for every store that has chosen to give my stories a place on their shelves. I'm also thankful for every store that has invited me in and asked me to share with their readers. I am grateful to the independent bookstores, especially those in the South, that made me a bestseller. Special thanks to Angel Wings Bookstore, Bookends, Cleary's Bookstore, The Country Bookshop, Fred & June's Books, Litchfield Books, M. Judson Booksellers, Main Street Books, Page 158 Books, Park Road Books, Pelican Bookstore, So Much More to the Story: A Bookery, and South Main Books Company.

Thank you to all the reviewers, podcasters, bloggers, and influencers who have read, shared, and championed my work. My appreciation runs deep. Special thanks to Bookstagrammers @aileenonbookz, @auburndawne, @bookwormbecky1969, @cristinareelyreads, @hazelgatorgirlreads, @katiereads.sc, @libraryofdallas, @livingthereaderlife_, @mollysbookedup, @readwithjennifer, @silversreviews, @stamperlady50, and @rochelles_reading_recommends (tell your mom thanks for the tips for the gelatin salads!). And a special thanks to Amy Allen Clark of @momadvice and the *Book Gang Podcast*. Your encouragement and friendship mean so much!

I must give a special shout-out to Annissa Armstrong (@annissabookishjoy). She has a passion for books and is a champion of authors. Thank you for all the shares and mentions on social media, the events you've attended, the countless books you've left in Little Free Libraries, the dinners we've shared, and the friendship that I cherish. And so many thanks to the Beyond the Pages book club. The traveling ARC of *The Girls We Sent Away* that you all so lovingly annotated, highlighted, and stickered is one of my most treasured possessions.

Writing would be a lonely affair if it weren't for my author friends, including Heather Bell Adams, Kristen Bird, Leslie Hooton, and Kelly Mustian. Joy Callaway, thanks for the countless hours of walking, talking, visiting bookstores, texting, lamenting, and celebrating. I couldn't do this without you! And to my book bestie, Terah Shelton Harris, your phone calls, texts, insights, laughs, and reassurances are a salve to this writer's soul. I'm grateful for you. Proud of you. And still want you to move to Charlotte.

And to the authors who read and blurbed, it is not an easy task, and the fact that you set aside time and then so thoughtfully crafted quotes means so much to me. So thank you, Sarah Penner, Kristen Bird, Kimberly Brock, Serena Burdick, Mimi Herman, Lee Kravetz, Kelly Mustian, Adele Myers, and Ashley Winstead.

So many hands worked behind the scenes to make this book possible. Ann McCain, thank you for having a recipe for cough and croup right at hand…and for the deep belly laugh when we read the ingredients. Maya Myers, thank you for sharing with me the delightful (notice I did not say "delicious") gelatin recipe book.

To Weymouth Center for the Arts and Humanities, I am grateful for the week I got to spend in residency at your beautiful, inspiring, historic home. A deep sense of community exudes from the halls to the grounds…and even the bumps in the night. Julie Borshak, I loved our conversations, and I appreciate all the history you shared with me. I will be back, but please don't make me sleep in the blue room!

To my early readers, I can't thank you enough for being willing to take a look at rough, messy, chaotic drafts and for offering me honest feedback: Heather Bell Adams, Dawn Beery, Jocelyn Chrisley, Heather Donahue, Jeanne Laney, and Nicole McConnell. Your insights helped make Lulu's story so much richer, deeper, better.

Many thanks to Kathie Bennett, a true author advocate and the founder of Magic Time Literary Publicity, for your boundless efforts in helping get Lulu's story into the hands and hearts of more readers. It has been a joy to make magic with you.

As always, I am grateful to the team at Sourcebooks and all you do to bring stories into the world. MJ Johnston, thank you for your sharp editing and nudging me to continue digging deeper. Also thank you to Dominique Raccah, Diane Dannenfeldt, Cristina Arreola, Kate Riley, Anna Venckus, Aubrey Clemans, Rachel Norfleet, Jessica Thelander, BrocheAroe Fabian, Monica Palenzuela, Heather VenHuizen, Stephanie Rocha, Erin LaPointe, and Diane Cunningham. And Kelly Winton for designing such a striking cover that I could not adore more.

To Rachel Cone-Gorham, my agent extraordinaire, thank you again for plucking me out of the slush pile. Your belief in me and my storytelling changed my life. Thank you for your constant encouragement, enthusiasm, feedback, pushback, and insights and for helping me find the delicious blend of broccoli and cheese that Lulu's story needed.

Thank you to Mom, Dad, my friends, and family for your continued support. And, Mom, thank you for reminding me of the importance of speaking about mental health and for sharing your own experience.

To my kids, thank you for being understanding when I'm on the road, away at events, or at home but still lost in the story world. Jonas, thank you for all the times you've checked in and asked how things are going. To my earliest reader, Kenna, thank you for being on the inside team with this one so I could bounce ideas off you and figure out the plot points. Adelyn, I'm grateful for your patience to stay in the dark and do a blind reading to tell me if I pulled off the reveal. You three are everything.

Matt, our adventure continues. Your support is constant. Your pride in me is obvious. Your love is unconditional. I don't deserve you, but I'm grateful for you.

And finally, Isabel, thank you for calling me to Weymouth. Though our times there were separated by decades, as Julie told me your story, I couldn't help but feel a deep calling beyond coincidence that I was telling a story of hysteria in a place where you spent your final moments. You wrote, "I loved life and living, but apparently not enough." I hope this story serves as a testament, not to the weight you carried but to the love and light you deserved.

If you, Dear Reader, have ever felt unseen, unheard, or untethered from the world around you, I hope this story reminds you that your existence, your presence, your voice, your heart is enough. You deserve to be here. You always have. Take care of yourself and each other.

ABOUT THE AUTHOR

© Bethany Callaway

Meagan Church is the author of emotionally charged, empathy-inducing novels, including *The Mad Wife*, *The Last Carolina Girl*, and *The Girls We Sent Away*, a Southern indie bestseller and North Carolina Reads statewide book club pick for 2025. After receiving a BA in English from Indiana University, Meagan built a career as a freelance writer. She is an adjunct for Drexel University's MFA in creative writing program and helps authors tell their own stories through editing, coaching, and workshops. A Midwesterner by birth, she now lives in North Carolina with her high school sweetheart, three children, and a plethora of pets. For more information and to follow her storytelling, visit meaganchurch.com.